K-Town Confidential

Brad CHISHOLM
&
Claire KIM

BLACK ROSE
writing™

SCHOLASTIC EDITION

The final approval for this literary material is granted by the author.

Second Edition – SCHOLASTIC EDITION

This is a work of fiction. Names, characters, businesses, places, events and incidents are either the products of the author's imagination or used in a fictitious manner. Any resemblance to actual persons, living or dead, or actual events is purely coincidental.

ISBN: 978-1-68433-885-6
PUBLISHED BY BLACK ROSE WRITING
www.blackrosewriting.com

Printed in the United States of America
Suggested Retail Price (SRP) $20.95

K-Town Confidential is printed in Plantagenet Cherokee

To Cole

Writers may work alone, but they rarely succeed alone. The authors wish to thank:

Linda Langton

•

Reagan Rothe

•

Richard Curtis

•

Hillel Black

•

Jessica Choi

•

Christina Campos

•

Special thanks to Dad for his stories

K-Town Confidential

"The truth is rarely pure and never simple."
Oscar Wilde

CHAPTER 1

Like snow, the night sky does not discriminate in what it will or will not cover. The streetlights above and the flashing squad cars below cast a light into the private office of the Phoenix nightclub.

Everything could be seen, from the mahogany desk where the Dumok sat, to the little drops of moisture forming on the forehead of a slight man who stood, with his head bent, next to an astonishingly beautiful and exquisitely dressed young woman.

She was a *domi*, a karaoke hostess who had worked for night clubs in Seoul and Hong Kong — and now K-Town in Los Angeles. She was seeking kiting money, a loan, an advance against the house. She called herself Cinnamon, though it was clearly not her true name.

The flashing squad car lights rhythmically changed the *domi's* gown from gold to red and back again. The slight man wiped his forehead. He had arranged this meeting. Cinnamon had asked for fifty thousand dollars, an extraordinary sum, more than double the usual advance.

"Why so much?" The Dumok wondered absently.

Mix stood in the shadows. He was the personal bodyguard of the Dumok. He had the physical strength of three men. He had been with the Dumok from the beginning and was fiercely loyal. He watched his boss out of the corner of his eye. He had a bad feeling about this

Cinnamon girl. She looked like the girl in the photo the Dumok kept buried deep in the right hand drawer of his desk. Mix had seen it once but that had been a long time ago. He didn't need to see it again. The girl in the photo had a face you could never forget.

The third man in the room was called The Enforcer and he was large, thick and his body was covered with tattoos.

It was said the Dumok was the most ruthless man in Koreatown. Of course the Dumok attracted rumors, the currency of whispers, because known facts about him were few. The Dumok was like that. He had the protection of the streets as well as the protection of the politicians. Even the whispers protected him.

The Dumok motioned slightly with his finger toward the bar. Cinnamon hurried over to pour him a drink, the scent of expensive perfume trailing. She poured a Cognac and walked over to the Dumok and held the snifter out with one hand, the other slender hand slightly holding her wrist in the deferential way of the *domis*. She looked up just as the flashing light outside cast a red hue on the Dumok's face, exposing an ugly disfigurement. The sight of it made her hand tremble, causing the Cognac to ripple. Only two men knew how the injury had occurred, and one of them was dead.

The Dumok studied the trembling girl. His face was a mask. Her resemblance to Nara Song, a woman whose memory still tortured him, was remarkable and unfortunate.

The Dumok stood and walked across the room to the safe where he removed five bundles of cash, fifty thousand dollars wrapped in treasury bands. Cinnamon smirked. She would get her price. Even the Dumok was just a man and she was an expert at working men. It was just her bad luck that the Dumok turned just in time to catch the smirk. He paused, then casually removed the treasury bands one at a time, slowly. He threw the money into the air like it was confetti and watched as the hundred dollar bills fluttered to the ground to form a thick green carpet at his feet. He then took the Cognac from her hand and poured it on the floor beneath him as if he were pouring chocolate sauce on a banana split.

If it took Cinnamon and fifty grand to get him to do something he should have done a long time ago, so be it. The Dumok opened the desk drawer and pulled out the photo of Nara Song and slipped it into his breast pocket and walked out. Mix followed.

Outside the door, the Dumok turned to Mix. "Call this number," the Dumok said, handing over a slip of paper. "I want to see this lawyer tomorrow morning."

Mix looked down. Holly Park. A female lawyer. And Korean.

"Yes, boss." Mix did not let his surprise show.

The muffled thump of music from the nightclub was punctuated by a crack as The Enforcer knocked the empty snifter off the desk and onto the floor, followed by the sound of crunching glass as he broke the glass into crystal shards with his heavy boot.

Cinnamon looked over at the slight man who had brought her. Do something, her eyes blazed. But the man stood, hunched forward, his eyes downcast and his hands folded humbly before him.

"Please," Cinnamon begged, clasping her hands and moving her body.

Stupid girl, the broker thought. Just... shut... up.

Cinnamon put her hands on her hips in surprise and indignation. She was not used to this type of treatment from any man.

Nobody moved.

With a bob of her head and a flutter of her eyelashes, Cinnamon slowly dropped to her knees, her long black hair cascading forward like a veil.

The Enforcer leaned back and watched. *Domis.* They were all greedy, but this one was arrogant, too. She needed to be taught a lesson. It was his job to protect the Dumok from these girls. Word would get around. The other girls would think twice before asking for so much.

Cinnamon worked steadily, her small cupped hands staining the hundred dollar bills with thin red lines as she gathered them into mounds. The Enforcer glanced at his watch. It was still early. Koreatown was just waking up.

CHAPTER 2

A large graphic of a beautiful girl with her lips painted red in a half smile welcomed the stream of drivers at Wilshire Boulevard and Western Avenue, the unofficial border of Koreatown. Other colorful wraps and giant billboards covered the rich collection of historical buildings dotted with advertisements for *soju* or Korean brands of beer. On the streets, storefronts featured Korean signs and menus for $3.99 breakfast specials. A visitor might not even know they were in America.

The streets were filled with people shielding themselves from the relentless sun. Pedestrians managed with baseball caps and sunglasses or by holding up magazines and newspapers. Women wore oversized visors or carried umbrellas to find relief from the early morning heat.

Holly Park banged at the elevator button in the front lobby. The elevators were still broken. She was irritated by the smell of old ketchup wafting in the air and the sight of a fresh footprint in the stale French fries littering the stairwell of the parking garage.

Someone had knocked a drink cup down the stairs. The fries and old ketchup packet had been there all week. The discarded cup was new. Yesterday, the fries had been on the top of the landing but someone had kicked them to the bottom steps. Holly carefully stepped over the mess when her cell phone rang.

"Your 9 a.m. cancelled. They've hired another lawyer." It was Mi Rae, her receptionist.

"Why?" Holly asked.

"They hired a Jewish lawyer, plus they said they didn't want a woman. Or a young one," Mi Rae clucked. Holly sighed, exasperated.

Holly banged at the elevator button. She was twenty-seven, exotic yet decisively American. She had a toned body from regular hours at the gym, with long dark hair, fair skin and full lips that easily broke into a smile. Not that she was smiling now. The air conditioning in the office building was broken and the moisture was forming under her clothes and sticking.

Holly sighed impatiently. It was a long step down from the days of working in a fancy downtown law firm. The dirty parking structure was a daily reminder. She had made an impulsive decision to leave the firm followed by a quick, painful descent to the wrong side of town.

It was the stairs again. Inside the stairwell, she caught up with an older lawyer, Johnny Gee, who was dragging a tired rolling briefcase up the stairs. "Good morning," Holly said cheerfully. "It's a good work out, these stairs."

"Morning." Johnny Gee grimaced. He was less sanguine than Holly about the stairs. "That was quite a verdict on that wrongful death case of yours." He whistled. "Twenty five million dollars. I imagine you got a nice piece of it," he added.

Word traveled fast. Holly just smiled politely without answering and sprinted past him. Minutes later, out of breath and sticky, she bent over to pick up the newspaper and loose flyers underneath the door and pushed it open.

"You're supposed to pick these up when you come in," Holly said lightly, handing Mi Rae the pile.

"Just put them there," Mi Rae said, not looking up as she picked at her breakfast. Holly opened her mouth to say something then bit her tongue, reminding herself as she did every day that she was no longer downtown, but subletting on the cheap in K-Town.

"Did my client drop off documents this morning?" Holly asked, but knew the answer. The smell of deep fried oil lingered in the air. Her

5

client owned a breakfast café.

"Yes. The papers are in your room," Mi Rae said.

"Office. It's an office. Not a room," Holly corrected.

Mi Rae ignored the comment. "Can I ask you something?" she said, her eyelashes fluttering with gossipy enthusiasm.

"Sure." Holly bristled inwardly. Mi Rae was so intrusive.

"Did you get fired — like from your last job?" Mi Rae asked. "This entire building is full of lawyers who are only solo because they can't get jobs, so why would anyone quit to work *here*?"

Holly braced herself. Mi Rae was always so rude. Like she was being now. Mi Rae looked up expectantly but Holly remained firm. She had yet to break her silence as to why she had left Stowe, Hubbell and Burg and she was not about to spill the beans to Mi Rae.

"I didn't get fired. I quit," Holly answered matter-of-factly.

"You would have been better off staying downtown if you're husband hunting, you know." Mi Rae glanced at Holly. "Everyone knows the guys who are the best husband material work downtown."

Holly offered nothing more, hoping Mi Rae's interest in her breakfast would win out over trying to elicit gossip.

"You know, you're not getting any younger," Mi Rae added, hoping to provoke a response.

Holly laughed, refusing to rise to the bait. She turned to walk to her office.

"Oh," Mi Rae chirped. "Someone called to make an appointment for the Dumok. He'll be here in an hour." Mi Rae was unable to hide the admiration in her voice. "How do *you* know the Dumok?"

Holly looked down at the phone message slip. "I have no idea who this is."

"How could you not know who the Dumok is? Everyone in town knows about him!" Mi Rae exclaimed.

"Except me," Holly said, shaking her head.

"Then why is the Dumok coming to see you?" Mi Rae mused. "Maybe he saw you on the news!" There was a twinge of envy in her voice.

It had been a fluke that Holly made the evening news. It was the largest jury award against the city of Los Angeles in the city's history. On the day the jury verdict was announced a news reporter caught Logan Burg and Holly leaving court. The clip made its way onto the wire services and Holly's face had appeared on news channels all over California.

"Really, Holly." Mi Rae sighed. "Don't you know anything? Everyone knows who the Dumok is… He is the boss in K-Town. He owns all the good room salons, karaoke bars, spas, and nightclubs on this side of town."

Holly shook her head. Her experience of Koreatown was limited to Korean barbecue. Mi Rae laughed. She enjoyed having one up on Holly and turned away, not offering anything more. Instead, she used her free hand to scroll through a shoe sale on her monitor screen. "You really should learn to speak Korean, too, if you are planning to work here," Mi Rae sniffed.

A cheap shot, but true. Holly was a transplant. Koreatown was not her true north. She, like other Angelinos, saw this part of town as a thoroughfare leading east towards downtown or west to the Santa Monica pier. Koreatown. It was the last place Holly had expected she would end up.

Holly went into her office and flipped on the light. She had a view of the building across the street, an almost new computer, and two 1940's oak client chairs with curved backs across from her desk. Most importantly, she had business cards that read Holly H. Park, Attorney-at-Law. The associates were somewhere in the future. Holly sighed and looked around. Had she jumped ship too quickly?

CHAPTER 3

"He said to remember you by your legs," a voice boomed at Holly. It was the lobby security guard. He smiled, a twinkle in his voice.

"Who said that!?"

It had been a twist of fate. Holly had started interviewing right after law school, and an interview at a different law firm in the same building had gone badly. Holly's only concern was whether she had enough money to get out of the parking lot when she heard the voice and looked up.

"Remember that girl, because she's going to work for me one day. That's what he said."

"Who said that!?" Holly asked again, taken aback.

"Logan Burg. He's the top dog on the thirtieth floor. He's got an eye for the ladies." "Then can you please let me up there?" Holly smiled impulsively. The security guard winked and conspiratorially waved goodbye as the elevator door shut and Holly rode up to the secure floor. The door swooshed open. Holly paused a moment outside the etched glass door that read Law Offices of Stowe, Hubbell & Burg.

Holly pushed the door open and went inside. "I would like to see Logan Burg, please," Holly announced. A moment later, Holly followed Robin, an attractive secretary, through a hushed maze of busy cubicles and small associate offices. Holly breathed inward, intimidated by the surroundings. Robin stopped in front of the corner office and gestured. Holly took a deep breath.

"I thought I should come introduce myself since you said I'd be working for you some day," Holly said bravely, smiling. "I'm Holly Park. Here is my résumé."

Logan Burg was the managing partner. He was in his early fifties and handsome. He had a light tan from regular golfing, sharp blue eyes, a hawk's nose and thick hair cut short. His suit was dark gray with a subtle texture, his shirt the palest blue behind a maroon tie with a tiny gray repeating pattern. He swiveled around his chair and stared.

This girl was slender, and dressed in a professionally feminine manner. Though she was conservatively dressed, it did not suppress her electric personality. Her sophisticated attire did not seem to quite match her innocent, almost child-like face. She wore no jewelry. Her hair was her only accessory, worn loose and long—the color of burnished embers—which looked real, although probably not her natural color. That and the legs. Logan Burg was rarely at a loss for words, but this time, Holly had caught him.

Logan was an imposing man in all respects. He always spoke to the support staff abruptly or just plain outright ignored them. They found him arrogant and chauvinistic, yet he was charming in front of a jury. He was known to come to the office every morning in a huff, galloping down the hallway towards his corner office, a large rectangular briefcase flying in his hand and *The Wall Street Journal* tucked under his arm. He never said good morning and with any luck would slam the door to his office and resurface only at lunchtime.

The nineteenth century fox hunting and polo playing artwork on the walls defined the traditional culture of the law firm, which primarily hired associates from privileged backgrounds whose families belonged to the right country clubs, knew their way around a golf course and never ordered blended scotch.

Logan barely gave Holly's résumé a glance beyond noting that she had gone to a decent law school. Not top drawer but accredited. As he sat eyeing the young woman sitting in the proper suit and heels and smiling broadly, he decided to play the recruitment game a little differently and go with his gut. He knew there was something about this girl even across the lobby where he had watched her walk towards the elevators. It was her energy. Untapped and bursting. He found her eagerness amusing and took an immediate liking to her. Logan Burg decided to reward Holly for coming to see him.

It was with great surprise to everyone when he hired Holly Park on the spot. Nobody was more surprised than Holly herself.

Logan Burg had gone to enough bar association meetings to see the trend of the bigger law firms in hiring a minority person to help get clients from that ethnic group. It was fine in theory, but the actuality of socializing in immigrant communities, with their mysterious food and cultural rules, made him anxious and would, more importantly, cut into his private life. The one he had worked so hard to build. It revolved around golf, the Hollywood Bowl, and dinners featuring good martinis. Chased with a dry-aged rib eye, just past rare, a Caesar salad, no anchovies, and a glass or two of a fat California Cabernet.

Logan didn't want to go to ethnic functions. Besides, he had no time. When was he supposed to attend these ribbon cuttings, grand openings, weddings, engagement parties and birthdays, flowers or potted plant in hand?

Send Holly.

Holly was personable, energetic and single. What did she have to do on the weekends except brush her lovely hair a hundred strokes? She would be welcomed. Holly was born in Los Angeles, would fit into the firm's corporate culture and, most importantly, she was eager to please. Yes, Holly Park was perfect. Plus her father had a church that served the Korean community. What a good source of referrals that would be. That afternoon, Logan Burg decided to take a gamble, which is how the name Holly H. Park appeared on the embossed letterhead of the Law Offices of Stowe, Hubbell & Burg as the first ethnic female hire in the seventy-five year history of the firm.

Perhaps one of his colleagues might call her a banana, yellow on the outside but white on the inside, but he wouldn't care. He liked her. Yes, Logan Burg was pleased with himself.

Holly floated out of the office and she even managed to buy her way out of the parking lot with the three twenty dollar bills carefully folded in her wallet in case of emergencies.

"Are you sure it's a *lawyer* position? Not a secretarial one?" Holly imagined her sister Christine asking. She couldn't wait to share her good news.

CHAPTER 4

The next Monday morning Holly was right on time. "Don't fraternize with the support staff, unless you want to be treated like a glorified secretary," Logan said sternly as he walked Holly down the hall. Holly was smart, worked long hours and made her billable hours. Logan was pleased. Exactly two years later, his gamble paid off when a man got hit by a delivery truck and died, leaving behind a young widow with three children and Holly brought the case to the firm, which turned out to become hugely profitable for the family and for the firm.

It was a night soon after the big win. The view of the downtown skyline was impressive from thirty floors up. Desmond Stowe, the senior partner, absently toyed with his cuff links as he spoke to Jill, his paralegal. He looked up just as Holly walked in with an armload of trial binders for another case, motioned where he wanted the binders placed, then turned away.

Jill buried her head and looked down at her yellow pad, focusing on her perfect cursive script, and giggled. Jill wore a crisp white button down shirt revealing a deep cleavage and the slightest hint of some elegant camisole peeking out, a recent gift from Desmond.

The senior partner had a refined and playful sense of erotic in his taste for lingerie and he couldn't wait to see the rest of it later that night. Jill glanced up at Desmond, who raised an eyebrow back at her, which made Jill toss her dark mop of cropped hair and suppress a laugh. Desmond was just like that. It wasn't personal. He made a point never to get too friendly with the associates.

"You can go," Desmond said, looking blankly at Holly. "Unless I'm forgetting something?"

Yes, he was forgetting something, Holly thought. To thank her. To give her a bonus, a referral fee, some acknowledgment for her contribution towards the multi-million dollar award. After all, hadn't she brought the case into the firm? And after the driver was found to be indigent and the trucking company uninsured, wasn't it she who had gone out and done her own private investigation while Desmond Stowe was busily preparing a letter of disengagement dismissing the case as a dog? It had been Holly who went to inspect the accident site, something no one had bothered to do. She noticed a large bus stop billboard on the northeast corner intersection where the decedent had been struck and killed. It seemed the placement of the bus stop bench and billboard impaired the vision of drivers negotiating the right turn until the turn had been made. Holly convinced Desmond to take a second look at the case, arguing the bus stop billboard created an unsafe road condition. Desmond agreed. The next day, the firm filed a lawsuit against the city of Los Angeles for creating an unsafe road condition.

The sharks circled around, wanting a piece of the action. Ambulance chasers and unscrupulous plaintiff lawyers appeared out of nowhere, offering the family of the decedent increasingly larger sums of front money to take the case away. Holly kept the sharks at bay as she worked up the case, propounding and responding to discovery, answering interrogatories, and taking depositions. It was Holly who dropped off food for the family—unreimbursed by the firm - and lent an ear to the grieving widow at all hours of the day or night to keep control of the case. Yes, Holly had no doubt how important her role was in the win. When it became apparent she would get no reward, she felt cheated, so she resigned.

Holly organized her desk and left neat notes in all the case files. Lastly, she packed a few personal items then quietly flipped off the lights for the last time.

"Where's Logan?" Holly wondered. But Logan Burg was nowhere to be found. In fact, he made sure not to be in the office on Holly's last day. Holly left a note on his desk, turned in her security clearance card and walked out of the polished lobby, dazed.

Downstairs she waved goodbye to the snack shop owners on the mezzanine level, passed a five-dollar bill to the maintenance man polishing the escalator rails, then she ran into Desmond Stowe and Jill in the parking garage.

"Where are you going to go?" Jill asked nicely enough.

Holly shook her head. "I don't know."

"You're Chinese, right?" Desmond asked abruptly, frowning.

"Korean, actually." Holly was polite but cool.

"Koreatown is a dump. And Chinatown's no better." Desmond wrinkled his nose in disdain. "Stay away from those parts. It's dirty in those places." Desmond smiled encouragingly and turned back to Jill.

Holly watched them ride up the escalators then turned away. She wished she had run into Logan Burg because she wanted to thank him for the job and say goodbye.

A little before midnight, a Jaguar sedan pulled into a driveway in the Pacific Palisades. The house was dark except for one-bedroom light. Logan Burg got out of the car and walked a little more slowly than usual up the driveway. The house was decorated in a nice, conservative manner. A Labrador bounced out to greet him. Logan put down his briefcase and rummaged through the mail before walking to his daughter's bedroom and bent down and kissed the sleeping sixteen year old on the forehead and turned off the light. Logan undressed and listened to his phone messages before crawling into his perfectly made bed. He couldn't sleep. He liked having Holly around, and didn't understand what had made her quit.

CHAPTER 5

Office rents downtown were so expensive that Holly found herself looking farther and farther west until she crossed the border into Koreatown. Crossing Vermont Avenue there were more billboards per square inch than anywhere else in the city. The signs were all in Korean. The strange combination of foreign and familiar excited her.

The building on Ardmore and Wilshire Boulevard was the only one with a *For Lease* sign written in English, so Holly went inside. The corridors were wide with marbled flooring and the doors were made of chipboard with oak veneer. It was the type of building loaded with accountants, lawyers, and dentists just getting by. The building manager wore an ill-fitting suit and chipped nail polish. She pulled out an application and handed it over with a dismissive look. In that moment, Holly realized that while she had enjoyed the status of a downtown lawyer, now she just looked like an unemployed one. She thanked the building manager and left.

For the first time in her life Holly found she had nowhere to go. She was not stuck watching the clock to make her billable hours, or hurrying in late after lunch hoping to escape notice. If she didn't feel like working or wanted to come in at noon, she could. Holly took a deep breath, overwhelmed.

"I can do jury trials or go into criminal defense. I can draft complex trust documents or file death row appeals. I can try to break into entertainment law or go into indigent defense. I can be anyone or do anything—only I have to be somebody!" Holly breathed aloud the freedom was both paralyzing and amazing.

CHAPTER 6

"So..." Neil Cooper's voice boomed across the cafe. "What you're essentially saying is that you're dispensing legal advice for free Chinese food." His voice was so loud others turned around. Holly's cheeks reddened.

"I didn't say that. I said it was an initial meeting. He owns a restaurant chain and wanted advice regarding new acquisitions. We met at one of his restaurants and servers brought out an incredible spread of dishes. Lobster, crab dishes, meats, everything!" Holly said, excitedly. "I think I may get my first client," she added, proudly.

"Precisely what I said," Neil snorted. "You're giving legal advice for free Chinese...er... Korean food," he corrected himself, winking. He reached for his coffee and took a sip.

Neil Cooper had broad shoulders and a booming voice. He had premature gray around the temples and when he furrowed his brows just the right way he looked reasonably intelligent. All his effort went into presentation. He had the perfect navy suit, the snappily polished lawyer shoes, the carefully conservative tie, the weekly haircut, all of which created the image of burnished experience that held up very well in front of potential clients. His face appeared in the local ethnic newspapers each Sunday. Neil Cooper was never at a loss for new clients—as long as they spoke no English. Whatever the language, he always had a translator present.

Now, he reached into his rectangular leather briefcase. It was suitably weathered with the look of many courtroom battles. Inside, there was an unused legal pad and three bottles of water. Balancing the yellow pad on his knee, he took a pen from his breast pocket, pulled the lid off with his teeth and scribbled a phone number and an address and ripped the page off the pad and handed it to Holly.

"I'm out of business cards," he said and added, "Do you know Kate Hong?"

Holly shook her head.

"Anyone who's anybody in Koreatown knows who she is. She's a good person to know." Neil smiled and patted Holly on the shoulder. "Don't worry." He laughed. "I'll introduce you to her. Isn't it funny that I have to introduce you to the right Koreans when you're the one who is Korean?" Neil guffawed. "Come to my office in the morning. I'll take you over there," he said, patting Holly. They walked out to the parking lot. Neil had a driver who was asleep in the Cadillac with his feet sticking out of the window. Neil cheerfully batted the resting driver's feet with his folded newspaper.

The next morning Holly sprang out of bed and rushed to Neil Cooper's office. She was exactly on time. In the parking lot Neil stopped in front, riding a Harley-Davidson motorcycle.

"Climb on," Neil said, handing her a helmet.

"A motorcycle?" Holly exclaimed. "Are you kidding me?"

Neil revved the engine and patted the seat invitingly. "Not just any motorcycle. A Harley-Davidson."

Holly hesitated. Neil patted the seat more firmly.

"You're impossible," she said, laughing, then climbed on the seat and gingerly positioned herself to be as far away from Neil as possible.

"Hold on tight." Neil squeezed Holly's knee and revved the engine and took off.

It was an old, rundown building. The sign on the door was made of cheap plastic and read *American Legal Services*. Neil pushed open the door. The sofas and armchairs in the waiting room had curves copied from Italian designs with cheap, garish and harsh fabrics. The coffee table was gilded in gold trim with a vase of tired silk flowers. A huge crucifix hung from the wall. Sections of a well-thumbed ethnic newspaper littered the end tables. Just inside the French doors of the first office a woman sat behind an imposing black desk. Hanging on the wall behind the desk were mail-order theological seminary diplomas and an elaborately framed certificate, which read:

West Los Angeles School of Law
Kate Hong
Paralegal

Holly peeked through the French doors and caught her first glimpse of Kate Hong, who was in her early forties, petite and quite pretty with dark eye makeup and long false eyelashes which swooped fashionably. She had alabaster skin and her dark hair swirled loosely in a bun with one strand curling prettily against her cheek. She wore a fuchsia silk blouse with an animal print skirt and high heels. She looked over and smiled with supreme self-confidence. Neil, who was standing next to Kate Hong's desk, bowed deeply in an exaggerated fashion, followed up by a wink.

"You must be Holly," Kate said. Her voice was modulated and clear. It was a statement. It did not suggest a response, a dialogue, a reaction. It was definitive. It was paired with a presumptuous glance, and then she turned away with a smile as the door opened and Choi walked in.

Choi was a broker of slight build who had once worked for the Korean diplomatic service in Los Angeles — just not lately. He wore a tired gray suit and an air of resignation, yet his eyes were sharp and anticipatory. Choi ushered in a middle-aged couple. Kate hurriedly motioned for Neil.

Kate Hong was an immigration broker and the owner of American Legal Services. She set up the office and employed various paralegals to process simple paperwork. But Kate was greedy. She also retained serious cases that she could not possibly handle and used lawyers like Neil Cooper to handle them on the cheap. Kate would introduce potential clients to lawyers, then take forty percent of the legal fees.

It was a perfect arrangement and highly profitable, except for one thing: it was illegal. Kate didn't care. Neil Cooper was the one with the law license to lose, and if he did, she would just replace him with someone else. Hungry lawyers were everywhere. She liked Neil, but she liked money more.

Kate Hong always knew when the moment was right. She spoke rapidly, her hands flying, her eyes brightening as she gestured to Neil, sitting with his eyes narrowed, deep in thought, looking off into the distance with his brow furrowed. Sometimes, Neil rested his chin between his forefinger and thumb and nodded gravely.

The couple listened, and watched, unable to take their eyes off Kate. Then, it was over as quickly as it had begun. The retainer agreement was signed and Choi and the clients left, a few thousand dollars poorer, but hopeful.

Kate splayed the tired hundred dollar bills across her desk as deftly as a Las Vegas croupier displaying a deck of cards. Kate Hong could count the money in a potential client's bank account, size them up with a glance, then extract fees equivalent to their net worth before they walked out the door.

"They're so damn willing." Kate sighed, then laughed, that tinkling laugh that everyone knew. Holly glanced tentatively at Neil, whose eyes were turned away as he slid his blank yellow legal pad back into his briefcase.

"There Holly! Now you've seen," Kate Hong said brightly. Her eyes glowed with excitement. "That's just how it's done. Let's go to lunch."

Neil chuckled and did a two-step and made a mock, swooping bow as Kate shimmied past him, laughing.

All types came to American Legal Services—men and women, young, old, middle class, immigrants—by ignorance or design, sometimes from too much craftiness or not enough, other times it was indulgence of drink or fists. Kate Hong could identify their greatest fear or anxiety, then, with one word, a phrase, comment or gesture, make that fear take on a heightened importance and urgency which emptied pockets. When Kate was around, there seemed to be no impossibility and it was astonishing how everyone around her believed it. Even Holly was impressed.

Kate looked at Holly—a quick careless glance that Holly missed. She could use Holly at a cheaper rate than Neil Cooper, instantly discounting her value because she was young and a girl.

Kate laughed a bright, high-pitched laugh, her signature. She linked arms with Holly.

"Neil told me all about you. Just always keep in mind that you have to look like you're worth the fees you're charging. Start by getting yourself a proper handbag." Kate turned away, but not before Holly caught a mocking, triumphant smile. It was in this way that the name Holly H. Park appeared on the door of American Legal Services.

CHAPTER 7

"Holly, It's the Dumok! He's here!" Mi Rae could not contain the excitement in her voice. A moment later, the Dumok walked in preceded by Mi Rae. Holly looked up with mild interest, then had to try and not react. The man called the Dumok had a mysterious charismatic force, as if the center of the magnetic poles moved with him. Holly felt strong electric currents pulling her to him. Her face reddened.

His eyes were dark, brooding and intelligent, measuring Holly, missing nothing. He had dark thick hair and a determined jaw, decisively European with the slightest hint of exotic in his eyes. His skin was smooth and would have been spotless but for the jagged scar that ran horizontally across his neck giving the appearance that his head had almost been severed, an alarming incongruity to an otherwise polished and flawless image.

Holly flinched. Their eyes momentarily met, but his were impenetrable and silent, refusing to speak of what his telltale skin refused to hide. Holly had never experienced a man like this. His height and the way he loomed in the doorway gave off an aura of impending, tempered danger. He was of an age where elegance and power had replaced youth. He had a patina of style that only taste and experience and substantial wealth could provide—a studied casualness, subtle yet distinct. He seemed utterly detached and alone as he stood, his large frame filling the doorway. If the Dumok noticed her staring, he said nothing.

"Please, won't you have a seat?" Holly gestured to a client chair and the Dumok sat easily, crossing his legs.

"How can I help you?" Holly spoke in a calm voice even though she wasn't calm at all. Her heart was pounding as she tried to avert her gaze, but it kept going back to the scar. It was an injury that refused to be ignored.

"I have a missing persons case which may require your assistance," he said. His accent was neutral, vaguely French, the product of private tutors, only faded and softened, like he'd been somewhere else for a long time and hadn't needed it. For once, Holly was glad of her Korean upbringing. It provided a formality and a reserve she did not feel.

"Do you have any information about the person you are looking for?" Holly asked carefully. The Dumok's eyes flashed and his gaze was unsettling yet Holly sensed he somehow felt better. She wondered how long he had carried this burden.

"Her name is Nara Song," the Dumok began. "I believed that Nara died many years ago, but rumors have been circulating now that she may be alive. If so, she has been flying under the radar. Trouble follows her, which is why I thought she might seek help in a place like this." The Dumok stopped, his shoulders even sagged ever so slightly. "I don't believe she is alive, but if she is, I want you to find her."

His eyes were piercing but lacked conviction. "Logan Burg referred you," the Dumok added.

"Logan?" Holly asked, surprised.

"Logan and I go back many years. He speaks very highly of you." The Dumok paused. "He believes you are the perfect lawyer for what I need."

"I've never handled a missing persons case," Holly started.

"This is not a complex case where that particular expertise is needed. Logan says you stand very firm on principle and discretion."

Holly blushed. It seemed the whole world knew she had walked out of her job. It was then the Dumok showed Holly the photo. The girl in the photo held two fingers next to her eyes in the double V-sign as she smiled, her head tilted girlishly to one side. Her large eyes had an artful innocence that gave away nothing. The coloring was unusual for a Korean—light hazel with a gray hue. She wore a necklace around her slender neck, the kind of necklace seen only in expensive magazines— not a necklace a young girl would wear. The Hermés silk scarf she'd tied loosely as a halter top looked as if the slightest touch would make it fall. She was a great beauty, flawless, feminine and exotic.

"It is an old photo." the Dumok laughed ruefully. "May I introduce Nara Song? Don't be fooled by the picture. She was a girl of contradictions and fiery impulses." He frowned, his voice contained. His eyes flashed as he glared at the photo. "I was told she died twenty years ago, but if she is alive..." he paused. "I want you to find her. " The Dumok handed Holly the photo.

"Hold on to this. I will be in touch in the next day or two." Then the Dumok stood and extended his hand, as though Holly had rendered him some profound courtesy.

After he had gone, Holly's office seemed suddenly empty. She picked up the photo of Nara and looked at it for a long time, trying to will Nara to speak to her, but she was as silent as her grave.

Holly left the photo on her desk and walked out to reception to find Kate and Mi Rae in a huddle, gossiping. They quickly straightened up when they saw Holly. Kate's eyes were bright, electric, as she marched up and down, unable, in her excitement, to stand still.

"Oh, I wish I had been here to greet the Dumok! He would have felt more confident if he had seen me instead of you," Kate declared in her decisive way. "The Dumok never uses Korean lawyers. He always hires strong male Jewish lawyers. I don't understand why he would hire you, Holly. You're none of those things!"

There was a contained hysteria as she mocked Holly.

"My old boss, Logan Burg, referred him," Holly answered.

Kate laughed her bright, impossible laugh, then paused. There was jealousy in her tone, but just as quickly, it was instantly supplanted with a perfectly docile expression.

"Did he pay you?" Kate was smiling pleasantly enough but there was a firm faint edge to her voice. Holly shook her head.

"No, but he said he'd come back."

Kate shook her head in frustration.

"You handled it all wrong, Holly," Kate said.

"Mark my words, I could have extracted a sizable retainer. A man like that doesn't walk into a place like this just any day." Kate put her hands on her hips and shot Holly an imperious look, shaking her head. "I would have promised him everything. Don't you know you should promise the sky — even if you can only deliver the dust from the ground?"

"He is searching for a woman from his past," Holly said, wanting to share the details of the new case. Holly couldn't help herself and added, "Who exactly is the Dumok? Do you know anything about him?"

Of course Kate knew of the Dumok. He was the favorite topic of Koreatown. "Do you want to see the photo of the person he is looking for?" Holly asked excitedly. Kate's face lit up. Like everyone else, she too had followed the Dumok's activities over the years. But in truth, Kate only knew the same gossip and speculation as everyone else.

"He is the godfather of Koreatown," Kate began. "Even the Korean gangsters protect him. I will tell you more later but we must go. A new client is waiting for us at the JJ Grand Hotel. They like to see the lawyer's face when they are paying."

Collecting fees was always Kate's first priority. Kate and Holly rushed out the door.

CHAPTER 8

Choi, broker and forger of documents, former operative of the Republic of South Korea's consular service, was a man of pale appearance, average build, and quick intelligence that carried some authority, though the charm of his youth had been worn away over the years by unrealized ambition and graying ethics.

It was morning rush hour in Los Angeles. The southbound 405 Freeway was jammed. Choi eyed the temperature gauge climbing towards red. He blasted his horn. The last thing he needed was his car overheating. His eyes darted nervously to the black leather messenger bag with the timeworn seal of a foreign government on the passenger seat. His stomach churned. It would just look bad if he got pulled over. He had promised Kate Hong he would deliver the fake passports first thing and he was officially late.

The pointer on the gauge moved to red. Choi reached over and turned the heat knob to high. As the hot air blasted into his face, the engine cooled and immediately the pointer began to drop. Rings of sweat formed under his arms as he unrolled the window and cursed at the traffic.

The traffic inched forward. Choi fumbled with the radio knob to find K-JAZZ. It was Slow Train Lexington playing "I Got It Bad (And That Ain't Good)." He fiddled with the volume, turning it up. Finally, the traffic began to move.

The flashing red lights came out of nowhere. Choi glanced at the rearview mirror and quickly pushed the black messenger bag onto the floor. He watched the flashing lights through the mirror and pulled over off the freeway and rolled down the window.

"Hello, officer," Choi said with his best smile as he nervously twisting the signet ring on his finger. "What seems to be the problem?"

An hour later and very late, Choi pushed open the door to American Legal Services. There was no one at the reception desk, Mi Rae's *Cosmopolitan* magazine was on her chair and her purse was gone.

"Hello?" Choi called out, but nobody answered. He peeked into the conference room, but it was empty and there was no sound. Kate's office was empty too. Choi thought of just leaving the package on Kate's desk, but he wanted to get paid. Maybe she was down the hall. He walked past what used to be an unoccupied office, but now there was a stack of files on the desk, a coffee cup and a cardigan on the back of the chair. Curious, he stuck his head in. The nameplate on the desk said Holly H. Park but nobody was there. He glanced casually at the desk while trying to decide what to do.

Then he saw it. His heart skipped a beat. His face drained of color as he looked again. There was no question. Choi drew a sharp breath and his eyes grew dark and flat as he picked up the photo the Dumok had left. Choi's blood ran cold as he realized with absolute certainty why the Dumok had come calling. There was no mistake. The Dumok was looking for Nara Song. Choi crumpled the photo into a wad and flung it on the floor.

"Holly H. Park!" Choi roared at the top of his voice, storming down the hall, his eyes bulging wildly. But the office was empty and nobody answered. He stormed back into the office and picked up the crushed photo from the floor. He hesitated, nervously flattened the photo on his knee, then jammed it into his briefcase, walked down the hallway briskly and stormed out, slamming the door.

Choi broke into a sweat as he searched, wild-eyed, for the emergency exit. He would take the stairs nine floors down to the parking garage. He was not about to take any chances of running into Kate Hong now.

In his car Choi sat, thinking, cracking his knuckles and clenching his hands into fists. He had hidden in the shadows for twenty years in dread of this day. The day the Dumok would come looking for Nara Song.

CHAPTER 9

An hour later Kate Hong and Holly sailed back into American Legal Services, happy with the fees collected and the client's anxieties assuaged.

"Mi Rae must have gone to eat," Kate mused. "She should have locked up."

"Let me show you the photo of Nara Song now!" Holly interrupted excitedly. "It's in my office."

Kate followed Holly down the hall. Once inside her office, Holly went to her desk, and stopped. "Was...someone in my office?" she asked slowly.

"I don't think so. Why?" Kate asked.

"It's...gone. Someone took the photo!" Holly said with a shadow in her voice. Her face paled. Something was wrong. The envelope was there, but the photo was gone. Holly pushed the papers aside on her desk, searching frantically. "It was here before we left!" Holly exclaimed as panic started rising. "Do you think the Dumok came back while we were gone and took it?" she asked, frantically.

"Oh, I'm sure it's there and you just misplaced it," Kate said, her condescending tone rising and falling in playful inflection. "You really should put important papers in a safe place, you know," she clucked in her bright voice.

Then the phone rang. Mi Rae was still not back, so Holly picked it up, taking a deep breath to sound professional and calm. It was a Kendall Taylor, a new referral from Logan Burg.

"Can you please ask Mi Rae about the photo, Kate?" Holly pleaded as she grabbed her purse. "I have a potential client who wants to meet right now, but I have to find that photo!"

Kate smiled. She liked Holly, no mistake, but she had to admit that she enjoyed watching her squirm.

CHAPTER 10

The name Kendall Taylor was no stranger to the Four Seasons Hotel spa in Beverly Hills. Disrobing, she lay down in the private treatment room and closed her sea-green eyes slowly. The lawyer had sounded so young, she thought. But she trusted Logan, so she would meet with her.

Soon, the scent of the mint lotion being massaged into her scalp relaxed her. She was naturally blonde, her hair the texture and color of corn silk. She loved the coolness tingling her scalp. She tilted her head back just a little and closed her eyes as the warm water rinsed through her hair. Spa workers loved to work on Kendall's body, which was pale like she had never known the sun, though in fact she loved the outdoors and was an avid equestrian.

An hour later, she loosely wrapped a big, fluffy white towel over her petite body and made her way to the dressing room. She dropped the towel at her feet before daintily stepping on the scale to weigh herself. The number never changed but in her mind she was convinced she had put on a few pounds.

Kendall helped herself to lime and strawberry flavored water before going to the mirrors to scrutinize her face. She stroked her forehead with one finger and pulled the skin back. Perhaps it was that time again? Kendall's focus shifted to the corners of her eyes. She was beginning to notice the ever so slight droop to her eyelids. *Maybe this is why people have been asking me lately if I'm tired*, she mused. She took a carefully manicured fingernail and prodded her eyelid. She let the towel drop again and pulled the towel wrapped on her head and let her hair tumble around her shoulders. She stood naked.

Yes, I'm still beautiful, Kendall thought. Her attention fell to her stomach, flat and taut. She had been wise not to let her belly swell with child. Now older and childless, she had regrets. Perhaps things would have been different if she had had a child with Wolf. Wolf. Not a good choice for going down memory lane. Kendall looked at the time. She should not keep Holly Park waiting too much longer.

A process server had knocked on her door late one night and Kendall had been carrying the papers around ever since, which weighed heavily on her. Luckily, Logan Burg had recommended Holly Park, a lawyer who had gone solo recently. That was all right, Kendall thought. She had gone solo, too.

The Four Seasons lobby was lush with beautiful, large flower arrangements and the hush of money. Holly took the elevator to the fourth floor and followed a sign towards the spa. She found Kendall Taylor in a cabana, reclined on a chaise for a pedicure. She had chosen a magnificent pink, perhaps coral, something that reminded her of flamingos and happier times. Kendall sipped a fruit drink and flipped through *Town & Country* while a spa attendant packed up her pedicure tools and slipped away.

Kendall laid down her magazine. Her eyes flashed green as she looked up at Holly Park, giving her the once over. "I'm Kendall," she said with a smile that gave away nothing.

Holly was intrigued instantly by the glamorous, husky-voiced woman who held out her hand. Holly didn't know whether she should shake it or bend to kiss it. Kendall motioned for Holly to sit down.

"How old are you?" Kendall inquired, kindly.

"Twenty-seven," Holly answered.

"You look sixteen."

It was a statement of fact and not a question. While Kendall was amused by Holly and took an immediate liking to her, her eyes remained neutral.

"How is it that you are a lawyer? Most girls your age are either out partying or planning a wedding."

There was a genuine curiosity which Holly didn't mind.

"After college, my father said I should get married or go to law school, and I'm not married." Holly laughed.

"Did you have a suitor?"

"No." Holly laughed again, embarrassed. "Not a real one. But through matchmaking there were several candidates."

"Matchmaking? I should have tried that." Kendall smiled. "Anyone suitable?"

Holly shook her head at the memory. "It's not so easy."

The glamorous woman suddenly brightened up and tossed her mane of golden hair and laughed, the light scent of coconut filling the air. After a moment, Holly smiled, too, both laughing easily at the common thread found.

"I had my share, too," Kendall admitted. "The first two times I married older, very wealthy men who wanted me. The third one I wanted and loved the most. That was my biggest mistake!" She laughed. "Never marry for love."

There was a frank honesty to this woman that was appealing and her laugh was infectious and disarming.

"You are so beautiful, I can see men fighting over you," Holly said simply, with the utter graciousness of truth.

Kendall accepted the compliment for the sincerity with which it was extended. She had the burnished look of a woman who, no matter what she had done to her previous husbands, and no matter how many millions she would cost them, would still stop to take her call and take her to dinner and grant whatever favor she had come to ask.

"Logan said you are Korean?" Kendall asked.

"Yes."

"Good. I need a Korean lawyer," Kendall said, settling into the chaise. "Wolf Linser is my husband," Kendall said in a tone which assumed Holly would know the social significance of the name. "Wolf Linser—husband number three—has spent the last seven years in prison—and he's still there now."

Kendall said it casually, like he was in a villa on Lake Cuomo for the season.

Holly nodded, encouraging Kendall to continue.

"I met Wolf when he was somewhere between down and out, spending the last of his charms for a bed and one more stake at the roulette table from a progressively diminishing pool of women. That pool being women who were less and less able to be selective in their escorts."

A shadow momentarily dimmed her eyes, then Kendall smiled, sadly. "Everything takes on a difference significance with time."

"What happened?"

"I was naive. I thought all men were like my previous husbands who were rich, generous, and kept me in a nice bubble. I gave to him as generously as I had received from my ex-husbands and never questioned anything. One day, I left for a business trip and when I returned he was gone. He just disappeared. He took everything I gave him and left. Expensive clothing, shoes, jewelry, money…" Her voice trailed. "Even the stables—particularly the stables—were empty. I couldn't get him on the phone. I even checked the obituaries. I waited to hear from him. I waited for some contact. For an explanation, which never came."

Kendall paused, her smooth face suddenly looking aged. "A year later, Wolf is in the society section of *Town & Country* magazine. The article described his wife, Alexis Lee, as the only child of a high society family in South Korea. Wolf was quoted in the article saying that if it weren't for his wife he would be a homeless has-been and he is eternally grateful to her. He conveniently leaves out that it was me, not this Alexis, that picked him up when he was down and out." Kendall's nostrils flared slightly. "I have the article somewhere. I'll find it. You can read it yourself."

"What did you do?"

"I did what any woman in my position would do," Kendall said. "I read the article a hundred times, studied the bitch's face, cried and took to my bed as if I had been shot through the heart."

Kendall shook as she spoke and her face paled. "I was married to the man for five years, Holly. He never mentioned he had a daughter."

She looked over to the counter. "Would you mind getting me a cup of coffee, please? Black."

It was not a question. Holly went over to the cafe area and hurried back with two coffees, anxious to hear more.

"One day he was just gone. Period. Gone without an explanation. He even took Lightning, the yearling I gave him for our third year wedding anniversary. Lightning was a special horse."

Kendall gingerly sipped at the steaming hot coffee. Her face relaxed. Holly's mental picture of this woman was of one sipping fine espresso with a lemon zest in some café in Milan or Geneva. "It's hard to accept the person you thought you knew and loved is a total stranger."

"What happened next?" Holly asked tentatively. Kendall was quiet and reflective.

"Often in life great drama is followed by... a great big fat nothing," Kendall said quietly.

"I thought I would die from a broken heart. Then, strangely, I didn't. Anyway, a year later when Wolf made the papers again—this time, for his arrest—I found out then the daughter was a stepdaughter."

Holly drew her breath in sharply.

"This Alexis woman accused Wolf of raping her daughter and she sent him to prison for fifteen years. He's served seven and has eight more to go."

She paused here and looked at Holly, coolly. "I heard from Wolf after he was arrested. He called, collect, asking me to post bail, if you can believe it."

"Did you?"

"Of course not," Kendall replied, indignant. "But I stayed on the phone with him, waiting for him to explain why he left me, but all he did was ask for money. I know when he needs something his charm comes out. But it didn't work. I didn't help him and never heard from him again. Until last week when I get this."

Kendall's eyes flashed as she handed Holly the manila envelope. "Divorce papers," she said, her lips pulled tight. "Seven years in a cell and he's still trying to put his hands in my pockets. I've barely slept since I was served these papers."

Kendall spoke softly but her eyes were mere slits. Holly felt a shiver go up her spine and she felt a little warm and faint.

"We were divorced ten years ago. I am no longer his wife. I think he did this to get a reaction out of me. Because he needs money." Kendall tossed her head and her tone was rueful. "I am telling you this perfectly horrible story for a reason. Understand that I would be the first to walk Wolf Linser to the gallows, but... something doesn't add up, Holly. Wolf is a man, and therefore weak, perhaps he is weaker than most men, yet... young girls are not his taste. I know what my men like in bed."

Kendall, as Holly was learning, was definitive. She lit a cigarette. Holly looked around to see if any of the hotel staff were about, but Kendall didn't care.

"I hired a private investigator to research the background of this Alexis Lee bitch and her daughter. The records came up blank. No records exist."

Kendall paused, dramatically, then continued. "Wolf is a precise, almost fussy man of particular tastes in cigarettes, horses, soap, folding his T-shirts, wine...very European. I know his tastes and it's not for underage girls. He is a lot of bad things but he is not that sort of predator." Kendall tossed her head. "I am absolutely convinced that Alexis Lee is not who she claims to be."

"What is it you want me to do?"

"I want you to find out why he did this silly thing of serving me with divorce papers, first of all. What it is that he really wants." Kendall leaned back and smiled. "That is the reason you will tell him you came to see him. What I *really* want is for you to find out everything you can about the bitch and his affair with her. When Wolf met her, when the affair started, how long it lasted, for starters. I want to know every fact and detail," Kendall growled.

"What will you do then?" Holly couldn't help asking.

"I will track her down, pull her hair out and scratch her eyes out. A catfight, which I assure you, will have but one winner. And it won't be that bitch."

Kendall shook her golden mane and watched the smoke of her cigarette curl and disappear. There was sadness in her eyes. "Holly, I need to know once and for all whether our entire relationship was a lie, or whether he really loved me at one point, and if so, why he left. Then I can forget about him."

Kendall stopped talking. She took a sip of her coffee and looked at Holly. Her eyes narrowed slightly, and she suddenly looked different in a way Holly didn't understand. She reached for a very expensive looking handbag and pulled out a thick manila envelope, which she slid it over to Holly.

"Since I was twelve years old, no man has ever left me. I get tired of them and move on. It's always my decision. I leave them. They don't get to leave me."

Kendall reached into her wallet and pulled out a roll of hundred dollar bills and folded them in half as she counted off a stack with her perfectly manicured nails and handed it to Holly. "You can send me a receipt and the retainer agreement." Kendall stopped and looked at Holly. "There's one more thing you need to do," Kendall added almost as an afterthought. Her face softened. Almost like velvet. Her next words were spoken barely above a whisper. She looked up, smiling. But it was not a happy smile. "I gifted Lightning to Wolf at a time I never dreamed of our marriage ending. I want Lightning back. By the time Wolf gets out of prison, Lightning will be too old to breed."

What could Holly say? She nodded her head slowly.

Kendall's voice was quiet. "It will take me about two weeks to get my files together. You'll hear from me then. In the meantime, you should familiarize yourself with Wolf's background."

Holly took a deep breath. "Is Wolf someone famous? Is he someone whose name I should know?"

"Wolf Linser is—or perhaps was—a household name in the world of equestrian sports," Kendall Taylor began. "I dreamed of the day I could have such mastery of horses and ride as artistically as he,"

Kendall said. "That was our common bond when we first got together. When I met him he was a penniless has-been. I didn't care. He was still handsome and athletic and charismatic and had a past that most men don't achieve in their entire lifetime. I respected that. He is an Olympian. Look him up."

After Holly left, Kendall Taylor lay back on her chaise and picked up her magazine and flipped through it absently then reached for her phone.

"Isn't she perfect?" the voice asked on the other end.

"Yes, Logan," Kendall Taylor answered, her voice relieved. "That was obvious within two seconds of meeting her. Wolf will trust her. Thank you."

CHAPTER 11

Kendall Taylor was right. Wolf Linser was a household name in equestrian sports and had won four Olympic medals. The photos were magnificent and Holly could see why Kendall had fallen in love with him. He was larger than life. As Holly sat in her office printing research articles, Mi Rae walked in carrying flowers from the Dumok.

"Oh my!" Holly breathed. A dozen perfect long-stemmed red roses from a florist in Beverly Hills. Even the smell of cheap Thai food drifting up through the vents could not overpower their exquisite scent and beauty. The card read, *"Thank you for your time today. It has been a long time since I met a woman whose company I enjoyed so much. Please join me for dinner tomorrow night."* There was an address and the time. The flowers somehow seemed out of place on the second-hand credenza. Holly hoped the Dumok hadn't noticed the coffee rings on her desk.

"Even roses have thorns," Kate cried, her eyes calculating.

The next night did not come quickly. Finally Holly pulled up to the blue and green valet umbrella in her black 3-series BMW coupe, a gift to herself when she got the job at Logan's firm.

It was difficult to imagine that this building had once been condemned, with boarded up windows and graffiti. Now there was new glass, wood and stone with a line of expensive cars in front. The elegant sign read *Anapji* in Korean and *Lake* in English. The graphic was a blue oval with three green dots.

Holly walked up the narrow ramp. Inside, a host greeted her, bowed low, and led Holly up a flight of winding narrow wooden stairs to a private room that overlooked the main dining hall. There was an outdoor patio shaded by palm trees surrounding a blue oval pond with three tiny green islands with dozens of floating candles. It was here at a balcony table where the Dumok sat, waiting.

The table was set with crystal and beautiful porcelain. He stood, and pulled out the chair for her. He was dressed in an exquisite suit of the darkest navy, as dark as his eyes, with a white shirt and a somber charcoal gray tie.

"The roses are so lovely. Thank you." The words tumbled out and Holly blushed, feeling shy. But the floating candles had a calming, hypnotic effect and Holly quickly felt herself relaxing in the Dumok's company.

"The design is an homage to an ancient Korean kingdom of a thousand years ago called Silla," the Dumok explained as they got settled. "Perhaps even older, long before the Joseon era. The pond, which is replicated here, served as a place of repose for poets. The King ordered that cups of wine be floated in the water, to inspire the quiet of the mind that poetry requires."

Holly nodded and took a deep breath and looked around. Dozens of tiny plates appeared by servers wearing *hanbok*—traditional Korean dress,—the women bowing low, invisible yet ever present.

"The design is authentic to the Korean tradition yet utterly modern in execution, a place of repose for all," the Dumok continued.

He sat back, studying Holly. She was natural, not at all shy, and certainly pretty, but without the hard edge often found together with great beauty. Most of all, though, it was her enthusiasm for life which he found attractive, for it was something he had lost long ago. Now, unexpectedly, the smallest flame flickered inside, and he was both amazed and curious about the girl who had lit it.

"If you don't mind me asking," the Dumok started, "how is it that you ended up at American Legal Services?"

The Dumok was polite in that very formal distancing way but his eyes were kind and concerned, and there was no malice in his question.

"Wh-what do you m-mean?" Holly stammered.

"Kate Hong is an immigration broker. She charges exorbitant fees to fill out basic immigration forms," the Dumok told her. When Holly looked up in puzzlement, the Dumok laughed in amazement. "Don't you know that? Kate Hong's only ability is that she can speak Korean to an illiterate clientele and English to the American attorneys she uses—and with immigration filings, it can take years for the mistakes to show up."

Holly shook her head and felt her face flush. "I didn't know that."

"Be careful," the Dumok warned. "People will have a bad impression if they think you work for that woman."

Holly's head jerked back. Her father had said the same thing. The small church where Holly spent her childhood was beside the freeway and served as a portal, the first sign of Korean settlement to the latest arrivals. They wandered in, heads bowed, looking for help and hope. The red brick church fit into the backdrop of the littered and troubled streets. It would have been easily overlooked but for the large red cross on the roof that lit up the blackness of the night. It was a lifeline for those searching for salvation or a handout. Tales of weariness, regret, longing, hope and disappointment were told in hushed whispers at a time when no one else cared or listened. Of those who came through the doors, some were ruthless and self-centered, interpreting kindness as weakness, their heads bowed in false humility while their furtive eyes darted around seeing what was there for the taking. They stayed, while their children went to public schools and learned to speak English with oddly stilted phraseology and carefully rounded vowels. These new immigrants were predictable. At the first sign of affluence they left the church as quickly as they came, peeling out of the parking lot for what they hoped was the very last time.

Pastor Park did not weigh intent. Modest meals of Korean soup and rice, instant coffee, oranges, and slices of watermelon were served each week, and an ear lent without judgment. There were others seeking fellowship and they were lifted. Somehow there were just enough of the faithful who stayed to make the soup and rice, sweep the floors, give guidance, and comfort those in need.

The Dumok had done his research on Holly Park and was attracted to her uncomplicated upbringing. He was weary of the artifice of his world and in Holly he found an innocence that he wanted to be a part of again. They talked. He enjoyed her lightness of heart, her rhythm and her ease as she moved from topic to topic.

"You don't know the world at all, dearest Holly," the Dumok said, amused, his eyes assessing her. "The poor rarely go uptown, but the rich will inevitably end up on the wrong side of town through curiosity, perversity—or sheer bad luck."

He scowled and reached for another cigarette and lit it.

His voice had a soft texture that drew her in. The deference and formality of the servers to her host made Holly realize she was the guest of someone who had a reputation and status she did not know. Light classical music played in the background.

"Have you noticed the streets of Koreatown resemble Dante's concentric circles of hell?" The Dumok asked. "The immigrant hell, of course, dreaming of freedom in America yet still constrained by the culture they left behind. Have you ever thought that when you enter this part of town, you have officially left America?"

Holly looked over to the rundown apartment buildings lining the streets. It was in these tired buildings the immigrants lived, moving around in their shadow world with blinkered vision, preoccupied with their misery and the squalor that absorbed them. Holly knew very well. She saw it in the church every week.

"Because the freedom they imagined in America is unfamiliar," Holly said, "so they begin to long for the comforts of home and they come back to Koreatown, searching." Holly found the Dumok's narrative intriguing and tried not to say anything that would break his mood, wanting to understand him.

"You were born in America so you are comfortable in your own skin, which means you don't feel the pressures immigrants feel. You sit here tonight with your polite manners, composure and charming speech. You politely pick at your plate but are not interested in the food at all. When I came to your office, I was looking for a lawyer. Instead, I find myself in the presence of a lovely girl. Your head is full of law and schooling but in some ways you know nothing."

It was then the Dumok reached into his briefcase and pulled out a manila envelope. "A retainer. There is ten thousand dollars. There is more if you need it." As he handed Holly the envelope their fingers brushed. At this slightest touch Holly felt a sudden rush of need, want, and longing deep inside. Perhaps he sensed this, perhaps he felt it too, because in the next moment the Dumok was almost abrupt as he said, "Shall we go?"

The glow of the lanterns cast shadows across the patio and they blew softly in the breeze. The Dumok reached over and brushed the windblown strands of hair away from Holly's face. The Dumok was a man's man, yet now, with the touch of his hands so gentle and light brushing against her skin, Holly could barely imagine the same hands in combat. The duality of the lightness in his touch against the jagged scar on his neck was exciting. Holly smiled inwardly, basking in his presence, wondering how the idea of his hands could be so sexy. It wasn't his hands. It was him.

"Go home, now," The Dumok's voice was quiet but decided as they left the restaurant. "Thank you for your company," he said. Holly could feel the warmth of his breath inches away. The Dumok reached down and kissed Holly lightly and then he was gone. Holly stroked her cheek where he had kissed her, stroking the spot where his lips had touched her.

Holly drove home, her head swimming with unanswerable questions, her heart filled with exuberance and the ache of the unknown. The streets were deserted. Two blocks away she saw a black and white squad car, parked, hiding and waiting, like a grizzly bear near a river scooping out salmon. The drunks never had a chance on this side of town. When Holly got home, she went to the kitchen and washed the coffee mug she had used that morning. She looked around. There was nothing else to do, so Holly went to bed but she couldn't sleep. She didn't know what it was but she couldn't stop thinking about the Dumok. She wondered whether it was about the scar or the sadness in his eyes that made her feel that way.

CHAPTER 12

"Can you join me for lunch?"

Holly had been walking out the door the next morning when the Dumok called.

"Yes, of course," she said excitedly. Immediately after the call Holly went back into her apartment and changed into her nicest black suit. Holly had trouble concentrating at work but finally it was time.

The street suddenly turned wider and the center divider became as broad as the roads. There were manicured lawns and palm trees waving high above. Everything looked bright, clean, spacious. Even the cars and light posts and street signs looked different.

"Oh, we are in Beverly Hills!" Holly exclaimed. While Holly's best friend Heather Hart hung out in Beverly Hills, for Holly it was her first time. The Dumok stopped at an alley on Dayton Way, a half block from Rodeo Drive. A valet opened the door. The sign read *Grill on the Alley*.

They walked down a few steps to a subterranean level. The restaurant was mostly white, with dark wood booths on three walls and tables in the middle. Opalescent glass further separated the booths for privacy. The linen was crisp white with black napkins, but the most impressive were dozens of perfectly framed and placed small sketches and watercolors on the walls. The variety was such that the collection could only have been accumulated over many years.

"It's a pleasure to have you back, sir," the host said as he showed the Dumok to one of the best tables in the restaurant.

An hour later their lunch plates were cleared away and they were relaxed.

The Dumok swirled his wineglass, contemplating the deep yet soft red and watched the translucent glycerin edges curve on the glass like waves breaking on the shore.

Holly was like the glycerin, he decided. She was translucent, about to skim the surface of his dark and rich past. The Dumok hesitated, enjoying her sweet smile and excitement. He realized he enjoyed her company and wanted to hang on to the moment, but the food was finished and the time had come.

The Dumok looked at Holly, the past separating them like the glass partitions that separated the dining booths, the light and shadows dancing on the outside but the details blocked by the white walls.

"Nara Song is my wife," The Dumok said, then immediately regretted his brusqueness. Holly's feelings for him were so transparent.

Holly's heart thumped in her chest, but she waited patiently for the Dumok to continue. The Dumok took a deep sip of wine, inhaling the rich perfume, and drank, his eyes flashing darkly. "Many years ago, I was the senior aide to a highly respected—and much feared— Ambassador in Korea. An imposing figure. Stern, quiet. I felt like I was being judged with a glance. Always formal and gracious but you never entered the room without being sure you had every possible answer ready in your back pocket. His mild disapproval was scarier than a regular person's rage, and could be communicated with a simple motion of his eyebrows or a change in his breathing. I learned to recognize the warning signs early on."

As the Dumok spoke, his face changed colors, from the clearest sake to the darkest vanilla-charred bourbon cask. "He asked my opinion on serious matters and always gave me his full attention and listened carefully, never interrupting until I was finished, whether or not my analysis was sound. If I was off base, he would find a way to make me discover the mistake myself, for which I was grateful."

Holly hung on to every word. She remained silent, afraid to break his mood of reflection, to lose this chance to understand the river flowing under the ice.

"Rumor had it he was quite fond of me. Trust was built from days of sitting in hotels and conference rooms and plane rides from one continent to another. I became his confidante and he in turn won my loyalty and trust. Nonetheless, it was still a great surprise when the Ambassador assigned his daughter to me and she became my charge."

The Dumok paused. The server poured more wine.

"Do you know of the late French film director Jean-Pierre Melville?"

Holly shook her head.

"Well, the quote I am thinking of is, *'Where there are two, one will betray.'* Melville had been in the war, and France was full of betrayal in those days. It is this quote that made me ponder my own relationship with the Ambassador. He was as wily and complex a man as I've ever known. I wonder, even after twenty years, who betrayed who?"

A dark cloud passed over the Dumok's face, but he continued. "Nara Song came from the kind of family who would arrange her marriage to an equally influential family. She was the only daughter of the Ambassador, and she was as wild and willful as she was learned and beautiful. My 'assignment' was to escort her to parties, galas and balls—and keep suitors away. She had no shortage of suitors with whom she toyed for amusement. She became weary of my interfering and resorted to pouting and defiance, and when that didn't work, she did the one thing I hadn't prepared myself for. She turned her charms on me. Soon enough I found myself drinking too much and having transient affairs with inappropriate women to distract myself. In short, I wanted her—and of course she knew it."

"Yes, of course," Holly said softly.

The Dumok smile ruefully. "That made things worse. Now that she knew she had my attention, Nara tortured me endlessly."

Holly fidgeted uncomfortably.

"One night, I had finished playing cards with a couple of my colleagues when she showed up in my room."

Holly stiffened, apprehensive of what was to come. The Dumok paused, searching Holly's face, but then continued.

"You're just a voyeur!" she taunted me with all the contempt a young girl can muster. "All you do is watch me. You don't do anything! You must not be a man. A real man would have done something by now.'"

Holly gasped. She couldn't help herself.

The Dumok shrugged with resignation. "She was absolutely maddening. I was fed up with her. Truly. She was exciting, infuriating, and demanding and I was under her spell. You can imagine the rest. There is nothing new under the sun. Soon her belly swelled. Finally, I mustered the courage to present myself to the Ambassador and tell him the news. Of course, I would do the honorable thing and ask for her hand in marriage."

Holly smiled slightly. "Of course."

"I was determined to marry her, not out of obligation, but because I was so damned besotted. I was tortured at having betrayed the Ambassador's trust and feared that I would gain a wife and lose a career with the same stroke of the sword. I was shaking when I talked to him."

"I have trouble believing that."

"Believe it. I was younger then, and yes, I was shaking. When I went to tell him, the Ambassador's face betrayed nothing. Judgment Day will come and his face will be stone, that one. I still remember as if it were yesterday. He walked to the sideboard and poured two drinks and gazed at me with his hard stone eyes. It was an election year and he did not want a scandal."

Holly nodded, clasping her hands.

"The pregnancy could not be hidden," the Dumok continued. "Nara was too far along. It was decided that I would be dispatched to Taiwan for one year. He had been thinking of it anyway. There was plenty of trouble between Taiwan and the mainland over our relationship with

Taiwan. While I was gone, Nara would quietly have our child. I remember drinking a toast to his future grandchild." The Dumok paused, reflecting. "I married Nara on Saturday and left for Taiwan on Monday."

The Dumok's mouth was a tight thin line. His hard eyes caught the glint of the light from a chandelier. He stared out into vast nothingness. "A year later," he continued, "I went back to Seoul to commence my married life and greet my child, only to find that I had been discharged from my position. I was also notified that my wife and my child had died during childbirth. Apparently, the news of their deaths had been withheld so as to not interfere with my performance of official duties."

Holly gasped.

"Korea after the war was exactly like that." The Dumok leaned forward. "The Korea of my youth...was hardened like a piece of burnt glass that you might pull out of a fire that has been melted and burned over and over again."

He pinged the edge of his wineglass with his finger, the perfect ringing sound faded slowly. His eyes flashed darkly as he stared into his empty glass. "That would have been the end of it — except the rumors that she was alive have never died."

The Dumok gestured silently for the bill. "I would like to bury them once and for all."

He folded his napkin on the table and rose. "Shall we walk a little and work off the lunch? I'm sorry I talked so long to say so little."

Holly smiled. She didn't mind. Given the choice, she would happily sit at the Dumok's table and listen to his stories for hours.

The Dumok and Holly walked towards Rodeo Drive, admiring the window display of Louis Vuitton next-door, pretty scenes of hot air balloons floating over the Ile St. Louis in Paris. Then, the Dumok surprised Holly by going inside.

"May I help you?" asked a salesgirl in a black blazer and slacks.

"May I see that one, please," the Dumok said, pointing.

It was the most exquisite handbag Holly had ever seen. Holly picked up the purse tenderly and stroked the beautiful leather.

"It's a monogram *vernis* leather and closes with a padlock," the salesgirl explained, "a classic of the House." There was a distinct perfume of expensive leather. "This one is Indian rose. It comes in four different colors." Holly peeked at the price tag and quickly handed it back.

"May I see that other one, please? The...smaller...red one?"

"The color is *pomme d'amour,*" the salesgirl said in her modulated tone. Holly peeked at the tag again. How could a handbag cost so much? It was more than three month's rent! Holly looked at the smaller handbag. Two month's rent, definitely.

"Why don't you pick one you like?" the Dumok asked. Holly politely declined, insisting she did not want such an extravagant gift, but the Dumok would not be dissuaded. In the end, Holly was careful to select the most inexpensive handbag she could find in the store, a lovely Speedy monogram handbag, insisting it was her absolute favorite.

"A little business next, if you can bear my company just a little longer?" The Dumok smiled at Holly. It was impossible to say no.

They drove to San Pedro, the port near Long Beach, and parked at the wharf, where a cargo container of very expensive cars was being loaded. The load included 7 Series BMWs, AMG Mercedes, Porsche 911s, a Panamera, and a four door Maserati. The last was a Bentley coupe in a dark green. The Dumok read over the manifest and signed off. He turned to Holly and said, "I am going to Seoul for a couple of weeks. The green Bentley is mine. I like to take it when I travel. One of my many idiosyncrasies."

"Thank you for such a truly magical day!" Holly piped happily as The Dumok pulled up outside her office and she climbed out. Holly waved until the car was out of sight. There was pure exuberance in her heart as she pushed open the door.

Kate Hong's bright, electric eyes swept over the handbag, at once mocking and dismissive.

"An entry level Louis Vuitton," she sniffed. "He bought you the cheap bag." Kate turned away with one of her infamous glances. It was so Kate Hong. "It will end badly, if you get involved with him," Kate said in her imperious way. "Mark my words."

Holly ignored Kate and walked down the hallway with her new handbag. Kate's laughter followed like the sound of tinkling bells.

CHAPTER 13

Kate Hong was not happy. Holly hadn't said a word about her lunch with the Dumok and instead closed the door to her office and had not resurfaced for the past two hours. Kate slipped Mi Rae a twenty-dollar bill to report any phone calls or visits from the Dumok. Kate said nothing to Mi Rae about the missing photo. "Watch Holly like a hawk," is all Kate had said. Then, Kate called Choi. "You didn't come today? I need those passports."

Choi mumbled something incoherent.

"Have you eaten?" Kate asked. "Let's go out tonight. I need to get those passports and pay you anyway."

"Okay," I'll pick you up," Choi said.

They went to a hole-in-the-wall restaurant on Oxford Street. It turned out to be a bad choice. It was crowded and the tables were not being bussed, despite the long line of people who were in front of them waiting. There was no hostess. There wasn't even a sign-in sheet. However, it was, as Kate could tell from the pictures of plastic food taped to the window, still cheap. Kate pressed her arms to her sides, stiffly, her nose tilted upward. One look at Kate spoke volumes. It was clear that she was past eating at old haunts. Plus, Holly Park, the nobody, having been taken to Beverly Hills for lunch and shopping by the Dumok was simply too much for Kate.

"I feel like lobster and prime rib," Kate insisted, pouting. Choi studiously ignored the remark, fixating on the menu on the wall with even greater intensity.

"Let's go to Lawry's Prime Rib over in Beverly Hills." Kate's voice was loud, and bright. She spoke in a way that everyone around her could hear, her bullying beauty ever present.

Choi sighed. It was in his interest to keep things sweet with Kate. "That's a fine idea," he said as graciously as he could manage. He had no energy to battle Kate, and if he angered her, she might change her mind about paying him for the passports. But having got her way, Kate's entire personality changed instantly.

"How delicious!" she exclaimed, as if she hadn't just bullied the change of plans. Kate put her hand through Choi's arm. "How I love Beverly Hills!"

Kate's mood shimmered over dinner. She carried the conversation in her bright, lively tone as she murmured over the thick cut of prime rib, poked at the lobster with her fork, and clapped her hands with delight at the spinning salad bowl, and soaked up the last bits of gravy and mashed potatoes with an extra helping of Yorkshire pudding.

"That's quite an appetite you have," Choi said with sincere admiration.

"We are in Beverly Hills!" It was her one opportunity and Kate ordered the most expensive items on the menu, planning to take the leftovers to lunch in the Lawry's take-out container for the girls to see the next day.

Choi ate a few thin slices of the admittedly excellent beef and his salad. He was a fussy eater at best, and this American restaurant was not his style, but it paid to go along with Kate. Choi watched Kate with a quiet absorption. Kate was fire. She had been since they were lovers. But that had been a long time ago. He appreciated the heat and the beauty of the flame. Despite their long history, for every stroke of the metronome, their beat came up the same. Kate eyed Choi between mouthfuls of prime rib. When he finally relaxed a little she slipped him an envelope with the cash for the passports. He relaxed even more, and actually sat back against the booth, smiling. The moment was right.

"The Dumok has hired Holly Park, the new lawyer in my office," Kate piped, her eyes dancing. The mention of the Dumok, spoken aloud, seemed to release a coil deep inside Choi. His face disclaimed any knowledge, and he continued eating but his smile vanished.

"He wants her to find someone named Nara Song."

Kate was like that. She liked to poke at embers to see what might catch fire. Choi had said nothing about having missed her at her office, or about the photo Kate was sure he had stolen. She wanted to know why. Choi took another bite of prime rib.

"I wonder who Nara Song is?" Kate said in her bright, metallic voice. "Perhaps a *domi*? But then, the gangsters would go after her. The Dumok would not need a lawyer for that."

There was still no reaction, but Kate knew Choi too well. He wasn't reacting, so she pushed a little more, her eyes fastened on his face, watching closely, and tried a different angle. Kate needled in her clear bright voice. "Holly Park is a nobody and speaks Korean like a four year old child."

Kate mimicked Holly's bad Korean then laughed, harshly. When Choi didn't laugh with her, Kate's tone changed. "Actually, the Dumok is quite clever in selecting her as his lawyer," Kate tried again, in her calculating way. "Nobody would suspect that she is doing anything useful. Holly may actually be close to finding Nara Song, too."

Choi picked up a fork and turned it around and around in his hand, rhythmically. Kate tossed a glance, and her eyes sparkled in victory. She had hit on something big. But it turned out to be the wrong thing to say. The coil deep inside Choi released. Even Kate Hong could not anticipate what happened next. In fact, she was too busy talking to notice. Choi moved around the booth to the other side where Kate was sitting and reached over and grabbed her by the arm.

"What are you doing?" Kate looked up, alarmed. "Let go of me! You're hurting me!"

"We're leaving!" Choi shouted.

"Lower your voice, please," Kate hissed. "You are embarrassing me."

"I said we're leaving."

"Let go—"

"Now!" Choi pulling Kate up, and knocking over a waiter. Glass shattered. Onlookers stared at the commotion but Choi didn't care. He tightly held Kate's arm as he led her through the tables. towards the exit.

"Let go of me!" Kate wrenched herself out of Choi's grip. "What is wrong with you?"

"Leave it alone, for god's sake," Choi thundered. "Please, just leave it alone."

Onlookers moved away nervously. Kate yanked her arm loose from his grasp, straightened herself and marched out, head held high, stopping only to grab a handful of after dinner mints on the way out. As mad as Kate was, Choi knew that part of her still enjoyed the drama.

Outside the restaurant Kate turned to Choi, eyes blazing. "I was kidding!" Kate cried as she swung at him. Kate's voice was metallic, loud and accusatory. "Holly didn't really find Nara Song! Can't you take a joke?"

"Let me guess," Kate continued, unable to let it go. "You screwed Nara Song, too, like you did me, once upon a time, playing the big shot to a helpless and innocent girl new to this country, and Nara Song turned out to be the Dumok's girl. That's it!" Kate laughed wildly, like a hyena, pelting after dinner mints at him. She should have let it go. But Kate Hong could never let anything go. "Let me guess. You're afraid of the Dumok because you screwed her. The big, bad Dumok, well, you should have kept it zipped!"

Kate's laughter rang into the night air. She was throwing blind but hitting soft spots.

"Just—shut up."

But Kate wouldn't. Choi was grim. He could not afford to have Holly—or anyone—snooping into his past.

"Call Holly Park. Now," Choi said, his voice quiet. "Tell her whatever you need to, but we'll pick her up. Just follow my lead."

It was the quiet in Choi's voice that scared Kate. She opened her mouth then shut it and did as she was told. Kate was quiet all the way to Holly's place, full of trepidation. She had never seen Choi like this.

"Where we going?" Holly asked, climbing in. Kate made the introduction, but gave no explanation except that it was urgent.

It was an eerie ride. Choi drove stiffly and Kate, silent. They got downtown quickly. On Mission Street Choi pulled into the parking lot of a large red brick and gray stone building and spoke briefly into his cell phone then hung up. The sign in front of the building read

County of Los Angeles, Department of Coroner.

Holly's eyes widened and she looked at Choi with surprise, questioning. Kate sat quietly with her arms crossed. Holly could tell they'd had a fight, but about what? What was their relationship? Choi got out. Holly and Kate followed quietly into the morgue.

The interior looked like a 1930s hotel, with an ornate staircase with art deco rails and marble floors and walls. The furniture was reproduction Mission. The architecture looked contemporaneous with the older courthouses Holly knew so well. A sign *read City Morgue— Quiet Please.*

Choi turned to Holly. "You are here because you need to know the kind of man the Dumok really is. No one should have to witness in their lifetime what I am about to show you."

Kate stood a little apart, with that superior look, but she shot a questioning glance that Choi ignored. It was after hours. The three stood awkwardly, waiting.

"Good evening, Choi." It was the night coroner. He was a tall very thin man with gray hair, wearing a lab coat. Choi had called in a serious favor to get them in the morgue that late.

"Come this way," the night coroner said.

"The coroner received the body this morning," Choi's voice clipped coolly as he explained. The three followed the night coroner in a single file, silent. Kate filled with regret of what she had started, and warily apprehensive of the immediate unknown.

They turned into a stark, cold room of aluminum furniture with walls lined with metal drawers. The night coroner pointed to a table. Choi walked over and looked at the body and motioned for Holly. The faintest grimace crossed his face.

Holly gingerly peered, steeling herself. But no one could prepare for what Holly was about to see.

"Not fresh," the night coroner said. "He was gutted at least a month ago, his intestines were falling out when we received the body. Also he was strangled."

"Tortured?"

"You can call it that. Alive when his intestines were cut out."

Holly felt herself breathing hard and her knees weaken. Choi grabbed Holly's arm, steadying her. Holly wrenched herself free.

"They called him The Enforcer," Choi said. "He is one of the Dumok's men. This is what the Dumok does to his own people. They say once you know too much, he gets rid of you. This is what the Dumok will do to you, and then to your family. This is how he repays loyalty. He will do this to Nara Song when he finds her. You will be next. Why do you think the Dumok came to you this time, instead of his fancy team of expensive lawyers? Because someone like you will not be missed after you disappear."

Holly's face went white. Choking and retching, she turned and ran out of the room with her hands covering her mouth.

"He will do this to your father and mother, too!" Choi called after Holly.

"That's enough," Kate cried.

Choi led Kate out of the building. The whole visit had taken less than two minutes.

Choi lit a cigarette and turned to offer one to Holly, but she was throwing up in the alley.

Down the street, in a blacked out SUV, Detective Mick Chang held his camera with the long lens as steady as he could and clicked the shutter. He watched through the lens. Click. Click. Click. Click.

The Enforcer had more visitors in death than in life, Mick thought. Chasing the Dumok was like hunting a ghost in fog while wearing sunglasses. Mick rummaged through the back seat for the file and studied the photo. Holly Park. Yes, it was her. Now he had caught on camera the Dumok's latest attorney identifying the body, and two others he didn't yet know.

Click.

Click.

How do you connect dots when there aren't any? Finally, he had connected a dot with perhaps more to come. Mick watched as the car pulled away. He put down his camera and looked at the time. Miller time. He wanted to call Mix, but no. It was something he hadn't done in years.

"Are you ready to call it off?" Choi asked into the back seat where Holly was sitting. He was parked outside of Holly's apartment. There was no answer. The shock had been too much. Holly had fainted.

"Honestly. You really take things too far," Kate said.

"Take her inside," Choi said. "Tell her it was for her own sake."

"I don't think you need to worry about Holly now," Kate said as she got out of the car and opened the back door to rouse Holly. Holly suddenly came awake. She was drained and holding on with the last bit of strength.

While Kate helped Holly into her apartment, Choi brooded. Stupid Kate, her eyes were always bigger than her stomach. And he had burned a big favor to scare off Holly.

The truth was that Choi and Kate were simply jackals, following the lion at a safe distance, hoping for scraps from its jaws. But Choi was much smarter than Kate Hong. He knew it was better to be the hunter than the prey.

CHAPTER 14

Detective Mick Chang walked into a bar off Alvarado Street. He was in his early thirties, tall, lean and muscular with a cowlick of thick black hair that fell over his eye. It was always during these times when he was alone at a bar that his thoughts turned to how the Dumok had cheated him and stolen his best friend.

The only lighting in the dive bar was cheesy red hot-pepper shaped lights that had been once put up for a cinco de mayo party and never taken down. Bad country music groaned from a 1970's vintage jukebox in the corner. The bar didn't even offer draft. In the farthest corner of the bar was an electronic poker machine.

The only décor was promotional posters for various American beers and a *Sports Illustrated* swimsuit edition calendar still showing August 1986.

Mick Chang sat. He'd seen worse bars on military bases in Afghanistan. He looked down at his arm and rubbed his tattoo. USMC—The United States Marine Corp. The few. The proud. The brave. Mick laughed ruefully. U-Signed-the-Mother-Fucking-Contract is what it really stood for. His humor turned sour. Yes, he had signed on impulse. He was pissed when his father ran out on the family leaving him to take care of his mother and sick sister—and then the Dumok had pissed him off. Then there was Mix. Fucking Mix. Mix usually went along with whatever he wanted, something Mick had gotten used to, until the Dumok came along. That was when everything changed.

Mick drank his beer and his thoughts wander back to when he had first met Mix, saved his ass from a beating, and given him his nickname. All in one day. Didn't that count for anything?

How many years ago was it now since Mick had decided to cut through that high school football field? He didn't want to be late getting home. It was quicker than waiting for the crowded bus. He jogged easily through the school yard. He was fifteen years old and tall for his age. He was not particularly big but he was wiry and quick and his child's body was fast maturing into a man. He turned a corner and saw three boys huddled over a shape. As he got closer it looked like a huddled boy, deflecting punches and struggling beneath blows.

The boy on the ground was Micah Jones. School for him was the same every day. He had no friends. Every day, he took out the lunch his mama had made him so carefully and sat by himself away from the other kids. His lunch was sticky rice flecked with flakes of Spam and carrot wrapped with seaweed, sticky anchovies, and sesame seed crackers. He took out his chopsticks and began to eat when several Korean boys came up behind him, laughing.

"Ever see a nigger use chopsticks before?" the first one said in Korean. Micah lowered his head even more and hunched his shoulders, hoping they would walk away.

"See, he understands everything," another boy said, eyeing Micah with curiosity.

"He's confused," the ringleader said in English, then flipped Micah's lunch box upside down, the food rolling across the table.

"I never saw a nigger who can't speak English," one taunted.

Micah kept his head down, and stared at the floor.

"A yell-ah nigg-ah—go figure. Hey, that rhymes!" The third boy laughed. They all high fived each other and took turns taking an airslap to his head. Now, off the school grounds, the attack turned physical.

Mick came closer. He recognized the tallest kid. It was Sam Kim. He had seen him at karate tournaments. Sam could fight, but Mick was not afraid.

"Hey, Sam, did you ditch math? Three on one ain't fair."

The boys turned and looked at Mick, keen on fresh meat. The turtled shape on the ground looked up. Through the blood on his face and cut lip, Mick saw mongoloid features—and almost negroid skin.

Sam Kim turned, his arms loose at his sides and looked Mick over. "You train at Blackbelt USA, I saw you at the Orange County tournament."

"Sure." Mick let his backpack slide easily to the ground. He was still warm from his workout. He would be fine. The boy on the ground sat up. He wasn't small, but against three he had taken a beating.

"You like Master Lee?"

"Sure. He teaches us to fight hard, but fair." Mick had added the "fair" part deliberately.

Sam Kim thought for a minute, then jerked his chin towards the street. "Let's get some noodles," he said to his buddies. "We were done anyways." The bullies walked away, laughing. They never looked back. Three on two wasn't as much fun as three on one.

The boy on the ground wiped his face on the tail of his shirt and sat up. Under the blood and mud he was still half black and half Korean.

Mick pulled a bottle of water from his backpack and a small workout towel and tossed them. The boy drank from it gratefully, and wiped his face with the towel.

"Anything broken?" Mick asked in English.

"No," the boy answered in Korean. "I fight regular enough. I can take two but not three."

"Bro, what's your name?"

"Micah Jones."

"Dude, you talk like an F.O.B. Do you know what that means? Fresh-off-the-boat."

"The Korean kids don't like me much and the brothers don't like me neither."

"Hey, I've seen you around school," Mick said, bouncing on his toes, making shadow boxing moves. "I'm gonna call you Mix. Cuz you're all mixed up, man," Mick joked. "I was thinking of calling you Mixed-Up Jones but that's too long."

"Mix" smiled hesitantly, peering out of the corner of his eyes.

"And you'd best follow me around at school and stay out of trouble," Mick said, doing upper cuts and jabs in the air. "Where the fuck are you from anyways? Are you really Korean, dude?"

Mix answered in Korean. "I came from Korea. But I don't speak English good yet."

Mick paused, not knowing what to say next. "Dude, when you speak Korean you sound like my grandma, but your English sucks. I'll look for you, dude. Shit, gotta go. I have to meet my mom." Mick jogged away. "See you."

"See you." Mix raised his arm and waved and stood there watching until Mick disappeared into the distance. He carefully pulled from his backpack the sesame crackers he had saved from lunch. He looked inside the zip lock bag. The crackers were only slightly broken.

The noise of the bar broke into Mick's thoughts. He ordered another beer. The bar was full of men milling around, noisy, loud, frustrated, with nowhere to displace their energy and frustrations. A hoot of laughter came from behind and Mick looked up to see a Mexican, standing, hands on hips and legs apart, clad in a saggy jeans and a close fitting white tank top that partially covered his tattooed skin. The man was staring at him.

"You say something, man?" Mick challenged.

"I said there's a gook in here."

Chang slid off the bar stool slowly.

"I'm not gook. Gooks were in Vietnam. You don't look old enough to have been in Vietnam. In fact you would have peed your pants in Vietnam, because those little gooks are tougher than any Mexican."

The Mexican swung. Mick jigged his head to one side to make him miss. Now the Mexican was off balance and Mick drilled his ribs with a left and followed up with a right to the jaw. The Mexican's head snapped back before he dropped like a sack. Of course one of his friends jumped forward. It was simply the wrong day.

Mick had long ago discovered the pain he carried was only

released when his fists flew out and he heard the cracking sound of contact against skin. It was only the sight, taste and smell of blood that could rid him of the heated rage inside. It was only when his fists flew and the punches meted out in mutual combat he felt like an equal and his fists became his ticket to social superiority.

"Bring it on! Bring it on! Who's next? Who's next?!" Mick was braying, pacing, fists clenched, his eyes shining bright.

I never saw a wild thing feel sorry for itself. A small bird will drop frozen dead from a bough without ever having felt sorry for itself. Mick thought about the D.H. Lawrence poem, told to him by his old gunnery sergeant. Mick always thought about the poem when he started feeling that way. Like right now. Fucking Mix.

If Mix had been with him, this never would have happened. They had been best friends and had each other's backs until the Dumok had shown up. Some best friend. Now, Mix was loyal as a dog to the Dumok, something that royally pissed him off. Mick would still be there, too, if he had been treated right. But Mick felt cheated. He had helped the Dumok from the ground up, sneaking *domis* over the borders in the middle of the night, and dropping money off to the crooked politicians. One day the Dumok and Mick argued. That very day he stormed off and signed up for the Marines.

Fuck everybody, Mick thought. He moistened his lip. He could taste blood. He looked at the time. Now, all he wanted was some hot chow and his bed. He hit the drive-thru and ordered a dozen tacos. Driving home, his thoughts again wandered to the Dumok, the man who had taken his best friend away and his resentment grew. He drove past the parking lot of a bar then pulled in when he noticed a pretty Latina in a tight peach colored dress fumbling with her keys. She dropped them, then wobbled in her high heels as she tried to bend down. She stood up again to hike up her skirt. It was just too tight.

"Let me." Mick deftly bent down and scooped up her keys and handed them to her. She was prettier than he expected, with a ripe body, but young.

"If you get in your car I'll have to pull you over." He glanced at her tired Civic. "You've had too much to drink."

The girl smiled nervously.

"If it's not far, I'll drop you. You can get your car tomorrow."

"Thank you. It's not far."

They got into Mick's undercover SUV. "Why are you partying on a Tuesday?" he asked. "Shouldn't you be home?"

"I just needed to get out of the house. My stepfather is a trucker. He just came home. The walls are thin. You know the drill." She shrugged, her resignation sadder than anger would have been.

"How'd you get the split lip?" the Latina asked. There was concern in her eyes. Mick smiled and tentatively reached over for her hand. She didn't stop him. He stroked her hand as they drove in silence. She let him until they pulled into a dark parking spot in front of a rundown, low-rise apartment building. The girl unsnapped her seat belt and leaned over and kissed him. She didn't want to go inside, yet. She looked up and they made eye contact.

"Thanks," she said.

"Don't mention it."

"I work. I'm saving my money to open a hair salon. I'll get out of this town, you'll see. I'm not like most girls, I just like to party sometimes."

She smoothed the front of her dress and popped an orange Tic-Tac as she opened the door. "Thanks for the ride."

She got out of his car. He watched her until she was safely through the front door of the apartment.

She turned and waved. He shook his head. These girls never got out of anywhere. Mick drove home in a more somber mood than usual, chewing his cold tacos.

A few months later, the pretty Latina girl turned up dead at one of his crime scenes. A shoot-out between the rival drug dealers. It was a stray bullet. Mick had seen dead girls before, in Afghanistan. Once, he had been in an APC when a civilian car in front of him hit a land mine and blew up. A girl was injured, but not dead, her leg blown off. He saw the locals dump her in the river and drive off. After that, he thought nothing could upset him.

Mick Chang knelt down beside the body and realized who it was. When no one was looking he took the pink ribbon from her hair and hid it in the palm of his hand. He didn't look in her purse to find out her name. He didn't want to know her name. He didn't want to say that he knew where she lived, because he didn't know her. He didn't know jack.

Later, he tied the pink ribbon to the belt loop of his favorite old jeans. It stayed there for a long time.

CHAPTER 15

Choi knew why the Dumok was looking for Nara Song. The Dumok wanted the truth about what had happened to his child. And if the Dumok ever found Nara, Choi would be blamed, because he had been part it. It was certain and simple. Choi also knew that the Dumok was no longer the same easygoing person he was when they were classmates and rivals at Seoul National University. He didn't want to think about what the Dumok would do to him if he found out the truth. For that reason alone, Holly Park must never find Nara Song.

Choi remembered the Dumok very well. They had been classmates and rivals at a time everyone called the Dumok by a made-up Korean name, because and no one could pronounce his true French name. Choi also knew the true reason that the Dumok left South Korea was because he had killed a man in a fit of rage over Nara Song. The rivalry that had consumed him for so many years seemed insignificant now. That was a long time ago. Today Choi felt every minute of his age.

When the Dumok returned to Seoul, he reported for duty only to discover his wife and child had died in childbirth and he had been terminated from his position. Choi knew because he was assigned to deliver the news. Choi did, but while doing so he couldn't help but add a lie. A small lie meant to be merely malicious and inconsequential, but it had ended up causing the death of an innocent man. The Dumok was thirty-five years old and suddenly found himself at the end of his career. As inevitably as the tides, the Dumok took the news hard and was ruined overnight, numbing his pain with alcohol and in the arms of women, the only solace of which he found himself worthy. A few weeks of debauchery makes a man feel invincible, but one day too many and he wonders if he will make it to the next hour. In the end, broken and friendless, he headed for America. It was the dark history of corruption and crime that drew him to the City of Angels. The Dumok wanted to disappear into it.

The year was 1992. Spring had brought trouble to the City of Angels when white police officers had been acquitted in the beating of a black man named Rodney King by an all-white jury. It became a turning point in history and resentment turned to violence. The mob mentality is a strange thing. It only took one act of violence to whip the crowd into a frenzy. A single bottle was thrown high into the air and came tumbling down with a crash. A roaring shout went up, a chanting war cry, and suddenly, the mob outside the courthouse turned into a single violent force—one voice that was heard for the next six days and nights, causing the largest riot in the United States since the New York draft riots of 1863. The rioters had no purpose, no plan, only rage. It was pure heat, stoked by years of resentment.

For six days the streets of Koreatown burned, as the Koreans were trapped geographically between the black and white neighborhoods. Then, it ended just as it had begun. There was no official intervention. No resolution. The fire had simply run out of fuel.

The Dumok arrived in Los Angeles only to discover that everything west of Vermont and east of Western Avenue had burned into the ground. He got out of the car on 8th Street and Western Avenue, and silently made his way through the streets, taking in the ruins. He felt like the streets inside, once energized and now ashes, torn, broken, and discarded. While pacing the streets, he saw opportunity and a vision came to him. He knew what to do. The town was full of frustrated men, caught up in their cultural and financial obligations with nowhere to go to relieve the pressure. He knew the formula to bring the town back to life. All he had to do was plant the seeds.

For his first career in international relations he had been trained to handle politicians. He would use all of that experience, he knew how they operated, only this time he would use it for himself. He would meet with the local politicians and convince them to loosen building codes and regulations in order to stimulate real estate development and businesses. He imagined the freedom and tolerance of the red light district of Amsterdam. The filtered grey luminescence of the Dutch sky reflecting off the clouds, the light complimenting the ancient stones of buildings compressed together as they hovered over the canals, the girls in the windows peddling their wares.

The Dumok began to feel a certain freedom. As the protégé of a senior Ambassador he had learned and followed every rule without question. Now, having been thrown to the wolves, he no longer felt any obligation to play their game. The plan was simple. He would build and they would come. Walking the scorched streets, he noticed two young men, their eyes hard. They were from a hardscrabble existence and two different breeds. One, called Mix, was a rottweiler, big and mean. The other, Mick Chang, was a doberman pinscher, skinny and mean. It was a delicate matter. If channeled wrong, they would wind up in prison or dead in an alley fight, having never understood that their fate was not fixed, but as malleable as clay in the right hands.

"I'll buy you a bowl of noodles," the Dumok called out. It didn't take much beyond free food to gain their loyalty. The young men looked at each other, shrugged, and followed. The stores on either side of the noodle shop had been looted, the broken windows boarded up with plywood. Mix and Mick stood awkwardly. The owner showed them to a booth. They sat and ate quietly. In the shared food a bond was formed.

In the basement of the first building he purchased, the Dumok trained the boys through boxing and martial arts to channel their adrenaline and surging testosterone into a tool, to be aggressive on the attack and tenacious on the defense, and at all times to go for the throat.

A web begins with a single thread. It was this chance meeting with the boys where the Dumok released the first length of thread, attaching the two other points of the Y structure. Mix and Mick found themselves at the center of the web, and eventually, what happened during those years came to change their friendship forever.

It was Mix and Mick who first brought in the girls who crossed the borders through Seattle, Arizona, Texas and Niagara Falls for the promise of work in nightclubs, karaoke bars and private room salons. The girls rotated from club to club, so there would always be a variety of fresh faces and never a shortage of men willing to pay for a few hours of distraction.

The ban on smoking in public places presented the next opportunity. Expensive citations were being issued to establishments that allowed smoking.

Next, the Dumok paid a visit to the Councilman of the 4th District, an old-timer African American named Willy McClellan. The next day Mix showed up at the Councilman's office with an envelope containing five thousand dollars in cash, an honorarium, Korean style.

"Damn, their money smells like kimchee," the Councilman chuckled. Suddenly, liquor licenses were issued, raids stopped, moratoriums were put in place against excessive regulation, and rules were bent and permission given with the Councilman's hand firmly on the rudder. Over time, the money stopped exciting him and his attention naturally turned to the *domis*. Temptation. It was everywhere and those young Oriental girls were so damn fine. Gradually, the lines began to blur and fade, graying until the lines washed away like the white chalk on a football field after a heavy rain. It was in this way Koreatown rose, like a Phoenix, from the ashes. Two decades later, Koreatown was booming and Mix was still with him. Mick, the Dumok lost, first to the military and then to the badge.

Holly Park was too young to know this history and Choi was not about to let her go snooping around to find out. Anyway, it had nothing to do with finding Nara Song. But if Holly found Nara Song, she would find out where the Dumok's story really started. From there the Dumok would find out about the lie.

Choi shuddered. One thing was certain. The Dumok must continue to believe Nara Song was dead—or at least never find her. Choi really didn't want to hurt Holly, but if the morgue visit didn't scare her off he would have to do something worse.

CHAPTER 16

"I lost." Holly told Mi Rae. She was back from court, pulling a rolling briefcase behind her.

"I hated your client, and I'm sure the jury did, too," Mi Rae sniffed.

"I didn't get paid to lose, Mi Rae." The case weighed on Holly heavily. Holly sat in her office nursing a Styrofoam cup of instant coffee. She watched the chunks of creamer floating on top, distracted.

Over her objections, the judge had admitted into evidence photos from the crime scene of bloodstains of the victim, the left shoe and broken eyeglasses scattered on the highway. The life of Stanley Gunderson, a college student, had ended in the terrible crash. Holly imagined Stanley's body laid on a shelf above the mutilated body of the Enforcer and shuddered.

Blake LeBlanc, the prosecutor, was seasoned, relentless and uncompromising. It was Holly's sheer bad luck to have such a formidable adversary. Blake LeBlanc painted her client, Jane Lim, as a Koreatown barfly, and the life of Stanley Gunderson cut short over her client's irresponsible decision to get behind the wheel drunk.

Holly watched as the jurors' eyes rested on the broken eyeglasses. She found her eyes kept going back to the glasses, too. How did they break? Was it at the point of impact or did the glasses fall off after the impact? Could he see as he waved for help? Did Stanley see the third car coming towards him at full speed? Were Stanley's last moments inexplicable terror or a merciful blur? Holly wondered, too, about the body she had seen at the morgue. She couldn't get the image of the body out of her head. Who deserved to die like that? What were the Enforcer's last moments before he was tortured and his body gutted? Were his last moments inexplicable terror or was it a merciful, quick death?

The parents of the victim sat on the front bench of the courtroom each day, their faces pained and aging with each day. Theirs was a sorrow that would never heal. Did The Enforcer leave behind grieving parents, too? Holly wondered.

When Blake LeBlanc played the tape-recorded confession for the jury Holly knew it was over. Her client's high-pitched giggling voice filled the courtroom, words slurred as she repeatedly asked when she could go to the impound lot to get her car back.

So Holly knew. Of course she knew. Even so, it was difficult to hear when the verdict was read.

"We the jury find the defendant guilty of gross vehicular manslaughter while intoxicated..."

Jane Lim's shrieks filled the courtroom.

The case, which had originally been filed as a single count of driving under the influence with great bodily injury, had been amended to vehicular manslaughter because the victim had died of head injuries. Jane Lim didn't help her cause. She had a prior driving under the influence conviction. No witness was more unsympathetic and Jane Lim found herself sentenced to ten years in state prison. A decade would be paid in exchange for a life.

Crime.

Judgment.

Punishment.

Justice.

"Oma! Oma!" Jane's screams for her mama rang out as she threw her head down on the table, weeping. The cries continued as she removed her jewelry and handed it to Holly as the bailiff handcuffed the screaming girl and escorted her out the back door.

"You lousy lawyer."

It was the boyfriend, his eyes hard, full of menace. He had been no help to Jane, as he sat glaring at the jurors, trying to intimidate them dressed in camouflage and combat regalia. He brushed past Holly, shoving her hard with his shoulder. Holly rubbed her arm as she watched him leave the courtroom. Her shoulder hurt a lot.

"Attorney Park!"

It was the client's mother, Mrs. Lim, a tiny woman, skinny as a steel rod, eyes blazing, summoning her. Holly walked and stood before her. The mother stared, angrily, then lunged at Holly to strike her.

"I trusted you! I trusted you!" she screamed. Fortunately, the bailiff, who was close, jumped up, and restrained the angry woman. "You'll hear from my lawyer! You'll lose your license, and I'll sue you!" The shrill words rang in Holly's ears. Then it was over.

Crime.

Judgment.

Punishment.

Justice.

Blame.

It was a case that should never have gone to trial. Irrespective of the bad facts, the unsympathetic client, and the relentless prosecution, the truth was that Holly had been preoccupied, lost her focus—and Jane Lim had gone down in flames. Now two families destroyed instead of just one. Holly's mood worsened. What if Choi was right? Would the Dumok put a hit on Nara? And her? Then the tears started. She would go away. Somewhere. Anywhere where the Dumok could not find her and where she would be safe.

She had traveled to Paris alone last year. She would go back and stand on the bridge between the Seine and the Ile St. Louis, the bridge with hundreds of padlocks, each padlock carrying a story. Shouldn't the weight of those stories plunge the bridge into the river? Were Holly to go back there, surely adding the weight of her heart would be the final straw, and she would suddenly be in the Seine's swift cold current. Holly looked up from these stormy thoughts to find Kate Hong standing in the doorway, watching her, and then turned away.

"Wait," Holly said, her eyes glistening. "Do you know what happened to The Enforcer? Did Choi ever tell you why he was targeted and who was behind his slaying?" Her voice faltered. "Was it really the Dumok?" She could barely say those words.

Of course Kate Hong knew it was not the Dumok behind it, but damned if she was going to tell Holly the truth.

The Enforcer drove up to a cheap, faux Hawaiian motel just off the 405 Freeway on Sepulveda, away from Koreatown. He was on time. A Korean girl opened the door wearing pink high fashion sweat pants and a white ribbed tank top and no bra. She didn't need one. She was young and beautiful as eye candy but too scrawny for his taste. Not that he had any ambition.

The TV in the corner was on, but muted. There were cop cars and choppers, yellow tape and chaos, some big car wreck. Welcome to L.A., he laughed to himself. Cops.

Too little.

Too late.

Always.

The TV was loud so he didn't see the other coming in from the adjoining room. A *domi*, scantily clad and barefoot.

"We meet again." It was a soft voice, which he recognized. His face registered surprise. It was Cinnamon. She was dressed so he could see the scars on her knees, and on her hands, which she held up as she walked towards him, as a large man came from behind and wrapped a black cord around the Enforcer's throat.

"You messed up my girl." They were the last words The Enforcer ever heard.

Kate Hong knew it was the Korean gangsters behind the slaying of the Enforcer, not the Dumok. But Holly was too stupid to figure it out and Kate was not about to tell Holly otherwise.

"I decided to drop the case. I will give the Dumok a refund when he gets back," Holly cried. It was all simply too much. Tears streamed down Holly's face. Kate came rushing over and put a reassuring arm around Holly. They talked for a long time and Holly poured out her heart. But somewhere during their talk, Holly caught a glint of pleasure in Kate's eyes, like victory. Holly didn't like it so she ended the conversation. A little voice had started to whisper in the back of Holly's head.

CHAPTER 17

Every Tuesday afternoon for the past three years, Holly had lunch with her best friend, Heather Hart. Driving back from the Biltmore Hotel, the road through Koreatown brought back memories for Heather. She pressed the window open and a gust of hot air blasted into the air conditioned sedan.

"Heather! It's hot out!" Holly complained.

Heather hung a toned arm out the window and slowed. "We're cruising! We have a minute." She looked reproachfully at Holly, who, in her opinion, didn't nearly have enough fun. She smiled, thinking about their first year in law school. Her dearest friend was exactly the same as the first day they met.

A bright light flashed and bounced off the glass as the doors to the law library swung open. Holly watched as an exquisitely dressed young woman came in carrying an armload of books. Heather Hart didn't walk, she "swept", so Heather Hart swept through the doors.

"Did you see that flash of light?" Holly asked, looking around the lobby. Heather smiled graciously and held out her hand.

"Maybe it was from this?" Heather said, holding out her hand and displaying a ring.

"That's the biggest and most beautiful diamond I've ever seen!" Holly gushed.

"Six carats," Heather shrugged, then matter of factly studied her hand. "Some people get a little over-excited when it comes to these things." She sounded as if she were trying to understand the fascination.

"It's so pretty." Holly sighed happily. "I hope I get one just like that some day," she added wistfully.

"You'll have to marry well then."

"I don't even have a boyfriend so maybe once I'm an actual lawyer I'll buy myself one," Holly replied, giggling.

"A law degree will never get you this kind of jewelry, my dear. You'll either have to inherit it—or marry it, like I did."

The strangely glamorous classmate was unlike any woman Holly had ever seen. Neither said anything for a moment, unsure how to react to the other. Holly found herself instantly intrigued. She had never known anyone like Heather Hart. Heather seemed so strange, so different, her manner of speech, the indifference with which she spoke.

Heather had very little in common with any of her classmates. She liked to learn for the sake of satisfying her own intellectual curiosity and found no pleasure in engaging in intellectual banter merely for the sport of it. She had graduated magna cum laude from Harvard and applied to law school because the sight of blood nauseated her, and accounting and finance were out because money didn't interest her, perhaps because she had so much of it. That there was more blood spilled in the practice of law than in any surgery didn't bother her because it was purely metaphorical.

Heather was married. She was expected to keep an orderly house, to live life without expending unnecessary emotion, and to maintain the status quo. The dutiful weekly visits to her in-laws were always the same. The content only varied with the shifting of the seasons and holidays, such as Thanksgiving, Christmas and Easter, which gave slight decoration to the usual conversations, which had, over the years, become as ritualized as the catechism. The ritual aspect gave great comfort to both mother-in-law and daughter. The interjection of any emotional family drama would have shattered the surface calm like a crack in thin ice and the carefully constructed truce in their relationship would have been destroyed. The mother-in-law and daughter-in-law had a difficult history and it had taken them years to reach this level of polished ritual. Despite her youth, Heather was a collection of expectations and social responsibilities that weighed on her heavily.

"Could this girl be for real?" Heather thought. She watched Holly burst out laughing, saying, "You're so funny," as if what she had said wasn't just god's honest truth. Had she once been like this girl, too? Heather smiled uncertainly and after a moment laughed too. And in that moment she, too, wanted to feel that innocence again. So she instantly attached herself to Holly and they had been best friends ever since.

Heather found a parking spot on Wilshire Boulevard in front of the long-shuttered site of the Ambassador Hotel, which was now a public school. Cars honked as she tried to parallel park along the busy boulevard. Heather left the engine running to keep the car cool and stepped into the heat and onto the sidewalk. She walked over to the high, chain link fence. She was a slender figure, tall and graceful, wearing a silk tank top, capri pants and loafers. A panhandler started to approach her but changed his mind and wandered off the other way. Holly, in her usual dark suit and black stilettos followed.

"I used to come here with my dad," Heather said wistfully. "Bobby Kennedy was one of his heroes. Now it looks like a prison."

"It's a school. They named it after him," Holly said. "Yes it looks like a prison."

Heather pressed her lips together. Her father had been dead for five years, but still she missed him terribly. But perhaps it was for the best. He had been so happy for her to marry into the security and status of Hancock Park after her boom and bust upbringing. But maybe it was better that he didn't know the truth: that life in Hancock Park was a corn maze dusted with gold and diamond dust, that it was inescapable. And for her it was barren and bore no fruit. Seven years into her marriage, at age thirty-one, she was childless with no prospects except more of the same. Duty without joy and heartache without passion.

Heather felt a hand on her arm. Holly smiled at her. "Are you okay?"

Holly had noticed Heather's thousand-mile stare and knew that she was subject to bouts of melancholy.

"I met someone," Heather blurted, her voice almost a whisper and her eyes glazed.

"Where?"

"At one of Gordon's fundraisers. No, it's not what you think," Heather quickly added. "He's not a donor."

"Then who is he? Isn't it a bit dangerous if it's one of Gordon's charities?" Holly looked at her friend with concern. She knew enough about her to know she wouldn't trade lives for one second. Heather giggled, which disconcerted Holly more than if she had started crying.

"He's a fucking cop, Holly. He was working security."

Holly gulped and her eyes widened.

"I live with bloodless old men and pinched mean old women, Holly. Can I help it if I fall for a man with blood in his veins?"

CHAPTER 18

Nara Song was not dead. In fact, she was still a great beauty, though the shimmer of youth was gone, replaced by sophistication and an intimidating poise. The scars of her hard—no, horrible—early years in America could be detected in her ice-cold eyes if you looked for them. Nara used charm to get attention. Beauty and brains to bait the hook, and the sexual prowess of a panther to get what she wanted. But trust? That had died a long time ago.

Nara was free to do what she wanted. It wasn't so much who she was that she wanted to leave behind, or even that she couldn't live with what she had done. She had already justified all that to herself. She didn't think about her early days often, and gradually distanced herself from almost everyone who had known who she was in the early years. Especially Choi. As far as Nara was concerned, she blamed Choi the most for what had happened to her other daughter, the one she didn't like to think about.

Choi grimaced. It had been a busy morning at the international terminal twenty years ago. Had twenty years gone by? Choi mused. Four flights had come in at the same time. Greeks, Italians, Indians and others were all speaking in languages foreign to him. He was late and hurriedly pushed the door open and walked through without regard to anyone behind him and pushed his way through the crowd.

He wore a blue suit with a Republic of Korea pin proudly on the lapel.

Choi bumped into a woman but kept walking without turning around, and soon took his place with the other drivers waiting to pick up passengers. He was on official duty by order of the Ambassador of Korea to pick up his colleague he most envied and admired.

Choi pulled out a makeshift placard written in the Korean language. He was embarrassed that he carried the only foreign sign and looked around self-consciously but nobody cared. It was too late to get back into the diplomatic clearance area. He tapped his foot nervously and waited. He expected the Dumok to appear at any moment, strolling out in that way he had, with that confident, devil-may-care smile. His easy charm had carried him through life, gained him every privilege and excused him from every trouble in school. He got away with everything, damn him!

What would he say to him? Could he conceal the jealousy in his eyes or would his friend see right through him and just dismissively laugh in that way he had, as if there was nothing grandiose at all about becoming the trusted senior aide to the great Ambassador of Korea?

Choi glanced at his watch, tapping his foot with impatience. Something wasn't right. They should be out by now. His stomach growled. He didn't care much for crowds. He eyed some Koreans standing together and casually made his way over, careful not to make it look deliberate, and absently listened to their conversation. Someone's brother was coming in on the same flight. At least he knew all the passengers hadn't cleared and others were waiting.

Choi held a package in his hand. It had arrived from Korea and he had been told to pass it on to the arriving party. Why couldn't his colleague just bring such a small package himself? Choi fumed.

Finally the delay and curiosity got the better of him and Choi carefully opened the package. Two passports fell out, and a fat envelope. He quickly thumbed through it, glancing furtively about. It was ten thousand dollars. The passports were of two young girls. At first Choi was confused. Why fake passports? It made no sense. He looked again at the passport of the girl called Sara. A black child. Suddenly Choi knew, with the certainty and dread of the damned. He had been tricked. The Ambassador, that wily old goat, had tricked him. Young Chun, who would become the Dumok, was not on the flight. It was the Ambassador's disgraced daughter and those damn twin girls. The money made sense too, for the daughter, Nara Song, to start her life in America—in exile, shame and disgrace.

Choi shoved the passports back into the envelope. His eyes changed from deferential to implacable, his disdain outweighing his conscience. Choi was old-school. Mere exile and dishonor was inadequate punishment. For all the family wealth and social position, it did not buy propriety for the only daughter of the great Ambassador who couldn't keep her legs closed before marriage and had dishonored the great family.

Choi clicked the bathroom stall door shut and leaned his back against it. Choi's fingers felt thick as sausages as he divided the bills into two stacks. Folding one stack in half he stuffed five thousand down his pants pocket. He would give her half only. Nobody would know. Nobody would come searching for her. Of that he was certain.

Both his stomach and his mind raged. But as he washed his hands he found he was getting even angrier. He shuffled back into the same stall and pulled out the second five thousand he had decided to give the daughter. She needed to be punished, and having to survive in America on nothing would do the trick. He stuffed all the money back in his pockets and shoved the envelope with the passports in his messenger bag. Choi straightened his shoulders and hurried out of the airport.

The terminal was crowded and hot on the day Nara Song arrived in America. Several flights had arrived at once. Nara Song wore no makeup. Her long hair was loosely tied in a ponytail. She was too tired to notice or care about the unfamiliar sounds and sights around her. Hunger gnawed at her stomach. She hadn't slept or eaten well on the plane. A group of older Korean men — *ajeossis*—were speaking so loudly throughout the flight she couldn't sleep.

Nara felt faint as she looked up at the great gold and blue seal of the United States looming high above. She stood apart from the crowd. She had an indefinable sense of entitlement as she stood waiting in line to clear immigration. Two little girls clung tightly to her. As the line inched forward Nara clutched so tightly to her passport it dented the cover. She felt nauseous. Nara covered her mouth with her hand and swallowed hard, tasting the bile in her throat. She rubbed the palm of her hands on her skirt to dry off the sweat and looked straight ahead, bravely. This was America. Everyone was brave in America.

"Daughters, Sari, Sara, come!" Nara loosened the ponytail and let her hair fall over her shoulders as she lifted one of the girls and quickly opened her blouse as her baby hungrily latched onto her breast as she tried to modestly place a blanket to cover the child's face. The other child Nara fashioned to her back with a large blanket. She noticed the uncomfortable gazes and the tight mouths of those nearby. She ignored them and focused on the strange voices and noises.

Even the smells were different. The warmth of the little bodies was comforting. As Nara moved closer to the front of the line, her hand clutched the strap of her handbag tightly. The immigration inspector spoke in English, a language Nara pretended not to understand, though in fact she spoke at the university level with very little accent and had read Western literature extensively during her long and expensive schooling.

The immigration inspector held an open palm gesturing impatiently for their travel documents. The public breast-feeding annoyed him. The child was too old to be sucking on his mama's titties. He wished he could yell at her to do stuff like that in her own country but he didn't speak any Chinese-y language. The inspector eyed Nara. There was something about her he didn't like. He would send her to secondary inspections where they would deny her entry and send her home on the first flight back. It was just his gut.

Nara's lip trembled as the immigration officer inspected the passports. Hopefully, he wouldn't notice the biographical information page had been altered and both of the girls' passports had the same photo. "Twins," Nara explained, pointing to the bundle latched to her breast, a bead of sweat forming.

As the officer was about to speak, a staffer with a clipboard from diplomatic services rushed over to her.

"Diplomatic clearance for Nara Song. Follow me please."

Nara followed, collecting the passports from the stunned officer whose mouth opened and closed like a goldfish. Her eyes smarted with tears. It had been a close call. It would be the last time Nara Song would receive a benefit by virtue of her family lineage.

Nara waited for two hours at the airport but Choi never showed up. Finally, she walked out and hailed a cab. Nara carefully adjusted herself on the worn vinyl seat. The potholes and trashed suspension of the cab hurt her back but soon she was distracted by the skyline of the mountains and the blue sky. After the grey and white skies of the cold Seoul winter, this was a reprieve.

It was a little after four in the afternoon, and the dry hot California air had a hypnotic effect. She felt herself relaxing as she looked out the window. Kissing the girls, she thought, gracious, gentle, forgiving America! She would buy American toys for the girls, they would sing jazz, pop, and take dance. They would be free from prejudices of the old country. They would enjoy the privileges of American children. Nara curled her toes, excited at the thought. When the cab pulled off the freeway Nara glimpsed signs in the Korean language. Koreatown at last!

The cab driver pulled into the parking lot of a church and grunted impatiently. They all stopped here. The little church on the border of Koreatown was the portal for the immigrants, the first stop from the airport. Nara tentatively held out all the American money she had on her, about a thousand dollars. The cabbie grabbed it all and motioned for Nara to get out.

Welcome to America, lady. There was no Lady Liberty welcoming Nara and the little girls that day. The only sign of America were the Golden Arches half a block from the church.

CHAPTER 19

Twenty Years Earlier

While beauty is celebrated among the affluent, it is like a disease to the poor. Nara felt like a weed trying to grow in a sidewalk crack stifled by the beating hot sun. In the summer, everything was stained a permanent ugly brown. The stench of raw meat was inescapable. She rented one room in an illegally constructed boarding house. The cockroaches went in and out of the walls in a steady stream.

At first, Nara wrote home dutifully every week but her letters were not answered. Through a church member, Nara found a job in a grocery store, a tiny market in South Central Los Angeles.

The shelves were cramped with merchandise stacked high on the walls. There was barely room for a stool behind the register. Candy, snacks, gum, condoms, cigarettes, disposable diapers, mouthwash, dried foods filled the small shelves.

Nara found a daycare. The cheapest one was an unlicensed rundown converted house off Arlington Avenue. It was dirty, crowded and full of dirty, crying babies — but it was close to the church.

"They must be potty trained," the owner said. Her lips disappeared in a thin line. A child cried in the corner. "No exceptions."

"Wake up, my daughters," Nara whispered the first morning. "You must wake up for school," she said, hurriedly, stuffing two pink second-hand backpacks from Goodwill with the girls' modest belongings. Nara put her things in a plastic grocery bag and sat up straight on the bus. She wore dark clothing and her hair pulled back in a ponytail. At the end of the day, Nara walked back to the bus stop. Her feet and back ached. She was the last to pick up the girls at day care and argued with the headmaster who charged double as a late fee.

"But they are twins," Nara protested.

"Yes. Twins is two. I charge two."

On the bus ride home she smelled a putrid odor and sniffed. "You didn't go in your pants, did you?" she asked sternly. But a check came up clean. That evening, as Nara mechanically went through their backpacks the bad odor became stronger. On the bottom of one of the backpacks was a tightly wrapped bundle. Poo. Nara sighed.

"Girls, you must use the toilet!" She was strict, so afraid the girls would get kicked out of the school. With her little earnings she bought rice cakes and took them to the day care, to bribe the owner to be a little more patient. She took a switch to the girls' behinds until the backpacks came home clean.

At night Nara dreamed of happier times, especially of the young man who had introduced her to the joys of love.

"Look," he said, eyes twinkling as he casually pulled two loose diamonds from his trouser pocket and dropped them in Nara's hand. Nara was eighteen. He was the son of a diplomat from South Africa. "Take me to the library and I'll show you where they came from on a map."

In the quiet seclusion of the library he showed her the origins of the diamonds and more. His hands were gentle and exploratory of her body as he explored the regions of the map moments before.

On his last night in Seoul, Nara slipped out of her bedroom window to meet her lover for one last time. They met behind the servants' quarters. Holding hands they ran into the guesthouse.

Just inside the door, he pulled Nara to him with a force that shocked and excited her. Suddenly, his mouth was on her and she felt her body arch towards him. His large hands tore open her blouse. He pulled her to the ground and he was on top of her, tasting and gently stroking her.

"This," he said, stroking Nara's face softly with his forefinger, "is nothing without this." He pulled her skirt up and placed his hand in her center and squeezed, finding the moistness between her legs. "I have the key to your jewelry box," he murmured into her ear. His voice was hoarse. "Nara, let me see your jewels."

He was beautiful, barbaric, savage and numbing. He took her from sublime to shrieking ecstasy as he thrilled her to unimagined heights. She kissed her lover for the last time as dawn was breaking and left, clothes disheveled.

Nara stared at herself in front of the mirror and barely recognized the face that had gracefully greeted so many dignitaries and diplomats in Seoul. The face that stared back was unrecognizable. The eyes once mischievous and full of life were now beady and mistrustful. Her eyes burned with tears and shame. She had been the subject of enraged turmoil, secrecy and plans for her exile had been made while her babes were still suckling her breasts. Life as she knew it had abruptly ended when she was handed a one-way ticket to America.

Now, stuck in Koreatown, in abject poverty with no prospects, Nara needed to do something. Fast. In the end, it was Mr. Choi who gave her an out.

It was a chance encounter. Nara saw him first. Choi saw her, too. His fingers tightened on the handle of the grocery cart. His mouth tried to move but nothing came out. He was a mere five feet away from her. He shuffled his feet nervously. Choi nodded, and barely gestured with his chin to the food court outside the grocery store. They left their carts with their modest freight standing in the aisle. The girls followed quietly and Choi bought them noodles. He carried the tray to the table.

There was little need for words, but they were drawn to each other like survivors of a shipwreck. Astonished as they staggered onto the beach, there was now a bond between them that neither would have chosen. The worn shoes, polyester clothing, rough hands and dirty purse showed how tough life had been. Choi did not look much better.

He had not aged well, even his clothes looked tired.

He finished his food and wiped his mouth and stood.

"I promise nothing," Choi said firmly, writing down her phone number, and walked away. Choi did not generally suffer from guilt, but in the end, his conscience gave way. He sometimes wondered if the bad times he had endured in America were because of the lie he told the Dumok and for stealing Nara's money. Fate walks on whispers, as softly as a kiss and deadly as poison.

In the end it was Choi who had come up with the idea, he had brooded on it, second-guessing himself a hundred times, and then, finally, convinced Nara that it was the best thing to do. "Save yourself," Choi said. "It is better to lose one child than two to the system. You are young. You can get remarried. But not with *that* one around," he said, pointing.

The day came when she had to give Choi her answer. Nara stared into the mirror. A death mask stared back. She had defied her father by not saving herself for an appropriate marriage, disgraced the family name, and was now less than nobody. There would be no death mask for her, only an unmarked pauper's grave. She was no longer in Korea. She was in America. She would change her fate to an American fate.

Nara did not go to work that day. Instead, she came home with a plastic wading pool for the tiny backyard. Choi came early and brought candies for the girls. He blew up the plastic pool and filled it with water from the garden hose while the girls shrieked with delight. The little pool thrilled the girls and their shrieking and splashing filled the air.

Two hours later, the terrible deed was done. Choi walked out into the sun-blinded street to his car. He could barely stand. Leaning into the car he started it, lit a cigarette and stood outside waiting for the interior to cool. An idea is light like a cloud, but reality has the weight of stones. His mind raced and his heart pounded. Gradually, his heart slowed, the forgotten cigarette burned his fingers. The ashes fell to the ground, and he smeared his gray ashen fingers against his un-pressed suit.

One month later, Nara looked out the window overlooking the

backyard. An hour had passed and Nara waited, watching. She saw her daughter, Sari, sitting alone in the small pool. Sara was gone. Nara was sure that soon, very soon, she would hear splashing and happy noises coming from the pool where the girl sat, motionless. But the afternoon passed and still she did not move.

Finally, Nara went and pulled her only child left out of the water and tried to feed her open mouth but the rice just fell out on the grass. Nara screamed, her fists clenched, the strength draining out of her legs. Soon after, Nara Song left Koreatown. She severed all ties, changed her name and never looked back. Before Nara disappeared, she made a secret pact with Choi to never tell anyone what they had done.

CHAPTER 20

Present Day

Holly's phone rang.

"Holly, you have to cover for me," Heather blurted.

"Details, details!"

"Holly..." Heather stopped. "I'm seeing him tonight," Heather whispered conspiratorially. "The cop. We're going out tonight," Heather confided, her voice excited.

"I can't believe it," Holly gasped.

"'Cover for me, Holly. Gordon thinks I'm going out with you!"

Holly laughed and tried her best not to let her surprise show in her voice as the words hung awkwardly between them. Heather never actually went out with anyone. She had limited her affairs and crushes to imaginary and emotional ones. Until now.

"Thanks!" Heather gushed urgently. Then she was gone.

"To you. The exception to all the rules." Heather lifted her glass. She eyed Detective Mick Chang merrily across the table. He was not in uniform tonight. He wore a dark corduroy jacket with jeans and faux crocodile shoes that were unnaturally long and narrow with square tips. Heather didn't care. The effort was enough. He was enough.

"I'll drink to that." Mick's eyes were full as he met her gaze.

Heather laughed as she studied him over the rim of her wineglass. She resisted her desire to reach out and touch his face. The skin was so smooth. He was so damn charismatic. There was something brash and daring that she liked, something she didn't understand.

"Top up, madam?" The sommelier was deferential as he poured from the near-empty bottle of a Premier Cru Chablis, a 2005. A busboy cleared the empty oyster shells.

"Try the scallops, dear," Heather said, as she reached over and pushed the plate across the table.

"Another bottle, please," she chirped to the sommelier. "Actually, perhaps a demi, please? We don't want to get pulled over."

As Mick told stories, Heather's laughter filled the room. She was at her most charming tonight. Not being the hostess, not on show, she relished the freedom to just enjoy herself.

Mick noticed the heels of her shoes, sexy and beautifully crafted by her favorite Italian designer. She, too, was distracted. She focused on his face, his strong and muscular shoulders, so disproportionately large yet graceful and smooth, deliberate and dangerous in his exactness. She stared at his forearm, wanting to stroke the muscles in his arms. His hair was black with an unruly cowlick that fell in front of his mocking eyes. The heiress loved her dining companion. She was happy tonight as she lifted the glass of Chablis to her lips.

At home, her husband Gordon would be finishing his evening cocktail of medication: a red one, a green one, a blue one and two yellows...or was it two reds? No matter, he would take his pills with a glass of ice-cold water from the pitcher by his bedside and put himself to bed, looking only for the dog. He would not even think about Heather, his mind everywhere else.

"Had to shoot a dog," Mick took another bite and swallowed, talking with his mouth full. "Pit bull. No choice. The suspect unleashed it and just started shooting." Mick shook his head. "What a cluster-fuck." Mick reached for his wine. "This any good?" He took a swig.

Heather sighed happily to herself. He was real. It was only him that made her feel alive. He was the cock-of-the-walk in her pinched, circumscribed, sterile, white-breaded, blue-blooded world.

"Darling, pardon me a moment." Heather lightly touched his arm and sprang up, turning all heads as she made her way to the powder room.

Two men, lawyers, watched Heather leave the table, then turned and stared as Mick tore off a large chunk of baguette and stuffed it into his jacket pocket with one hand while texting with another. They shook their heads and exchanged glances.

Mick's phone rang. The exchange was brief. He gulped down the last of his wine. He helped himself to some more bread and wiped his fingers on the tablecloth just as Heather reappeared.

"I got called out. I gotta go, sorry, babe."

He was unapologetic as his mind was already calculating the shortest route to the crime scene.

"Go, dear," Heather demurred, reaching for her wineglass. "But text me later so I know you are safe." Heather crossed her legs absentmindedly and nursed her wine.

Mick gave the valet a dollar tip and was gone. He had chowed. His mind was elsewhere now. He made an illegal U-turn, tires screeching, and peeled away into the night.

Mick knew well the parking lot that had once served as a meeting ground for drug dealers and prostitutes until the city had cleaned it up and made the owner put up a fence. He parked and climbed out of the car. His nostrils flared as he kicked open the door and walked into the Club Kiki to investigate the source of the call.

Off to the side there was a narrow flight of stairs. He skipped the stairs on his toes two and three at a time, kicked the door open and stopped, surprised at the sight of marble floors, a French chandelier and a large lobby with no furniture. The lights were off here, too. He unclipped a small flashlight and looked around. On each interior wall were doors. Just doors. One, two three...ten, he counted. As he was walking down the corridor, he saw a room with ornate brass handles. He knew instinctively that the call had come from behind those doors. He drew his weapon and kicked it open.

It was dark, but the city lights were coming in now through the windows. Something had happened here, everyone had left, the last person out had shut off the lights. Smoke curled thinly from an ashtray, and Mick saw an abandoned cigarette with a very long ash.

Out of the corner of his eye he saw the fleshy buttocks of a large man in a dark suit laying face down, his pants down around his ankles. He shone his flashlight over the body, and caught the red soles of a woman's black high heels sticking out between the legs of the fleshy white buttocks. It was then he caught sight of the girl underneath the man. She gasped for air, then shielded her eyes from his bright flashlight with her thin arm. Her blouse was open. She had straight long black hair shiny with blood. The bloodstains on the man's dark suit were wet. The suit looked expensive. There were hundred dollar bills stuck to the blood like Post-It notes.

"Micky?" It was that little girl voice that triggered his memory. "Remember me?" the girl said, playing with her hair. "It's me. Naomi Linser."

Mick started. He knew the voice instantly. It was the distinct voice of Naomi Lee Linser. He looked up. She was beautiful, even in a blood splattered sequin dress. The curve of her pale spread legs, hips and tiny waist from under the half undressed body had a strange hypnotic effect.

"Can you help me get up?"

Mick lifted the body while Naomi wiggled her way out. Naomi sat, leaning on her hip, dazed, oblivious to the fact she was splattered with blood.

Mick had first known Naomi when she was an adolescent, a minor, victim of a sex crime. Her hair was longer now, loose and flowing, which accentuated her finely carved features and her unusually large and impossible gray eyes.

Naomi wore dark purple lipstick, which was smeared like a clown. Yet the melancholy of her youth remained. Now here she was, hesitant, her eyes uncertain. That hadn't changed.

Mick shook his head and stood up, glanced around, and grabbed a glass from the large table that still had booze in it. He took a quick sniff and passed it to Naomi who took a hard swallow, then passed it back to Mick, who left it on the table.

Naomi Linser pushed her hair around nervously, rubbing her chest while Mick took in the scene. It was then the detective noticed the small box next to the body. The box was open. Inside was a solitary diamond on a simple gold chain. He used his flashlight and shone it hard; the jewel's inner light refracted patterns on the creamy plaster ceiling. For a moment the perfection of the simple beauty of the glimmering jewel overcame the horrific crime scene.

Sirens were in the distance. Naomi caught the look from the detective and their eyes met.

"My chest hurts so much," Naomi whined.

The sound of a solo trumpet came up in the distance. Some guy up on his roof practicing, Mick thought.

Finally, they heard the sound of squad cars wailing in the distance, then the thump of boots on the stairs, the beams of flashlights crisscrossing on the walls.

A crowd had gathered, walking in and out of the room. Someone took a blanket and covered the sad nakedness of the late Councilman Willy McClellan.

More sirens grew louder in the distance, competing now with the plaintive trumpet. Mick was getting dizzy himself. There was no oxygen in this place. That was the problem. He went and opened a window.

"Up here," Mick called out to the cop cars arriving below.

"Mick, you'll help me again, like last time, won't you? Say you will?" Naomi pleaded, prettily. Mick's head turned. Their eyes met and spoke in silence.

"You have the right to remain silent," Detective Chang began his catechism.

CHAPTER 21

It was on this hot summer night that the highly respected politician Willie McLellan was found dead in the VIP room of a Koreatown room salon, and Naomi Linser arrested and charged with first degree murder.

Los Angeles, the ever-hungry city, badly needed a sensational distraction. Even Hollywood was not enough.

Charles Manson.

O.J. Simpson.

The Olympics.

Rodney King.

Arnold.

Christopher Dorner.

Los Angeles, heir to Rome in its decline, perpetual bread, corruption and media circuses, and now it would be the summer of the sensational trial of Naomi Linser.

Beautiful murderess.

Victim.

Seductress.

Chameleon.

Whore.

Lamb.

Slut.

Classy or trashy? Even Holly didn't know.

By the next morning, Naomi Linser caught the attention of the American public. She was an exquisite, petulant party girl, photographed handcuffed, with a half smile, being pushed into the back seat of a police car wearing a sequined dress and clutching a Chanel handbag. The photo became ubiquitous, and Naomi Linser was crowned the poster girl for every sin of Koreatown—both real and imagined. The mug shot pictured Naomi wearing a fiery purple shade of lipstick that summer when the heat was the worst in California history. She was arrested for first-degree murder, yet there was a melancholy that the cameras captured and which captivated the Americans.

The councilman's untimely demise became a media circus. Beloved bridge-builder and peacemaker between the whites, the blacks and the Koreans now murdered by a beautiful young Korean girl in what was described, charitably, as a "house of harlots". The papers were just getting warmed up. The public fascination was endless. Holly, too, hung on every word and grainy photo.

CHAPTER 22

"The accused in the murder of Councilman McClellan is a young girl, Naomi Linser..." Holly spoke out loud the words that scrolled across the bottom of the screen, which hung over the coffee bar on the roof of the Four Season as Kendall's back was to the screen. "Do you think that girl, Naomi Linser, could possibly be Wolf's?"

Kendall leaned forward across the café table and said in a hushed whisper, "I'm certain it's her. The thought simply gives me the chills," Kendall took a sip, pensive. "If it's her, then it proves my instincts were right that Wolf was framed. Is she a victim or a murderer? Or can she be both?"

Holly hoped Kendall wasn't expecting an answer.

"It's karma, is what it is," Kendall decided in her usual definitive manner. "The apple doesn't fall far from the tree. Naomi Linser is a bad seed. Just like her mother."

Kendall's green eyes were those of a hawk, Holly thought. Why it mattered so much, even Kendall probably didn't know, even after all these years. Jealousy, revenge, spite, ambition, the full quiver of arrows that humans rely on.

"I don't know how common the name Linser is, but I want you to go visit Wolf and find out if it's the same girl who had Wolf put away." Kendall's eyes were sad. "I gave to him unconditionally. All I wanted in return was his loyalty. I never knew about the other woman. It never even crossed my mind that he would cheat on me, much less leave me..." Kendall's voice faded.

Holly liked Kendall, her brusque style didn't bother her at all.

Kendall sat silently, pensive, thinking about Wolf in a detached sort of way. "May I smoke?" she asked Holly. Without waiting for an answer, Kendall took a slim orange cigarette case from her bag and lit up. She took a long drag and watched the thin curl of smoke until there was nothing more. "Put a little money on Wolf's books. Just enough for snacks and to win him over—but not too much. Keep him hungry and win his trust."

Kendall had a funny pained look in her eyes. "Holly, have you ever been in love, betrayed and left for another woman?"

"No," Holly said, wriggling her nose.

"I hope you never experience it, because vengeance is insidious. And it becomes an obsession and fills your heart with hate. I want to destroy her the way she destroyed my life. I want to know every detail of that other woman. You find yourself wondering what she had that you didn't have."

"Kendall, you can get any man," said Holly, sincerely. "Why not just move on and forget about him?"

"Pain," Kendall began, "is better than nothing. When I feel nothing, I question whether I'm alive. With pain, at least I know I'm still here. That woman is going to rue the day she ever touched my man," Kendall growled.

Holly speared a slice of mango as she tried to contemplate the depths of Kendall's fury. The morning news shows were still on. Holly's eyes were drawn by the already ubiquitous photo of Naomi Linser. The latest graphic read *The Virgin Whore*.

Holly left the Four Seasons and went back to her office. A homeless man wandered by shaking a cup for coins. He then turned and Holly watched as he headed the other way, restless, searching the streets. She hoped he would find whatever he was looking for, or perhaps the searching was the point, and there was nothing to find.

CHAPTER 23

Alexis Lee Linser, a woman of *une age certain* walked into the American Legal Services lobby and sat wearily in an equally tired vinyl wingback chair. One look and it was obvious why Wolf had left Kendall Taylor. She was willowy and beautiful, dressed in Italian knits and carrying an Hermés bag. But her face was tense and slightly contorted and her eyebrows furrowed. She moved as if she were floating, unhurriedly, her clothing moving with her body. She had hair as black as a raven falling softly around her shoulders. Her face was unmarred by time. She looked as cold as a diamond until you saw her eyes, warm and liquid and sad. As great as her beauty was, her eyes told a story that it had been far more of a curse than a blessing.

Kate Hong's eyes narrowed, watching, calculating. Even Kate was stunned by her beauty—and the resemblance to her suddenly notorious daughter.

"Hello," Kate greeted, her chin out and nose high, her voice in that sweet professional sales pitch that worked so well. "You are more beautiful than your daughter — if that is even possible."

Neil Cooper was comfortable in his office that morning. He had just poured himself a short glass of Johnny Walker Blue and leaned back in his executive chair and gone back to watching on-line porn. Then his intercom buzzed.

"Come join us in the board room," Kate said, her voice shimmering with prospect.

Neil drained his scotch, found a breath mint in his desk drawer, picked up a fresh yellow legal pad and pen, and stood up. As Alexis Linser walked into the conference room, her heel caught the edge of the carpet and she suddenly stumbled. Neil had just come down the hall and caught her elbow. Alexis looked up with a helpless smile. He was instantly charmed.

He pulled out a chair for her and then took his place across the table beside Kate. Alexis looked Neil over with her tired eyes and found instant comfort in his powerful build, hair slicked back, with just the right amount of gray at the temples, and his sleek impeccable suit. A powerful, charismatic—and American—defense attorney—exactly what she needed. She knew instantly that she would be able to get him to do whatever she wanted.

Mi Rae tiptoed in with a cup of coffee and left it for Alexis, eyeing her curiously.

"Naomi Linser...is my daughter." Alexis sighed. "She made the papers once before, eight years ago in an... another unfortunate matter."

One statement, and it took all the wind out of Alexis. Oh, the enormity of it! Her body sagged and she crumbled forward as she talked, her head bowed, black hair covering her face, revealing the pale back of her neck, which waited, as if for the executioner.

She absently played with a long gold necklace, which had different colored gold rings dangling from it. Neil sat across from her with his arm spread over the next chair.

Occasionally, he would shift positions and cross his legs towards her, his strong big hands steepled at chest level, his spread—and carefully manicured—fingertips lightly tapping as he watched and listened.

Alexis spoke for the next hour, her fingers nervously toying with the rings on her necklace. It took every ounce of energy she had.

"I have a copy of the police report," she finished, handing it to Neil with both hands, Korean style, who received it with appropriate solemnity.

"She was covered with the Councilman's blood," he read ominously. "The knife entered his body with such force he died upon impact. It cracked his sternum." Neil bobbed his head up and down slowly, impressed with the strength of the blow.

"Was she involved...romantically...with the Councilman?" Kate couldn't help herself. She hoped that adding the word "romantically" would soften the question, a gesture which was totally out of character.

Alexis shrugged. "All men like my daughter, that is nothing new." Her jaw tightened and her nostrils flared a little. "He was infatuated with her and convinced himself that he was in love. Every man fell for my daughter's beguiling ways. The late Councilman McClellan was no exception. He was just the first to die from it."

Alexis's eyes were dark and sad and rested on Neil. Would he like her, too? And handle her defense, pro bono, in exchange for the publicity? She wondered. Well played, it would make him famous. He looked photogenic, had a deep voice. It wouldn't even matter what he said.

"What about the father?" Neil asked. "Is he in the picture?"

"Stepfather," Alexis corrected, bristling, but then stopped herself. "Wolf Linser is in prison, so I will be making any decisions about my daughter's case."

What a mess, Alexis thought and then couldn't help but think of Wolf. She bit her lip. "Human capacity for self-deception is unfailing, isn't it?" Alexis said as she looked up. Neither Neil nor Kate commented.

"I was an immigrant without a dime but I made my way. I was aware of every nuance of social distinction and tried so hard to adopt the Western influence for Naomi and myself. In due course I married Wolf Linser and took his last name, the gateway into the 'American' world. I wanted Naomi to belong to the other world and not the immigrant world. I insisted Naomi go to private schools, she took modeling classes and rode horses—I wanted her to belong to a world where nobody could look down on her." Alexis stopped and glanced at Kate, not wanting to offend, but not really caring either.

"All of us who are immigrants struggle with such choices for our children," Kate said as neutrally as possible. Kate had no children, but lack of direct experience had never stopped her from having an opinion.

"There are thousands of tales of successful immigrants which all end with them looking back at their beginnings with a feeling of nostalgia and cheap sentiment. They are fools." Alexis tossed her hair, an almost equine move. "I realized too late, that Wolf, for all his charms, was past his time, no more than a gifted horse wrangler living off his wife's wealth.

But he liked Naomi from the moment he saw her. Of course, she was just a little girl when they met. He was enchanted by her and took care of her and I was grateful, I was free to do as I pleased. Sometimes I felt they didn't even want me around. But somewhere along the way she grew up..." Her voice trailed off.

Neil stared, he wanted to say something intelligent, wise, comforting, she was so damn beautiful, but nothing came out.

"It happened so quickly." Alexis sighed. "At the end of the day, he was just a man, and men are weak. Naomi was under age, and he is still in prison for it."

Alexis took a sip of coffee and leaned back, deep in her story, deep in her sorrow and rage.

Even Kate Hong was intimidated by Alexis Linser. By her beauty, her articulate and perfect English, and her dignified manner, even in such profound distress. She was like a leopard to be disturbed at one's peril.

"I always wondered what men saw in her," Alexis said, frankly. "But I suppose mothers are always a little dismissive of their daughters. To me she was ordinary and I never gave her too much thought. I always wonder how different life would have been if I had borne a son."

Kate nodded. There was no need to elaborate.

"Does Naomi have any type of criminal record?" Neil's loud voice broke the hushed tones. He had never been involved in a murder case but where he lacked experience he made up in volume.

Alexis's eyes widened then her pupils quickly constricted and she squinted slightly, her arms stiffening for the slightest second. "No," she said, her hands trembling as she lifted the coffee cup to her lips.

Neil pressed his fingers together and was about to speak when Alexis turned her body towards Kate and slowly twisted a ruby ring from her finger and placed it in the middle of the conference room table, exactly half way between them. "I've had this for twelve years," she said softly, a single tear forming and running down her cheek. "It was given to me in Istanbul, at a very special time in my life—a happy time."

Kate could barely conceal her delight as she had been eyeing the ring since Alexis walked in and had not been fooled by Alexis playing with the Cartier trinity rings around her neck on a chain. Kate had never seen such a big stone in her life. It took every ounce of self-discipline for her to not grab it. Instead, she leaned forward and spoke, in her best, most sympathetic tone. "Of course we can help you."

Outside, Alexis fumbled for her cigarettes and car keys as she crossed the street to the $7 All-Day parking lot. She badly needed a cigarette. Finally she steadied her hand enough to light one with a gold Dunhill lighter. The lighter had once been Wolf's, but he didn't need it where he was. She was pleased. She had her strong Jewish-American lawyer. The ruby ring was a very good and expensive fake, intended for women who kept their real jewelry in safes and rarely wore it, wearing the copy, but a fake nonetheless. The case would be well underway before the true value of the ring was discovered and Neil would be stuck as her counsel. In their greed they hadn't even asked to have the ring appraised. Alexis knew a greedy woman when she saw one.

CHAPTER 24

The next morning Kate burst into Holly's office eager to gossip. "At one point, I thought Alexis would spill her coffee she was shaking so badly." Kate's eyes were electric as she marched up and down in front of Holly's desk, unable, in her excitement, to stand still."

"Oh, I wish I hadn't been in court so that I might have seen her!" Holly breathed. "Is she truly so beautiful?"

"Yes, though that family has been the subject of rumors for years— all kinds of rumors." Here Kate dropped her voice to a confidential whisper. "Alexis Linser appeared all over headlines one day, a Korean, married to Wolf Linser, a former Olympic Equestrian," Kate went on, excitedly. "Five years later, the family hit the headlines again, this time accusing Wolf Linser of molesting her daughter."

"Were the accusations true?" Holly drew a breath sharply.

"Only Wolf and Naomi know the truth. Wolf took a plea deal. Fifteen years. Could have been worse." Kate was never so happy and animated as when she was gossiping.

"The problem is Alexis didn't foresee the firestorm of publicity, though to be fair, nobody did. Naomi couldn't leave the house, so her mother sent her to Korea."

"But..."

"Yes, she came back. Mother apparently not too happy about it, especially now, of course."

"Why did she come back?" Holly asked.

"Nobody knows." Kate smiled smugly. "For all their beauty, wherever they go a trail of destruction follows them. I told you, they are a family of witches."

Holly felt shivers.

"Neil can't do much, but I don't think anyone can under these facts," Kate snorted. "There's no defense, just a deal to be made," Kate rendered her verdict. "And no bail, she's a flight risk, certainly. Anyway, who would pay it?"

"What if she's innocent?" Holly frowned.

Kate whirled around. The air froze between them. Kate Hong was old-school Korean. How dare Holly Park question her or even speak before spoken to? The jealousy deep inside unleashed. The anger had nothing to do with Naomi or the case. It was about the Dumok. Kate's expression contorted and changed to ugly. All Holly offered was the bloom of youth, and that faded quickly enough. It took time for a woman to ripen and truly beguile a man. Holly could not compete. Kate felt slighted. The high profile murder case of Naomi Linser had just walked through her door and Kate Hong was not about to let Holly steal her thunder.

Kate's face puckered into a forced half smile. "Now Holly," she began. "I just retained the case of the century. I am going to need you focused. You know how Neil is. The clients love Neil because they are separated from him by their own ignorance. But Neil doesn't actually work. You know that. So I need you. I know you have been focused on the Dumok lately but—Holly, he is old enough to be your father, never mind all the other reasons you should stop thinking about him. He has *domis*—much prettier, more charming and younger than you—lined up for his taking."

Kate stopped and leaned in. "You haven't even gone to bed with him, have you?"

The expression in Holly's eyes made Kate push more. That was Kate. Always pushing. She would never leave things alone. Then her voice changed. Kate was always engineering, manipulating the situation. In a hard voice that tangled with cold admiration Kate said, "The Dumok is using you and will tire of you quickly. So stop being silly. He is a worldly man and sees you as an amusement. Nothing else. Now, I need you focused." With that, Kate left, her rude words tingling in Holly's ears.

Holly watched Kate and suddenly felt sorry for her. Kate Hong was a middle-aged, hardened woman, full of coarse words with eyes that softened only at the sight of dollars. For all of Kate's roughness and unfeeling talk, it was really only a cover for her loneliness. Kate had no man and she didn't want Holly to have one, either. The world seemed suddenly small, bitter and troubled.

CHAPTER 25

Choi walked softly on his toes up the threadbare stairs to the second floor of a cheap hotel around Alvarado and 7th street. The sign over the entrance said Color TV. Inside it was dark and he wondered if the place were kept that way on purpose so they wouldn't have to clean it.

Outside of room 214, which was on the backside of the hotel, Choi leaned on the door. The key he had coerced out of the desk clerk made only the slightest click, then opened. There was a daybed by the window and Huck Stryker, a skinny white intermittent junkie type, who was in fact a very good software hacker from a decent home, was there. He could have easily passed for dead, except he was snoring like a chain saw.

There were two other people in the room whom the snoring didn't seem to bother. Raoul, a tough looking Mexican, maybe twenty, in a tank top to show off his tattoos and baggy striped boxer shorts, and a pretty Mexican girl, very naked under a cheap dressing gown that made no effort to hide her ripe puppy fat body. She didn't look more than fourteen as she played cards at a small table with empty beer bottles between them and a messy stack of ones. Raoul's wallet was on the table. The single greasy window let in some light, if not much air. The stuffiness of the room was nothing a Santa Ana wind couldn't have fixed. The girl, whose back was to Choi, turned and put a hand to her mouth, not as if she was happy to see him, but not like she'd never been rousted, either.

"Hey, Chiquita—throw some water on this guy's face." Choi pulled a hand-rolled cigarette butt out of the ashtray and sniffed it. Mexican marijuana. Must have been some party. Choi had no interest in drugs. His nervous system was so, well, nervous, that an occasional beer or one drink was all he could handle.

Meanwhile, the Chiquita wiggled her way over to Huck and threw a filthy glass of water in his face. She looked like she enjoyed doing it. God knows what he and Raoul had done to her—and each other—last night. Huck sputtered and opened his eyes.

"Hey Choi," Huck groaned his greeting. "This is what I get for playing at being immortal."

"Don't die—yet," Choi responded. "I'm here on business."

Huck sighed, sitting up. "Would you please pass me my pants?" Huck asked politely, struggling to get it together. "Nothing kills faster than immortality."

"How much money do you have in your wallet, Huckster, when you got here?" Choi pulled Huck's wallet from the pants and flipped through it. It was as empty as a promise.

"It looks like I came at the right time," Choi said, tossing the wallet. Raoul shrugged and shuffled the cards.

"You got a job for us?"

"Big job." Choi nodded.

"Then you can fuck her no charge, if you want. She likes it." Raoul cut the deck.

"My medical insurance isn't that good." Choi looked down and studied his fingernails and instantly regretted wasting the joke on Raoul.

"Who is it?" Raoul asked.

"A lawyer. Female."

Raoul shook his head. "I got my standards, man. No women or children."

"Think of it as a social service. It's a lawyer," Choi said. "And it has to look like an accident."

"That's harder. Ten grand. Half up front and half after the job's done."

"You're one sorry ass motherfucker," Choi said.

"When?" Raoul asked, suddenly serious again.

"Friday." Choi kept looking awkwardly around.

"You ain't wearing no wire, are you?"

Choi ignored the question and stared out into empty space. He was gone, wandering down memory lane, passing his fingers over the edge of the card table, drumming his feet to an imaginary beat in his head.

It was that one excited phone call from Kate Hong, of course, bragging that Neil Cooper had been hired to represent Naomi Linser that made him finally snap. The walls were closing in. It would be no time at all before Holly figured out that Nara Song was living under the alias of Alexis Linser. Up to now, everyone had been fooled.

The Dumok had always accepted that Nara Song had died in childbirth, until now. Wolf Linser had never questioned Alexis or Naomi's identity. Now with Holly poking around and Alexis walking into American Legal Services, the truth would all come out and the Dumok would surely find Choi's hand in all this. Especially when the truth of the other daughter came out.

It was all too much for Choi and he began to shake as his face clouded over in memory. Damn Nara Song. After they had gotten rid of the other daughter, Nara had lived for five years under the alias of Alexis Lee then Alexis Linser. Choi had put her out of his mind until she had called again.

"We agreed never to speak again," Choi said, his voice tight. Time certainly had passed quickly.

"I need a favor," she said, refusing to take no for an answer. "Not for me, for Naomi."

Finally, Choi capitulated. It was Choi who made the 911 call to get Wolf Linser put away. It was Choi who coached Naomi on what to say to the police about what Wolf had done to her.

Now, with the Dumok involved, there was no way Choi could capitulate a second time. There was only one thing to do. He would get rid of Holly. Choi sat up and methodically organized his thoughts.

Once and for all, he would free himself from the rocks that hid between the waves. His voice was hollow, and his face contorted as he spoke. Raoul listened while playing solitaire. Huck drank a Coke and slowly came back to life. The Chiquita was bored and had fallen asleep on the bed.

Choi made the deal with them, in careful detail, their voices fading, like people leaving shore in a small boat. Soon the soft sound of the waves were all that would remain. Only in getting rid of Holly would he truly be free. There was only one problem. Slight, incidental, a mere annoyance—yet potentially disastrous. He didn't have the ten grand.

CHAPTER 26

Big office buildings have a different feel at night, empty, silent. It was just sunset and American Legal Services had a warm glow. The security guard sat in the lobby flipping through a magazine. Kate Hong was wearing a white dinner jacket and black pencil skirt and standing looking out the window at the bruised orange sky.

Choi was in business. He'd caught Kate at the office dressed up with nowhere to go. He said he would pick her up. In the car, Choi refined his strategy, working until it was simple as possible.

Kate got in the car, and as he drove she spoke without looking at Choi, as if he'd been there for hours.

"I believe each of us has a problem, and each of us have a solution. Shall we see if we can match them up?"

"I think we can do better than that, Kate. Shall we go somewhere for drink?"

"God, yes."

Choi drove a short block to Taylor's Steak House on 7th Ave. It was an old-school place with red vinyl booths. And very busy. They cooled their heels at the bar waiting for a table.

"What are you drinking?" Choi asked, hoping a stiff one would calm Kate down.

"I'm having a martini, and you'd better keep pace," Kate teased delicately.

Choi gulped, he was no drinker, but he had no choice. Kate Hong's moods—her insecurities—Choi could read her. Kate Hong was jealous of Holly Park, for capturing the Dumok's attention, when she could not. Competition never fares well to a vain woman and Kate Hong was certainly that.

"The Dumok has fallen for her," Kate announced, solemnly, as she stabbed her pimento-stuffed olive with the little plastic sword that had come with the drink. "I have never seen such flowers as he sent her, that first day."

"Vigorous, careful, judicious youth is all Holly Park has. The bloom of youth is fleeting, then she will have nothing while you will remain the great beauty you are." Choi leaned forward, his eyes glittering in the dim light of the bar.

The host came by and said their table was ready. They were seated in a booth upstairs, unfashionable, where the families with children were corralled, but the booth was private enough, the waiter amenable, and Choi ordered another round of martinis and filet mignon for both of them. Kate was impressed. Choi seemed more assured lately, more manly.

Kate seemed happy. The steakhouse was fashionable, and that was what pleased her. Choi made sympathetic noises as Kate complained about the Dumok and Holly. Choi gently reminded her that she, Kate, was the one who had retained the high profile murder case, not Holly. And that Holly's missing person's case for the Dumok was like hiring her to look for a lost dog, compared to that. If the Dumok had hired a nobody such as Holly, how important could this missing person be?

Kate liked Choi's logic, that and the icy martinis put her in a happier mood, and she agreed to Choi's loan request. She didn't ask what the money was for. She knew it was better not to know. Anyway, his credit was good. He had always paid her back.

Choi drove carefully, to Kate's place, of course. There was a need deep within Kate to feel desired that night. She invited Choi in, it was her new place and he'd not seen it yet. She made them another drink at the wet bar. Her eyes were half-closed as she nursed her drink, but

Choi knew the mood she was in. He shut off the lights and they stood in front of the floor to ceiling windows of her bedroom looking out at the glistening downtown. The lights from the city glistened against her white jacket. He remembered it for a long time after.

Choi stood there, looking, but he only saw what all his hard work and cleverness helping Kate had bought — for Kate. The condo was large and in a good building. Beautiful, decorated with Persian carpets, leather sofas and expensive artwork on the walls. It was then he realized that all the years he had worked for peanuts and done without, Kate had feathered her nest. Anger gurgled in his throat like blood. But she had agreed to the loan and so he was there.

When they finished, it was after midnight and Kate was sound asleep. Theirs was a sexual compatibility built over a long time. As he was leaving, Choi spotted Alexis Linser's ruby ring carelessly flung on Kate's dresser. Kate wouldn't miss it. To her, it was all about the hunt, the carcass was left in the tall grass for the carrion feeders. Choi quietly slipped out the door. He might be a carrion feeder, but he still had some teeth.

At home, Choi put his *Train Wreck* album on carefully as he dropped the stylus into the first groove of the vinyl. He took a cold beer from the fridge and opened it, then sat in his only comfortable chair and let the music roll over him. He glanced at Kate's money on the table next to him and a bad feeling came over him. He concentrated on the music, and the jazz helped. It seemed like a long time ago, where it had all begun. Where had all the time gone?

CHAPTER 27

Heather Hart rarely left Hancock Park, the tiny enclave where serious money had settled ninety years ago and saw no reason to move. It was a neighborhood where the dogs were better cared for than the help. Tall shrubbery, fences and iron gates surrounded it. Graceful, imposing, intimidating from the outside. A secure and utterly private refuge from the inside.

Heather lived the kind of life where quiet perfection was expected. At twenty-one, when she had returned from her summer abroad, she had learned the hard way not to step outside the social fences. Since then, she rarely allowed herself to even imagine it, and when she did have those thoughts, she had terrible headaches.

The chance meeting with Mick Chang changed all that. She found her thoughts wandering. Mick Chang was exciting. Her husband Gordon… She tried to think of the last time she had been excited to come home to him, and couldn't.

Some families claim to have come to America on the Mayflower. It was rumored that Gordon's family had owned the Mayflower—or at least financed it—and gone on from there to flourish in America. The Hart family took for granted their name would be on a discreet brass plate or cornerstone on wings of universities, hospitals and museums to which they contributed, or even founded.

The family never traded on their wealth and influence, but strangely, the more discreet they were, the more powerful their influence became.

As expected, Gordon Hart went to the same prep and Ivy League schools as his parents, grandparents and great grandparents. He could converse expertly on any topic, adding an interesting and unusual perspective without coming across as pompous or arrogant or even academic. His learning was natural, resulting from a pure and sincere intellectual curiosity. He read everything, from cereal boxes to white papers and subscribed to many esoteric publications.

But his abiding fascination was golf. Perhaps it held his interest because, inherently, golf does not allow for perfection or absolute mastery because of the deliberate amount of chaos and randomness built into the game. Having mastered everything else, no challenge sustained his interest other than sports in general, and golf in particular.

Gordon saw no challenge in women, so he was agreeable to marrying Heather, who had a background sufficient to understand what was expected and not to rock the boat too much.

Heather admired Gordon's brains, and was young enough to think that passion would come with time. In other words, she was too young. But she undertook the marriage in good faith, learned to dress appropriately, smile on cue, volunteer for her mother-in-law's favorite charities, was never late to events and never made public scenes. She was a perfect wife. Even when it meant coming home to an increasingly medicated husband who was in bed with his dog by 9:30, long asleep on a cocktail of pills. Whether they were for ailments real or imaginary didn't matter, because either way the pills precluded Gordon from being much of a husband. And the idea of becoming a father became one of the things not be discussed because it might upset him.

Strangely, her mother-in-law put no pressure on them to start a family, and Heather was too innocent to wonder. By the time she began to want to ask questions, it was too late. Questions of that sort would just upset everyone.

Nonetheless, Heather's perfection lasted ten years. Then, one night, it stopped, and finally her heart pounded, and her blood raced at the thought of being with a man.

CHAPTER 28

"Over here." Mick Chang leaned over and opened the passenger door of the undercover car. He wore his usual rumpled plaid shirt, baseball cap crushed to his head. He chewed gum and looked around casually. There was a badly folded map on the front passenger seat next to a Bible. Heather slid into the passenger seat wearing jeans, a sweatshirt, sneakers and dark glasses, even though it was midnight.

Her hair was piled up under a baseball cap. The dashboard had cracks in the vinyl from the sun and the cloth seats had worn thin and had dark stains. The springs were a lumpy memory. If Heather noticed, she didn't let on.

"Hey baby." Chang pecked her on the lips.

"A Bible?" Heather exclaimed, taken aback.

"Just open it." It was pocket-sized with a worn leather cover and gilt edges that looked worn from time. But the pages had been hollowed out and there was a small audio recorder inside where the pages once had been.

"I was on an undercover assignment last night. Spent the night in the can. It's the perfect size for a back or front pocket. The crooks like to brag about their crimes to pass the time. I sat in a cell all night waiting for my cell mate to talk."

"Did he?"

Mick shook his head. "Nope. He just sat there for fourteen hours with his arms crossed on his bunk. He never said a word."

"What if he asked if he could borrow your Bible?"

"Guess I'd be dead. Shit. I never thought of that."

They turned the corner to San Pedro Street and stopped next to an outdoor soup kitchen. Mick reached under the seat and pulled out a flashlight and switched it on.

"Stay inside, don't move and don't open the door for anyone."

As soon as he left, Heather immediately rolled down the window so she could hear what was going on. Plus she hadn't counted on the car smelling like stale tacos. Mick walked up to two men in line at a mobile soup kitchen, next to some old picnic tables. Another man sat nearby softly playing the saxophone. Heather leaned forward, her eyes adjusting in the dim light. It was getting darker and the sound of the saxophone soothing, it's tarnished metal virtually glowed.

Mick knew a couple of the fellows in the soup line. He waited until they had their food—soup and large chunks of bread—and had settled at a picnic table, discretely away from others. Mick perched on a corner of the table.

"What's the soup tonight? Smells good."

"Wishbone soup," grunted the first fellow. "Makes you wish you had a bone for the soup."

"Cops don't eat soup," said the second man. "I hear donuts."

"You fellows tell me if Snapper comes around and I'll stand you a bottle. It'll cut the damp."

"He was working the docks last week but he don't come around." Mick handed them a few crumpled one dollar bills. "You see Snapper, you let me know. I need to talk to that boy." Mick strutted back to the car, slid into the driver's seat and started the engine.

"Done. Next stop gotta head downtown to return the property."

"You're done? What have you done?" Heather asked. "You just talked to those homeless men for a couple of minutes."

"I'm cultivating informants. I'm looking for a guy that's a friend of theirs. Snapper, he goes by. My main snitch. I need him to complete my warrant so we can bust down some doors, but he's disappeared."

"And if he doesn't resurface?"

"Then I'm fucked. These guys will tell him. I toss a few dollars and someone bites. It's like fishing. You have to bait your hook, and most of all, be patient. Everybody in this life wants something that someone else can get for them."

Mick peeled away from the curb and made an illegal U-turn, tires screeching. Heather looked around for a cop, then laughed out loud, realizing she was with one.

CHAPTER 29

The sky flamed orange behind her and Holly felt the sudden chill in the desert air as she got out of her car in the prison parking lot. She tucked the Wolf Linser file under her arm. This was the inland empire. Over a hundred easily by day in the summer, yet plummeting to forty overnight.

The jail deputy had a precise sneer. "Who you here to see, Counselor?" The deputy drawled. The words rolled slowly off his tongue like he had marbles in his mouth.

"Linser, Wolf Linser," Holly said.

The sheriff deputy gave Holly the once over and his eyes gleamed. "You know what your boyfriend is doing time for, don't you,?" His mouth frothed at the corners as he spoke, his voice as cold as the A/C in a 7-Eleven. "We don't like his type to begin with, if you know what I'm saying."

He spoke carefully with a curl to his lip. "We don't ask for much here other than to go quietly to the right cell and stay there. But not your boy, he don't get it at all. Our prisons are full of innocent people. Ask around. They all say they didn't do it. Every single one of them. But your boyfriend? There's something different about that one. He's cuckoo." He made slow circular motions with his index finger next to his head.

The deputy's eyes were vacant as he wandered down memory lane, a thin smile on his face, remembering when Wolf Linser had first been imprisoned, the night they couldn't find him and went into lock-down. "Linser, where the fuck are you, boy?! Don't make me come and find you."

It wasn't pretty when they found him. When the jail deputy came back from the memory his eyes glistened. "We don't much like grown men diddling little girls here, understand? And we don't play nice when the lights go out. They're on a timer, see. It's real dark, real sudden." He cracked his knuckles and smiled but his eyes were lifeless. The deputy straightened his shoulders.

Holly knew it was important for the jail deputy to feel he was better than the men he guarded, so she just waited patiently. Finally, bored with his game, he motioned towards a steel door. Holly stepped forward, the mechanical steel door clicked loudly and opened, which made Holly jump. She stepped gingerly inside and the doors clamped loudly shut behind her. A second door opened into a large room with steel tables and identical low steel stools on each side separated by a plexiglass window.

Another lawyer sat at the far end with a folded newspaper working on a crossword puzzle, legs crossed. He had wavy black hair with a few gray stray ones pulled back into a ponytail. He wore a paisley print tie, a summer weight plaid flannel shirt and a worn Harris Tweed jacket over ancient gray flannel pants and brown Wallabies. A messy stack of legal files spilled over piled at his feet. Holly looked at her unused legal pad and shifted her feet. She thought of Wolf. She was about to meet the great Wolf Linser, former Olympian. The thought excited her.

"Ms. Park?" The voice was accented, high pitched, tentative. Holly looked up. The man calling her was tall and thin with long blond-gray hair. The prison denim and his skin hung from his bones like they were on a coat hanger. His eyes were hollow and his cheeks were gaunt from poor nutrition, abuse and neglect. He was skittish, like a rescue animal. His head bobbed and twitched nervously as if expecting a blow at any moment.

Holly flinched, trying not to let her alarm show. There must be some mistake. They must have brought out the wrong man. Kendall Taylor would never have married this man!

"I've had no visitors in seven years. Not one." His eyes flitted about, full of fear and suspicion. He had some sort of unidentifiable European accent, with a musical lilt. "How's my baby? She never wrote to me, not one single time."

His speech was slurred, incoherent at times as he spoke. Perhaps he rarely spoke in here. "Even one letter, so I would have something..." He spoke, but not to Holly. She sat in front of him but he could only see inward.

Buzz! The buzzer rang every twenty minutes. This time Wolf jumped, then, muttering apologies, he darted out of the room, hands cupped in front of his genitals on his tiptoes, his shoulders hunched over. He looked like a castrated centaur. He was so effeminate and Holly bristled. Is he gay? Holly couldn't believe the man who stood before her could be a man Kendall Taylor would marry.

"Kendall Taylor sent me, Mr. Linser." Holly steadied her voice as she spoke, then watched him and waited. He did not respond. "I was hired to come see you regarding the divorce papers you mailed her last week. She feels there was a mistake and asked that I come speak to you. You and Ms. Taylor have been divorced for over ten years. Did you mean to send the papers to Alexis and got your ex-wives mixed up?"

At the mention of Alexis's name his eyes widened. His eyes narrowed as he spoke.

"I didn't do nothing bad to Naomi to belong in here. You have to believe me. Nothing," Wolf repeated. His eyes were piercing, desperate, furtive. "I made my baby happy." He leaned towards Holly. He stopped and reached into his pocket. His long fingers quivered as he took out a piece of paper and smoothed it. "I saw my baby's picture in the newspaper and read the articles. I don't believe it. Alexis framed my baby, too, like she framed me. She was a horrible mother. I was always protecting her from her mother. They were like two dogs each with one end of the stick. See my baby, isn't she so beautiful?" He kissed the paper before holding up the picture of Naomi. His eyes became focused. "Sometimes, when I think I am suffering...in here—" he waved his hand like a host introducing an act—I think of Naomi, and remind myself we are going through the same thing. She never hurt no one. Once there was a bird that fell out of a nest. She carried the bird and nursed it back. We did things like that, she and I. I never hurt my baby. I made her forget the bad things that gave her nightmares... What happened later is just a natural thing between a man and a beautiful woman."

Wolf babbled nervously, twitching his fingers as he talked. Holly watched his yellow jaundiced fingernails and his fractured nervous energy, and felt afraid. She wanted so badly to jump up and run.

"Are you saying it was a false accusation?" Holly asked quietly, with a calm she didn't feel at all.

Wolf stopped moving. Madness was seeping into his eyes and he looked feral. His brows furrowed and he squinted his bird-like eyes, suddenly bright. He stood, craning his neck at Holly. His eyes hardened, glacial blue in their coldness and she winced and let out a cry. When he spoke, the high pitch was gone and in its place a nasal snarl.

"Do you really think that we were a nice little family out there on the ranch? Or shall I tell you what you came here to hear?" He crossed his wrists and rocked back and forth, gathering his strength for the task. "Alexis was never home. I cared for the little girl. I took care of the horses. Naomi liked being around me. She was kind, good with the horses—everything her mother was not. Then life changes happened. The little girl became a young woman. Perhaps it did not happen suddenly, perhaps it only felt sudden at the time and I was a fool and did not see it. And then, too late!! Pah!!!" He spread his hands and opened his fingers wide, like some magician with a trick. "Like rushing water, you cannot push it back up the river."

Holly held her silence and waited, scared out of her mind but too afraid to move, trying to follow the tumbling thoughts, trying to glue fragments together, dreading the buzzer would interrupt.

There was defiance in his eyes, daring judgment, like a magician who defies the audience to spot his slight of hand.

Holly sat silently, careful not to throw wood on this fire. "Mr. Linser, it doesn't matter if there was consent. She was underage. There are laws and you broke them, which is why you are here," Holly explained. "It also doesn't matter what I think, personally."

Wolf raised his eyebrows and shrugged his shoulders and gestured with his hands. "Legally she was my daughter. Was it incest? Of course not. She was not of my blood. If she was underage, it was a mere technicality. She was a woman, she was a child, she was my baby, she was my love." He paused, withdrawing into himself, then put his fingers together like a teepee and pressed them against his forehead.

"Aarrghh!" Wolf growled in mockery as if he would grab her. "You're exactly like Kendall, no wonder she chose you," he spat. "I see how you sit prim and proper with your knees pressed together but you are paid by the hour, so here you are. You might be disgusted by me but you disgust me, too."

"You are a user and a hustler and a hypocrite, that is all," Holly said, her cheeks hot. "What did Camus say about hypocrisy?"

"No man is a hypocrite in his pleasure." He looked pleased as he waited for the surprise to register. It was a tiny moment between them, a connection where Holly had only seen madness, but Holly resisted.

He shrugged, using his entire body and leaned back, stretching. "I see you make assumptions about me, too. You see me as an uneducated man, a man of no social standing deserving to be locked up and forgotten. Why did Kendall Taylor marry me? Maybe she was slumming. Or tired of dressing up in fancy lingerie and jewels for those billionaires she married. Camus may equally have said that no woman is a hypocrite in her pleasure either." His eyes had a challenging glint, his mouth a hard line. "Do I offend you?"

It was obvious he was trying to push her every button. Holly wanted to turn and walk away and let him rot in the hell of his mind and this place, but she didn't. Holly couldn't stop herself from saying what she said next.

"Yes, Mr. Linser, you offend me," Holly said hotly, her voice tight. "But what offends me the most, is that you are a coward. You have no hope, so you are rude and vile. You are selfish. You hurt Ms. Taylor. You used her and then left without any explanation. You are a user. That's why you offend me."

Holly's chest was heaving as she spoke. She didn't like this man. Down and out, hungry, penniless, yet proud and defiant. Had she turned away at that moment, she would never have been responsible for what happened next. She would never have been faced with the moral and ethical dilemmas that lawyers face after learning the truth of their clients' lives. Instead, she looked directly into his eyes and saw a rawness that had not been there. His shoulders slumped and he bent his head. The truth of her words hung between them.

The horror! Holly had stripped Wolf Linser of the last of his human dignity because she could not hold her tongue and gave way to her temper instead. In this place, he was not Mr. Wolf Linser as she addressed him, he was prisoner 985426, who would be stripped naked and made to bend over and cavity searched before going back to his cell, back to a room full of nothing, to memories that became more remote each day.

"Forgive me." Holly bowed her head, her eyes wet. The superficiality of any other words would create only more damage. Holly meant it with all her heart and he knew she was genuinely sorry. In that moment trust was cemented and a friendship sealed.

CHAPTER 30

"I'm not proud of what I did. I was in a situation, isolated, where my judgment...decayed gradually." Wolf Linser looked up at Holly as he spoke. He sat back with his long legs stretched out as he spoke.

At thirty-two years old, Wolf Linser had found himself divorced and mourning the death of his infant daughter from leukemia. The slow, cruel death had squeezed every ounce of hope and faith out of him and destroyed his marriage in the process. He was newly divorced from a model who had graced the covers of fashion magazines and the swimsuit issue of *Sports Illustrated.* He partied hard to numb the pain. The divorce settlement didn't last long. The marriage had been brief.

When his money dried up, Wolf found himself alone with nowhere to go. He made his way to Las Vegas to distract himself with the bright lights. His good looks and muscular shoulders caught the attention of a woman whose husband, twenty years her senior, lay bedridden back in Manhattan. She coolly slipped him several thousand dollars with which to gamble and amuse her.

He won. They drank good Champagne, and nature took its course. After a few days, she went home to New York, and Wolf sat on the hotel bed and counted his money. He had a stake, and the stunning realization that older women in Las Vegas would pay to be charmed, amused—and fucked. In fact, that was exactly why they came. And even better, they would make no other demands on him, no scenes, no "talks," no planning his future, no trying to change him.

It was perfect.

From that point he was hooked. Wealthy older women became his lifestyle and the means to support his gambling.

Unfortunately he did not have the personal means to support the inevitable dry spells. In actuality, he was just an average lover, but his good looks and charm and seemingly exotic European style perhaps made the women's memories better than they really were. If they went home happy, who was he to pass judgment?

Wolf Linser walked through the casino perusing players until he spotted a woman playing alone.

"Want a tip?" He leaned over playfully. She hesitated but was amused by his boldness.

Wolf woke up at 2:30 p.m. the next day with a splitting headache. His recollection of the previous night was completely fragmented. The girl had wanted to drink mixed cocktails, which he never did, and in bed she had been demanding but not interesting. He remembered the craps table, and something about winning big on the field even though it was a sucker bet.

He was completely dehydrated from the shitty bar drinks and felt awful. He picked up the Champagne bucket full of melted ice water and threw it on the girl's naked back. He heard her shriek as he entered the shower, then realized as he was looking for shampoo that he was in the girl's room. He showered and left quickly.

After two Tylenols and a nap it was time to collect himself and get ready for the night's action. He was down to his last money, his last few comped meal coupons.

Four months later, he had survived, but barely. The blue and white smoke was the same, but the cigarettes a generic brand. The careful manicure, the fussy hair styling, the pressed suits and shirts and carefully knotted ties...the expensive watch...the ritual nightly shoeshine, the gracious tipping—these were only a memory. Worse, they had been his work tools, the way a carpenter needs a hammer and a fisherman needs a boat. How many rolls of the dice did he have left?

CHAPTER 31

Wolf stood at the table cursing himself for losing almost every penny that he managed to extract from his last conquest's jewelry at the pawnshop, but not all hope was lost. He had a few chips left.

Reflexively, he had started spinning his charms on the woman gambling at the table with him. A smile here, a comment there—he knew she couldn't take her eyes off of him. Then a man, probably her husband, came to her elbow and said something to her. Wolf played one more hand, pissed and distracted, and lost. He threw his last chip to the croupier, hoping the gods would bless him for it. He cursed himself further for misreading the woman. It was because he was hungry. The real truth was that screwing the girl the night before had taken more out of him than he had thought, though he was not happy to admit it.

He went to the café restaurant in the hotel and used his last meal comp ticket on breakfast. He knew he had less than a hundred dollars left in his pocket, not counting his money clip, which was untouchable, but felt better after eating. He could focus now. He strolled through the casino in a more relaxed mood, when he noticed a stunning blonde with the most unusual of qualities—she was alone.

It was Kendall Taylor. Spotting Kendall Taylor in a Las Vegas casino was like walking through a used car lot and seeing the owner's Porsche 911 purring patiently while he gutted another fish inside.

Wolf could see that this was a sophisticated woman. Her silk-draped body was full of promise. Wolf could identify almost any high-end Italian brand, and this woman's clothes were a confident mix. She had not just walked into a store and allowed herself to be dressed. She had an eye and worked at it. She had long blonde hair, but it was wavy and casual and touchable. The shoes were glossy black heels with a zipper at the back and small gold lock at the top. She had confidence and a sense of humor. And, of course, the jewels. Around her neck they were whimsical, high quality costume, chosen for color to compliment her outfit. The money shot was on her finger, a brilliant cut diamond, at least five carats. He could be wrong about it, but he didn't think so.

Wolf needed an angle, a way to connect, a plan on how to get that pretty looking woman with the big diamond on her finger to turn into another notch on his belt. He would be patient. He watched her long enough to make sure she was truly alone. He was not going to blow it.

The dealer shuffled the cards, and she was about to play when Wolf Linser touched her arm and whispered discretely in her ear, "Pass this hand, then ask for a new shoe."

Kendall did as she was told and asked for new cards. Wolf ignored the dirty look from the croupier. Kendall immediately won again. After only ten minutes, Kendall was up $5,000. She was so thrilled she tipped the dealer a hundred dollar bill and turned to Wolf. "Here," she said, holding out her hand. "How did you know?!" She held a grand in it for him.

"No, no, no," he said, in a manner that only encouraged her to try and stuff it in his pocket, laughing.

There was something different about this one. His typical choice of prey were the older, married lonely women, but this one, there seemed to be more than one night's worth of cashing in, and she wasn't hard on his eyes. Even more unusual, it didn't look like a plastic surgeon had been anywhere near her.

Kendall was thinking that this was really turning out to be her lucky day and not only because she was winning money, but she was doing her best to seduce this handsome young man with an interesting, lilting European accent. Not German. Dutch? She felt she would like to be on his arm, having already burned through two very wealthy husbands.

"Thank you, " Kendall said and extended her hand, and after a handshake, walked towards the elevator. She flashed a smile.

"Perhaps we can meet up later and you can share your luck with me again?"

Wolf put on his best smile and walked towards her.

"Perhaps we can go to your room now and we'll see about later, later?"

The look in her eyes told him that he got her and now it was time to get to work.

"What a lucky day," Kendall thought to herself. She had a handsome young man at her side, free money in her pocket, and a private suite where the carnal possibilities seemed limitless. Kendall Taylor was on top of her game.

Two hours later, her suite was a mess. The shower door handle and coffee table had broken in their romp. Wolf barely took notice of the look of satisfaction on Kendall's face. He was used to pleasing women in bed via any means necessary. He wished though, that he hadn't spent half the previous night screwing. No matter, he knew many ways to keep Kendall purring.

They lay naked on the bed, content, passing a bottle of mineral water back and forth, discussing what to order from room service. It was only then he noticed her beautiful handbag on the dresser, and the metal horse stirrup that joined the leather straps. He remembered also that she had been wearing a bracelet with the same stirrup design. His heart thumped a little in his chest. He took a chance.

"Is your handbag just fashion? Or are you actually interested in horses?"

Kendall raised an eyebrow. "That's their theme, Hermés. It's a French company. They use a lot of horse and tacking images in their designs. They make actual saddles, too. I'll buy you an Hermés tie, with a stirrup design, so you won't forget about me."

"How would I forget about you? How would that be possible?" He kissed her ear, which, yes, had diamond studs that matched the ring he was sure now was Cartier. Wolf had shocked himself with his sincerity, and immediately changed the subject.

"Tacking?" Wolf smiled, lighting two of her Dunhill cigarettes with his Dunhill lighter, and placing one carefully between her full ripe lips. "What is tacking?"

They talked about horses, and a bond was made.

CHAPTER 32

For three more days Kendall and Wolf enjoyed themselves. Each day Kendall disappeared to the hotel spa for a few hours and always looked great when she came back. Whatever she was doing, it worked. She made sure Wolf never saw the same outfit twice, which considering the small suitcase she had brought meant she was shopping. She had also attended a couple of meetings with the owners or sommeliers of several high-end restaurants who were clients of her finest Napa Valley winery and needed to be assured they were getting a fair share her very popular but limited production Cabernet Sauvignon which she had whimsically named *Indiscretion*.

For his part, while Kendall was in the spa Wolf swam hard lengths in the hotel pool and felt better for it. He had been too stressed in recent weeks to take care of himself. There was probably no place on earth with more pools than Vegas, he thought—and nowhere were they less used.

Otherwise they gambled only a little, would quit when they got ahead, and then go back to Kendall's suite and have paint-peeling sex. Kendall was demanding in bed, but also generous, and after she liked to listen to his stories of dressage and jumping horses for the Olympic games.

"The way you tell the stories, I feel like I'm there," Kendall said. She snuggled deeper into his arms enjoying his scent, the touch of his hard, taut skin and muscular arms. It had been a long time since Wolf had actually talked to a woman, at least one who had some idea what he was talking about. He shrugged. Kendall loved Champagne, sex and horses, and for now, that was enough. Inevitably, the idyll ended, and surprisingly, it was Wolf who ended it.

"I have to go and see a producer in Calgary," he said, as he carefully unpacked his new shirts and placed them in the dresser drawer. "Not a movie, but something for the Calgary Stampede next summer. Produce some stunts, get back in the groove, you know."

Kendall stopped fussing with her make up. "When do you go?"

"Day after tomorrow, so we should make bread while the crocuses bloom."

And so they did. Kendall's luck at the tables continued, and as she dropped him at the airport two days later she pressed a fat envelope into his hand. "You'll feel more confident with this in your pocket."

Wolf kissed her warmly and promised to call from his hotel.

"Do more than call. Come to L.A. after your meeting."

Wolf's nerves were calm and excited at the same moment. She was hooked. He had taken a risk, but like a smart fisherman, letting Kendall have some line to run with had been the wise move.

Of course there was no horse-show producer in Calgary. The only way Wolf was going to the Stampede was if he bought a ticket. He waited patiently until Kendall's limo was out of sight, then waved down the next cab. He did not go back to the strip, but to a modest but decent family-friendly motel closer to the airport, where aircrews often stayed.

Wolf had decided not to drink for a few days. He had a case of sparkling water, a carton of Dunhills, a deck of cards, and the ice machine was down the hall. His plan had been to hook a woman like Kendall, and he had. Nonetheless he admitted he was kind of in shock at his success. Now what? The problem was he really enjoyed Kendall's company, but it complicated things. In his first marriage he had been a young idiot, signing what was put in front of him like a fool. How often would he get a clean shot at a woman like Kendall? It was getting late in the game to make mistakes. He had to play this hand perfectly.

CHAPTER 33

Kendall Taylor lived in Beverly Hills, in a three thousand square foot house of Spanish style covered in white stucco with a terra cotta clay tile roof and little turrets with midget-sized balconies with wrought iron railings.

Kendall had fussed over Wolf's arrival. They had an early dinner by the pool, which was more of a dipping pool, decorative, rather than anything for actual swimming, with a pretty waterfall and a Jacuzzi. The surrounding foliage was lush, wild, with soft-rooted palms.

Kendall couldn't get enough of him. She couldn't stop thinking about him anyway. He was more than a fling. He was special. She wanted to mold him into a perfect partner. She felt sorry for him. Wolf never talked about his days as an Olympic equestrian but Kendall had looked up the records and there he was, winning medals for the Austrian national equestrian team.

Olympic medals, he loved horses and was great in the sack, what else did she need? She had money. Tomorrow they would visit the horses. He would love the ranch. She enjoyed luxury, but now she ached for something more. Kendall fell asleep dreaming of their new life.

Four months later they were married. "By the way, Mrs. Linser, you look astonishingly beautiful."

Kendall sighed happily. "I got my man. What could possibly go wrong now?"

The final jail buzzer rang. Holly watched Wolf walk away. He moved like an old man. When Holly got outside the air smelled like manure. Holly bought bottles of water at the gas station and got on the 60 Freeway heading back to Los Angeles. A pickup truck blasted by on the inside lane and blew a tire, swerving from left to right and back and barely missed hitting Holly. Shaking, she slowed down to a careful fifty-five.

CHAPTER 34

The three young men were nervous. One wore a pale raincoat. Two of them had brought pillows and stuffed themselves carefully into the crappy gray Ford Taurus. The driver, a tough looking Latino named Raoul, had paid each of them fifty dollars in advance. There had been a scrawny white guy lurking in a doorway, but he had not participated in the transaction. Maybe a lookout. And a big Mexican named Christobal who said nothing the entire time.

A few days before they met Raoul on Alvarado Street and worked out the details. Their job was to show up on time. For that they got another $100. They had done it before. Been passengers in staged accidents. They would split the insurance money with the doctor and lawyer who got the most from the insurance settlement. That was just the way it was. This work took courage and desperation, but desperate men were not hard to find.

The passengers looked worried. If they had known what was really going on they would have worried more. Raoul didn't have to ask if his passengers were all buckled in. He looked in his rearview mirror, one of them was fingering a gold crucifix that hung on a thin chain around his neck.

He got on the 10 Freeway from east L.A. and headed west. The exits to Koreatown came up fast.

Beep. Beep. Beep. The black BMW. There she was. Raoul spotted the black BMW. He stepped on the accelerator and the weary Taurus gave its best. The plan was to cut her off and force her into the guardrail and cause her to crash, but she was going slower than expected. Raoul caught up to Holly and cranked the steering wheel hard to the right. But Holly wasn't on the inside lane yet. An 18-wheeler carrying a bed of cars was making up time when an old gray Taurus swerved in front of him and cut him off. The driver hit the brakes, but there was just nowhere to go. The 18-wheeler T-boned the Taurus and the smell of burning rubber filled the air.

"Christ!" shouted the driver at the sickening sound of the cars falling forward off the flat bed, one by one smashing the Taurus.

"This was suppose to be just an accident," Raoul moaned, punching a pillow in disgust. He didn't have to look. There were no air bags. All he could see through the blood-spattered windows was the huge grill of the truck.

The three others were either dead or close to it. That hadn't been the plan. He twisted his neck and looked for the black BMW. His shoulder hurt like hell. Raoul banged his head against the headrest. He could hear sirens now. He wanted to unhook his seat belt, but somehow his arm wouldn't work. Sirens howled, getting louder.

Choi was sitting in a white plastic chair on his tiny balcony drinking brandy. He should have had a phone call by now. He went inside and put on the local TV. An 18-wheeler had been cut off on the 10, near the Koreatown exit. There were fatalities. The news chopper camera showed a crushed gray car, up against the guardrail, the 18-wheeler's trailer at a bad angle. Cops and fire department vehicles everywhere. And Choi could see it clearly. The black BMW parked safely on the shoulder with Holly talking to law enforcement. She was on TV. Clear as day. Not dead. Not even injured.

Choi's phone rang. It was Huck. "That truck came out of nowhere," Huck's strained voice managed. Choi poured another brandy and drained it in a gulp, grimacing.

CHAPTER 35

If the visit to the morgue and Kate Hong's threats were meant to scare Holly off from the Dumok it had the opposite effect. The Dumok called and Holly jumped to see him.

"Promise me something."

"Sure."

The Dumok frowned. "That you'll be very careful." His eyes flashed.

Though he didn't tell Holly, he had a strong suspicion that the car wreck was no accident. There was a contract on her life. Why? He didn't know but would get to the bottom of it. Soon.

Last night, the Dumok had opened up to Holly. He had completed college and also obtained a law degree before going to work for the Korean government, he said. At eighteen, he had enlisted in the armed forces, and later worked as a liaison with the armed forces in Britain and eventually was dispatched to South Korea. He was in good health although he had been seriously injured, the only direct reference to the scar on his neck. He said nothing more about it and she did not ask. His father was of French descent and his mother was Korean.

"So, because of my dear mother, I have an appreciation of Korean women," the Dumok shared, his eyes twinkling.

He had the beautiful French manners to go with the beautiful eyes. Holly could see clearly that genetics had strongly favored his father, his coloring, his height, and the soft curly black hair on his chest and legs. His eyes and cheekbones showed his exotic Asian side, but in general the contributions of his mother's genes were subtle.

"Don't draw attention to yourself. Put the search for Nara Song aside for the time being and do your other work. Safety is the top priority. There is only one Holly," the Dumok said softly. "Go, but stay close, and you must distance yourself from me for now."

CHAPTER 36

It had been a long drive for Holly and the entrance to the ranch was poorly marked. The wood sign was splintered and faded and off the main road. The paint was cracked and blistered by the hot Malibu sun. It said Dry Creek Ranch. There was a caricature of a horse standing on its hind legs, and an arrow pointing right through an open rusted wrought iron gate.

The road was long and dusty and full of ruts. The fences surrounding the property had once been white but now a weathered grey. Holly peered as far down the road as she could see but the road twisted and turned out of sight. Soon Holly could no longer see or hear the highway behind her. The road wound around ancient trees. Half a mile more and there was a clearing and two large circular metal fences with, horses. Beautiful horses! Holly cautiously turned off the engine and opened the car door. There was no sign of human life.

A dog ran up. The only sounds were of birds and the ticking of the car engine cooling. It was just as hot out here as in the city, in fact, even hotter. Holly gingerly pushed the gate to a riding ring with two fingers. It didn't budge. She tried again, harder. The gate swung open and she stepped inside. The ground was sandy, dry and uneven with deep holes. There were lights placed carefully around the ring. Off in the distance, a hawk dove from the sky against the backdrop of dusty mountains. Holly folded her arms over her head to block the sun, looking around.

"Can't you read a dang sign?" a gruff voice said.

Holly whirled around and squinted into the unrelenting sun. It took her a moment to focus on the man's face. He was tall and lean and the creases in his skin looked like riverbeds, the skin rough as leather from years under the sun.

"I'm Holly Park. I'm a lawyer," she quickly added.

"Then you should know best what the laws are on trespassing." He squinted at her, his eyes narrowing.

"I'm sorry, but I didn't have a phone number."

"It's unlisted."

Holly said nothing and tried to smile encouragement. He was probably not used to people just showing up. Finally he relented a little.

"The name's Earle. Travis Earle. He quirked his finger for her to follow him over to a tacking shed next to the riding ring. "Long way to come, missy, presuming you drove up here from L.A.?"

"I'm looking for a horse named Lightning," Holly answered. "Is he boarded here?"

The old cowboy turned around. "You Wolf's lawyer?" he asked, suspicious. "Wolf can't afford no lawyer, not even a young one like you."

"No, I'm Kendall Taylor's lawyer."

Travis Earle didn't say much after that. He gestured to the open door. The old cowboy stood aside politely for Holly to enter first. She hesitated and cautiously peered inside before going in. There were worn leather straps, and metal bits hanging on the walls. Her heart was pounding. Loudly. Why did he bring her here? If she was murdered here nobody would know and if she yelled for help nobody would hear, she thought frantically.

"My office."

The flypaper hanging from the ceiling swung gently in the afternoon breeze. The dead flies were stuck like raisins. A refrigerator? Holly thought, and laughed. Of course, a refrigerator. It was so hot outside.

The ancient cowboy opened the small fridge and helped himself to two beers. He cracked them open, the quick hissing sound interrupting the quiet. Holly looked up at the cowboy and in that instant secretly christened him "Riverbed" — for the deep etches in his face, which told stories. Travis Earle, now officially Riverbed, stood directly before her, handed her a beer, and looked down at her feet. He went into a closet and pulled out a pair of women's hiking boots and held them out.

"These should fit."

The boots were a little big, but at least she could walk. Holly hadn't been near—or smelled—horses before. Especially in the heat, the smell was unbearable. She tried to breath shallowly as they entered the stables. Holly forgot all about the smell when, from the large corner stall, a magical creature rose gracefully. Holly clasped her hands, bright eyed. It was Lightning! She just knew because the creature was as graceful and beautiful as Kendall herself.

Travis Earle eyed Holly. Young, pretty, modern. Astonished at the everyday magic of his dying world of men and horses and the silence of nature, which wasn't silent at all, really.

His hands were weather beaten and callused but gentle as he guided Holly's hand up to Lightning. He showed her how to cup her hand when offering the small apple.

"This way he won't accidentally bite your fingers," he said gruffly.

Holly smiled up at him. She stroked Lightning's head, softly, murmuring, and in the smells of the hay and earth, the sound of dogs barking and birds chirping high above, Holly forgot all about the dirty sidewalks, the intrusive smells from food carts lining the streets, the homeless man she gave money to each day, and the sight of the ketchup stained stairwell. Holly had even got used to the smells a little. And she had made a new friend. Maybe two. She smiled and kissed Lightning on the nose.

CHAPTER 37

The next day, Holly got to the prison early. The prison guard was different this time. There were two, one was blond and watched Holly carefully. He had a long elegant nose but a pockmarked face and his eyes were a pale cold green. The other one was younger, shorter, but hard and dark, and had propped himself against the wall as Holly walked through the clanging gates into the attorney visitation room where Wolf was waiting.

Wolf Linser swung his feet off the desk and onto the floor and leaned forward, his hands folded, elbows on the desk. Today he looked more like a bank manager than a prison inmate. The sleeves of his prison blues were rolled up. He stood to his full height and had smoothed his wavy gray-streaked fair hair. The furtive look was gone, his blue eyes clear. Holly could now see traces of his old good looks and charm. Wolf took a seat across from Holly. He grinned with his arms behind his head.

"No one has an attorney as pretty as you," he said. "It's made me a minor celebrity around here."

Holly blushed. She liked the compliment and the slight musicality of his Austrian accent.

"I have a present for you," Wolf said. There was a hint of pride in his voice. He sat upright in his chair and proudly pulled out piece of carefully folded paper. It was a pencil sketch of a horse's head with a white lightning bolt on his forehead. Holly took it with both hands, holding it carefully by the edges.

"This is beautiful. Is the horse yours?" Holly asked.

"Yes," Wolf answered. "The beauty of a horse comes out from the rider."

If Holly wasn't mistaken, she detected the slightest bit of flirtation in his voice. She laughed to herself as she put the drawing carefully to one side of the table. After their horrible first meeting they had become an odd pair. They balanced each other's moods. When he was despondent and brooding Holly could cajole him out of his dark moods. He in turn rewarded her by giving her his trust and telling her his story.

"Let's start with something easy." Wolf smiled.

"Wolf, I want to know how you met Alexis," Holly said. "Is that easy?"

"Once upon a time," Wolf started. He stretched his arms over his head and his eyes got a faraway look.

"Cut! Cut!" The director yelled. "Shit!" The horse neighed and fell in a quivering mass of torn flesh and blood. Wolf ran over to the horse. "There, girl, it will be all right." He soothed the horse, holding its gaze, petting its nose. The horse had run through a wire in a fall and sliced its leg. Wolf glared quickly at the director who said nothing. The vet was there quickly. Fifteen minutes later the decision was made. Wolf did not break the animal's gaze as the vet used his needle. The horse, named Charcoal, had trusted him. He had trained her for two years. Trust. Time. Patience. Even love.

And now, a life. A horse, but still a life. Dead for no reason. Horses died, but never so stupidly as this. Wolf stood to his full height and sighed. An intern brought over a bottle of water. She was crying. Flesh and blood. Feelings.

He walked over to the hotshot young director who had insisted, despite Wolf's warnings, that the scene was too difficult for the horses.

"How do you plan on shooting this scene now?" Wolf asked in a flat, lifeless tone, then stood and waited. The others stood around staring at the ground. The silence grew like a wave. Wolf bit his lip, digging his own nails into the palms of his hands. The silence said it all. He had never wanted to kill a human being as much as right now.

The director looked at his shooting schedule, avoiding eye contact with Wolf, looked at the sky and squinted. "We have another hour of this light. I'll talk to Tony and see if there is a way we can shoot around this for today."

With that, Wolf was dismissed. No apology. As Wolf walked away his cell phone rang.

"Hi. A client wants to buy a horse." It was Kendall on the line, calling from Texas.

Irritated, Wolf said, "I can cut her a deal on a dead one, otherwise, I'm busy." The phone rang again.

"She wants to buy a horse today. I need you to meet with her today. Obviously I'm not there."

There was that harsh undertone to her voice again. How he hated it. He sighed. He had fought with the director all day, then the accident. The heat had made the horses surly and uncooperative—like his wife. The last thing he needed this late in the day was another fight.

"Baby, I'm busy now. We have big problems. Charcoal got injured and we had to put her down."

"Then we need to make a sale so we can replace Charcoal. The buyer can come late. I'll tell her nine. Be there at the show corral."

Click.

The line went dead. Kendall didn't understand. She was as hard as the diamonds she loved when it came to business. Somehow Wolf got through the rest of the day, everyone was somber and just wanting to get it over with.

Wolf was fifteen minutes late. Two fancy cars were parked side by side near the show corral. It was nearly dark, no matter. There were lights. Wolf's mood had not improved, neither had he eaten since breakfast. He sipped a bottle of warm water as he drove, not even time for drive-thru. Wolf pulled in and parked next to the cars.

The woman eyed Wolf as he made his way to them. He had long

confident strides and a swagger. How she liked that.

Wolf looked at the woman, she was beyond stunning. She was tall, particularly for an Asian, slim and dressed in distressed jeans, a plain black T-shirt and expensive boots. She carried a briefcase and the jewels on her hand shone even though the summer light was virtually gone. Her left hand rested lightly on the man next to her. An actor who Wolf thought he recognized, but he wasn't sure. Wolf didn't watch much television. Wiping his right palm on his jeans he extended his hand. They were Michael Allen and Alexis Lee.

After an hour, Wolf made an excuse to end the meeting. He had an early call, he apologized, gave them his number and said if Alexis wanted to come and ride a couple of horses on Sunday, he would arrange it. The cars disappeared into the night.

Wolf drove back and parked by the corral. He badly needed a shower but he needed to be with the horses for a few minutes. He was pretty fed up with people.

Then his phone rang. A strange number. He didn't want to answer, but maybe it was someone from the set.

To his surprise, the caller was the Asian lady who wanted to buy a horse.

"Can we talk?"

"That's how I met Alexis." Wolf's tone was mild, cautionary, even still astonished, his mind a cacophony of things past.

Holly smiled bravely but felt nothing of courage. The twists of fate, impulsive actions, a roll of the dice... It made you want to stay in bed with your head under the covers.

CHAPTER 38

"It was a beautiful life once upon a time," Wolf began. Hot steam curled up and over the shower door and coated the bathroom windows with a light fog. The sound of Wolf singing came through the door.

"Oh what a beautiful morning, oh what a beautiful day, I've got a wonderful feeling everything's going my way!"

The voice rang merrily. Wolf was happy. The night had been idyllic and the ring of the early morning phone had made the day even brighter. It had been a month since his first wild encounter with Alexis. He had money in his pocket, he drove a Range Rover, traveled first class with Kendall and had his hot Korean girlfriend on the side. He considered himself a simple man; it was like alternating bottles of red and white wine.

Now Alexis was calling to offer to come over and make him a home-cooked meal. He tried to remember if Kendall had ever cooked anything. In fact she regularly joked that she made only one thing well: reservations.

Before that he had lived in casino hotels, and before that with the model, who did even less than Kendall. She had hired some food service to bring three meals a day, and while expensive, all three were not even adequate for one meal for Wolf's frame and activity level.

He could not remember his last home-cooked meal. Certainly not since his dear mama had cooked him his favorite Austrian dishes. It was an exciting prospect. The timing couldn't be more perfect. Kendall was out of town—again. Still, he wasn't going to take any chances. Rather than have them come to the house, he suggested meeting at the ranch. They could go riding first.

Instant family. Just add water. Wolf smiled to himself as he watched Alexis and her tween daughter Naomi tacking the horses. Naomi loved horses and wanted to learn to ride.

Wolf taught Naomi to ride on Lightning. She should have started earlier, but she had her mother's long legs and perfect posture. She was a quick learner and soon was cantering and jumping fences. The daughter was a dead ringer for the mother.

Wolf couldn't help but notice the swell of her breasts against the thin fabric of her T- shirt and the shapely swell of her legs, which reminded him of a young wild colt. As Wolf spent more and more time with Alexis Lee, the crazy thing was he began to find himself enjoying the package deal, and somehow, it was Naomi that kept tugging at his heart.

"The next morning I woke up to find Naomi standing over me," Wolf continued.

"Can you give me a ride to school? I'm late already," Naomi said. It was seven thirty. He never slept in. Alexis's spot in the bed was empty. The girl shrugged her shoulders and looked down.

"Where's your mother?" Wolf asked, trying to clear his head.

"How am I suppose to know? She left!"

"Yes, don't panic. I need two minutes. Go in the kitchen and wait."

Wolf peed and brushed his teeth, pulled on his boots and a clean T-shirt. He looked at his phone, no messages. There was no note in the kitchen. He grabbed two apples as they went out the door.

"Eat this." He tossed one to Naomi as they got in the Range Rover. He took a large bite.

"I never eat breakfast."

Wolf hit the brakes on the car and sat there staring at her. Naomi said nothing, then took a bit of her apple.

"This is good," Naomi admitted.

"Where's your school?"

Naomi told him the cross streets. Wolf stepped on the gas. They were there quickly.

"I get out at 2:30." Naomi opened the car door and stepped down, not looking at him.

"Does your mother know, or do I need to tell her?"

"I think you should come." Naomi ground the toe of her shoe into the gravel.

"Please." She looked up at him. He saw fear in her eyes, and pleading.

"Okay, okay," he said, wondering what was going on.

"Wait! Do you have lunch money?" Wolf asked.

"My mom's real busy. Sometimes she forgets," Naomi said without looking at him. He had left without his wallet, but there were crumpled bills in the console. He flattened them against his thigh and then folded them and handed them to her.

"Thank you, Wolf," she whispered, and then she was gone. Wolf watched a small group of teenage girls crossing the street in front of him, their carefully done hair, their smiles and laughter, the outfits they had put together, their general aura of confidence. Naomi was prettier than any of them, but she seemed so fragile, like a little bird that had fallen out of its nest.

At 2:30 Wolf was waiting outside the school gates when the bell rang. There was still no call from Alexis.

"Hey, Naomi," he said as she climbed into the dusty black Range Rover with a smile. "I did not hear from your momma," Wolf said mildly. "Did you?"

Naomi didn't answer.

"Shall I just drop you at home? I'm sure your momma will be there shortly."

"Um...I don't think there's any food." Naomi stared out the window, not looking at Wolf.

"Ok...let's go shopping," Wolf decided, trying not to show any frustration. But in the end he had fun with Naomi, perhaps it was the sweet way that Naomi chose some particular food or snack that she knew her mother liked, or that she imagined Wolf would—the girl just tugged at Wolf's heart.

It happened just like that. Wolf wasn't looking to move on from Kendall or change his life forever. It wasn't that he didn't love his wife or was madly in love with Alexis, either. It was just that he found himself liking the family life.

At one point, Wolf had decided to end it with Alexis, but he found he couldn't, because his heart now belonged to Naomi, who moved into his orbit like the moon around the earth.

It didn't help that Kendall was always flying off. Investing in a vineyard in Chile. A wine tasting in Bordeaux. Charming celebrity chefs in Aspen so they would promote her wines. The woman was never still.

Wolf was confused, yet suddenly happier than he could ever remember. Naomi. Math. Cookies. Riding lessons. Grooming the horses. Short of when he was taking a piss or shoveling horse manure, outside of school, the kid was stuck to him like glue. Going to buy hay? She was first in the truck. Getting a horse ready for a client? She was happy just to be with him. She chatted happily about kids at school, mean boys, teachers, her friends, horses. It was music to Wolf.

His first impression of Naomi had been of a quiet, lonely girl but she was blossoming now. Suddenly it seemed the days became weeks, the weeks turned into months.

Time passed, and with it fate turned the impossible into the possible, and then, finally, to the inevitable.

CHAPTER 39

The white wooden fences could be seen from the freeway. How Naomi loved them. They seemed to go on endlessly into the hills with promises of horses nearby. She looked out her bedroom window at the white fences in the moonlight, remembering what had happened earlier by the stables, her body tingling in happy memory.

"One day I'm going to jump bareback onto a horse and jump over the white fences and canter off into the hills and just keep going until I disappear," Naomi said, decisively. It was dusk and Naomi was keeping Wolf company as he brushed out the horses.

"No, no, my dear," Wolf corrected, his voice stern and serious. "You can't teach the horses to jump over the fences or they will all run away!"

Naomi's face flushed, red. She hid her face behind her long hair, turning away. He had never reprimanded her before and her eyes welled up with tears. She had upset this tall stranger who had moved in with them, bringing his horses and his wine and his clothes and his black Range Rover that he never washed and his pickup truck that he did.

Wolf eyed his new little charge thoughtfully. She had the awkward beauty of a newborn colt. After a moment he said, "Come here, come here." He stopped brushing out the horse and put down the brush, the bristles uneven with strands of the course horse hair caught in the bristles, the handle, worn and cracked with use and time.

He got down on his knees so he was eye level with Naomi. "I'll teach you not only to ride, but to jump high fences." He gestured at his own height, over six feet tall.

Naomi looked up at him and could scarcely believe it.

First, she didn't believe for a second she could ever learn to jump a fence that tall, and second, even if she could, she could never imagined him sticking around long enough to see her do it.

None of her mother's boyfriends ever stayed. But she really wished this one would. He was kind and never yelled like the others, and he knew how to ride horses. And he kissed her on top of the head and said things like "good morning" and opened the car door for her. She loved that.

Now, as Naomi looked out the window, she wondered how her mother had met him. He was an American after all, well, sort of American. He said he was from Austria and to Naomi it was the same. He looked like the Americans. She couldn't tell the difference. Her mother had never dated an American before.

Naomi tilted her head to one side and resting her head on her arms, stroking her shoulders slowly as she imagined his forearms, thinking of how the muscles tightened as he pulled the saddle, tight, showing her the trick to make the horse exhale as you cinched the strap. He said otherwise the horses thought it was funny to hold their breath and then the loose saddle would roll upside down.

Naomi looked down at her own forearm and flexed. Nothing. Squeeze and tighten as she did there was no muscle movement. Maybe it was different between them and girls.

Another day, Wolf had brought her a gift.

"Thank you!" Naomi breathed, grabbing the diary he presented to her, and a tin of good drawing pencils, holding it just out of her reach. Naomi sat back, her eyes shining. The diary was red. Its cover was a bouquet of hearts.

"You can write and draw about horses, even," he said, winking. When he winked, she turned bright red with happiness. It was

Christmas every day with Wolf around. Naomi loved to talk about horses and Wolf with her friend at recess or lunch.

"You should see how easily he can mount a horse," Naomi had confided. "You can see his quadriceps through his jeans," she said knowingly. She was proud of herself because she knew that word. Quadriceps. She had slipped into the library at lunchtime one day to look up the word because she wanted to know the name of the muscle that moved when you mounted a horse. "I need to know important words like that," she continued. "I'm going to be an equestrian one day." That was another word she liked. Equestrian. That had a "q" in it, too, which was funny, as so few words did. She knew she had started late, but she would work double hard, as long as Wolf was coaching her.

"Naomi, be a love and open the gate for me, will you?" Wolf had called out to her. Naomi's heart pumped as she ran to the gate as if it was the most important job in the world.

Her heart was racing. Nobody ever called her "love" before.

Wolf noticed Naomi never asked for her mother. He also saw that the more time he spent taking care of Naomi the less her mother stayed home, which led to huge fights. One day, after a particularly bad fight, Wolf decided he'd had enough.

"I know you have to leave..." Naomi said, standing in front of him and snuffling, "... because it always ends this way. But I want you to know you were the best daddy I ever had."

Naomi flung herself into his arms and sobbed, her little body shaking and heaving against him. Wolf stroked her hair, soothing her, his heart melting.

"I'm not going anywhere," he whispered over and over until the sobbing stopped and the heaving of her body stilled. "I promise."

The prison guard opened the door. Holly looked up, so caught up in Wolf's story she hardly remembered she was in the prison visiting room. She smiled weakly. "Just thirty more minutes, please," Holly begged prettily. Holly looked at Wolf, his face pale. He didn't even see her. But he began speaking again.

"There were children in big cities who had never seen such stars,"

Wolf began. "Starlight, star bright, first start I see tonight, I wish I may I wish I might, the wish I wish tonight. I wish I may..." The childish rhyme trailed off unfinished to the fates as the teenager dared not say aloud the wishes of her heart. The stars twinkled brightly high in the black sky above the ranch house. Naomi sighed wistfully as her eyes followed Wolf as he moved around the stables, turning the horses in for the night. The horses knew and trusted him and snorted and snuffled when he came near. She wished she were one of them.

Her young heart yearned for him and she stole a picture of her mother and Wolf and cut her mother out of it and hid it in the inner pocket of her wallet. Sometimes, when nobody was looking, she would take the photo out and look at it. How she missed him. Lately, he spent less and less time with her.

Naomi started sleeping with the night-light on and her bedroom door wide open, saying it was against the heat. But really, she liked to hear when Wolf came home. But from the bedroom, Naomi always awoke at the sound of car wheels on the gravel road and the sound of the keys turning quietly in the front door. She could hear him hang his keys on the key hook near the door after he had checked the horses, which he always did, and his footsteps were quiet as he made his way to the empty master bedroom.

Her mother was rarely home these days, either. It was in these lonely days and nights she kept company with her memories of her lost sister. How her heart ached for her.

"Goodnight, Wolf." Her girlish voice echoed faintly in the quiet night. The first time, Wolf stopped, surprised. His footsteps paused, and then he turned towards her bedroom to find Naomi wide awake.

"Why are you awake?"

"I can't sleep."

"Go to sleep my beautiful princess," he said to her affectionately. "You don't have to wait up for me, baby," he added, kissing her forehead. Her face burned with embarrassment and delight. "Go to sleep now, love." His voice resonated in her heart.

Naomi snuggled deep into the duvet with a peacefulness that warmed her body. She loved how he called her princess and love.

Naomi felt her body tingle warmly. She tried to sleep. But she could never sleep. She could usually keep her mind busy during the day but it was always at night when she thought most about her twin sister, Sara, and when her heart ached the most. Her mom had said she should never mention Sara to anyone, ever.

She once had accidentally mentioned Sara to Wolf.

"I told Sara she could ride Lightning one day," Naomi said, softly. "She's my twin sister."

But Wolf only smiled. "I wish I had imaginary friends," he teased in his gentle way. "They don't try to borrow your truck and bring it back dirty and with no gas, or forget it's their turn to buy the beer."

It was perfect. She could talk about Sara and Wolf thought it was make-believe and they would laugh. But at night she did not laugh. At night Sara always visited in her dreams. They talked in their own secret language that no one else understood. And often Naomi would have bet the moon and the stars that Sara was right there with her and she would wrap her arms around her sister's waist, tightly, the way they used to, with every ounce of strength in her young body to keep her there. But when she opened her eyes, Sara was never there. She always would find herself staring at her pillow in her arms. That's when the tears came because the hole in her heart was so big she felt like she would fall in.

Then there were the other nights, when Naomi just woke up screaming.

CHAPTER 40

Holly's back hurt. She was thirsty, but if a meteor had been about to crash into the planet she would not have stopped Wolf's story. Holly silently willed Wolf the strength to keep going.

Naomi's body was changing, too. It was developing curves and the more it changed the more she wrestled with her feelings. Lately, she was always looking in the mirror and cried over nothing. Life wasn't any fun at all. She didn't like the way her breasts swelled and the way her hips were rounding out. None of her other classmates were developing so early. which made Naomi even more ashamed.

"Go on a diet, you're getting fat." Naomi was standing with Julie, her best friend. Naomi tugged at her shirt self-consciously. Her body was betraying her. Julie made fun of her and teased her endlessly so Naomi started wearing sweatshirts to hide her changing body, even when it was hot.

One particular day, the summer heat was so unbearable Wolf worked outside, his shirt off, mopping the beads of sweat from his forehead with a towel. He looked over and noticed Naomi in her usual spot, watching.

"Princess," Wolf called out. "Aren't you hot? Why don't you change into something cooler or go inside where the air conditioner is on?" he said. He walked over to her. Perspiration gleamed on his forehead.

Naomi hung her head in deep shame. She couldn't even manage to speak, her frustration was so deep.

"What the matter with you?" Wolf asked. Naomi burst into tears and ran into the stables. Wolf followed. "What's wrong with you, princess? Is something the matter?" he asked again. "I just don't want you fainting in this heat," he said, helplessly. When Naomi buried her face in her hands, he picked her up and hoisted her on top of one of the corrals. Wolf cupped her face in his hand.

"Look at me," he said. "Look at me," he repeated, this time a little more gently.

Naomi blushed.

"Tell me," he said, quietly. "I can't help you if you don't talk to me," he coaxed her, murmuring as if to a colt, softly, until her emotions broke like a dam.

"I hate...my body," she cried.

"Why, princess?" Wolf asked, astonished by her confession. He was genuinely perplexed. "Why do you hate your body?"

"It's getting...it's changing... I just don't like it," she whispered, her head hung low.

"That's... how it started," Wolf stammered, his voice hoarse now, the energy draining out of him. "It was like that. The two of us alone. All the time. She was nice. Her mother was different. I don't understand women. Not at all. Her mother was always angry and gone all the time. And I didn't know what to do."

"It was always the two of us," Wolf said nervously to Holly. "We spent an awful lot of time alone. She was a skinny little thing. Always had an upset stomach. She never finished a meal and was prone to vomiting easily. So I started cooking for her when her mother was away," Wolf said with a thousand yard stare.

The kitchen was busy with activity. Wolf hummed merrily as he sprinkled flour on the marble kitchen counter and placed a mound of chilled pastry. Aluminum bowls of melted butter and a brush and another of an apple mixture sat ready to one side. And they had already made a custard from scratch.

"Come, dear, and lend a hand," he beckoned. "I'll teach you how to roll out the dough. Naomi dusted the rolling pin with flour as she had been taught and set to work.

"Don't be afraid of the dough!" Wolf laughed, putting his arms around her to reach the outside edges of the rolling pin handle. "Put some of those new muscles into it."

Their fingers overlapped as he showed her just the right pressure, just the right rhythm and motion to roll out the dough. His fingers clean but rough and large, her fingers long and delicate with the palest pink polish.

Wolf loved Naomi's company. Cheerful with drifts towards melancholy, but that matched better with Wolf's temperament. Even her teenage eccentricities and growing pains amused him. The drama with her friends, the urgency of everything. Even her make-believe twin sister amused him.

By the end of the second glass, the intoxicating effect of the wine and the girl were the same. He rolled the bottle over in his hand. He drank deeply with the girl on the other side of the table watching him, vicariously sharing the moment. She had no idea how beautiful she was. Her mother never told her.

Wolf stopped abruptly. Suddenly he looked very tired.

"Please, just a little longer," Holly begged. "Then I promise I'll go.

CHAPTER 41

"Everything changed after Seoul," Wolf began. "Alexis's father was dying, so we all went to Korea to pay our last respects." Wolf shook his head, still mystified. He pressed his hands against his face.

"What happened in Seoul?" Holly asked, her breath sharp.

Wolf shook his head. "I don't know. Alexis changed after Seoul. After her father died. There was something, the dark cloud over her got even darker. I could hear Alexis and her mother speaking angrily but I understood nothing," Wolf said, shaking his head. "I don't understand you people," he added.

"Shall we take a break?" Holly asked, exhausted herself.

"I can do it." Wolf sighed. "You don't stop an exorcism in the middle." Wolf grimaced, shaking his head.

It was the month after he returned from Seoul that changed Wolf's life. Alexis had been home for a couple hours and had left again. Her bags were still unpacked upstairs in the ranch house. Wolf had given the bags nothing more than a passing glance when he had come home that evening. Right now, he was preoccupied with getting ready. It would be an exciting night. It was Naomi's sixteenth birthday and he was going to take his little girl out.

Naomi chose a deep red lip liner and carefully followed the curve of her lips with precision, copying her mother, who had done the same just hours before. Her face was a canvas and her work flawless.

"I can't go. I have a business meeting tonight," Alexis tersely told Wolf

"But it's Naomi's sixteenth birthday," Wolf protested.

Alexis ignored Wolf and left.

Naomi finished her face and sprayed her mother's Chanel perfume on her neck and sprayed the insides of her knees. She wore her mother's black camisole and a pair of her mother's thigh high hosiery with French black lace, which made her look so beautiful and sexy. She wanted to look that way, too. She had waited for this night. She could tell the nights her mother would not be coming home.

With her heart beating rapidly, she dared look in her mother's full-length mirror. In her mother's dressing room there were many shoes. Naomi knew the right ones.

Her breath was sharp as she caught her reflection. Her breasts spilled from the thin camisole and the French lace on her thighs and the stiletto heels elongated her legs. The shoes were a little large and she wobbled, and caught her balance.

The *Penthouse* magazine was under the bed. She had seen it. She reached for it and flipped through the pages. The full-length mirror was positioned in front of the king size bed. She positioned herself on the bed and copied the girls on the pages, giggling. How long she stayed in the darkened room she didn't know. She was lost in her own thoughts and strange trembling when she heard a noise from the bedroom door. Wolf was standing at the door. Naomi's heart beat wildly. How long had he been standing there?

Naomi stared at Wolf with curiosity and trust as his eyes move over the curves of her body.

Wolf could feel his blood rising. Here she was, laying on cool white sheets, curiosity and trust in her eyes. She was his daughter. She was not his daughter. She was a stepdaughter. She was not a stepdaughter, even. Naomi was constantly following him around giving him long looks, and it was getting harder and harder to stop his mind from wandering from mother to daughter. Naomi was like an untamed colt, daring him to ride bareback. Enough was enough. At the end of the day he was just a man.

In the early hours of the morning, Alexis came home to a dark and quiet house. As Alexis undressed and climbed into bed, had her mind not been preoccupied otherwise, she may have noticed the faint sweet smell of strawberry lip-gloss coming from her snoring husband as he slept on the other side of the bed.

"Was that the first time?" Holly whispered.

"Yes." Wolf's voice was strained. "The first time was on Naomi's sixteenth birthday."

Holly exited the gates. The yard was empty. A half a dozen prison guards walked in a disconsolate circle under the setting sun. She rooted through her purse and slipped them a few twenties.

"God bless your heart, Counsel."

Back in Los Angeles, Holly turned on Crenshaw Boulevard and raced past the ten-story orange and white public storage unit off Pico and Crenshaw Boulevard. Today, the building looked an ominous gray because it was the summer and it had not rained in months. As she pulled up to the church gate, police sirens howled and several police cars screeched up. Four cops burst out of the squad cars weapons drawn and surrounded an overexcited homeless man on the sidewalk.

"Please leave him alone. He just wants dinner and the church is closed tonight. It was my turn to be here and I was late," Holly pleaded.

CHAPTER 42

The historic homes of Hancock Park were built with thick walls to withstand the hot California sun. Usually that and the beautiful tree-canopied streets kept the temperatures moderate. But not on this night. Instead, the hot air swirled, trapped and stifling, ever present and taunting. The night before had been equally unrelenting and Heather had gotten no sleep. She quickly packed an overnight bag and left.

The instant relief of air conditioning calmed Heather as she walked into the lush flowery lobby of The Four Seasons Hotel. Comfort and respite. Gordon had been having one of his episodes. It was better for Heather to leave than stay and fight.

Culina Restaurant offered a seductive and tantalizing slow dance of the palate of the subtle and fine flavors of Northern Italian cuisine. She started with white grapes sprinkled over bitter greens, olive oil light to the taste and touch, then ate a simple piece of fish baked in parchment with herbs. It was served with grilled zucchini and she enjoyed two glasses of a perfectly chilled Gaja. By the end of dinner, she had completely forgotten about the heat and how stressed she had been.

Heather slipped upstairs and walked in as housekeeping was leaving. She loved the turn-down service, especially the treats left on the pillows, which she never ate but liked to see anyway. The plushness of the pillows and fine linens seemed so inviting.

Finally, she thought. Highly indulgent but worth the price. Undressing, she slipped between the coolness of the perfect white sheets and felt her body relaxing for the first time in forty-eight hours. *Sleep, sleepy sleep*, she thought. *Tomorrow will be better.* She closed her eyes, allowing her body to sink deeply into the plushness of the bed. As she felt herself relaxing the phone pinged. She smiled to herself and reached for the phone. A text.

She smiled. It was Mick. "Hi ;-)" the text winked.

"Hi back," she texted.

"Are you melting from the heat and turning heads?"

"Earlier, yes. But not now." Heather quickly typed. "I checked into a hotel," she wrote.

"Do you have air conditioning?"

"Yes, do you?"

"No. But I was born cool."

"Remember tomorrow. My charity event is at 1 p.m. sharp. Park in the back, drop my name like a grenade down a hole." Heather hit send, quite pleased with herself.

Heather put down the phone and snuggled deeply in the covers and looked out the window towards the twinkling lights.

Downstairs at the Four Seasons Hotel, Kendall Taylor wandered into the bar, drawn by the music of an acoustic guitar playing a song she remembered from happier times. A musician sat on a stool in the corner. Very young, Kendall thought, as she sat on a black leather couch close enough to hear him.

What did he know of love and loss at that puppy age? Kendall laughed wistfully. The song had probably been written by someone much older. Nonetheless his singing was convincing. The melancholy songs were like a time machine, and she decided to order a drink. Tonight she had no plans, and though it was late, she just wanted to get out of the house.

She ordered a Grey Goose vodka. Vodka, no hidden agenda, no reticence, and straight to the point. It suited her mood. Sharp, but with a smooth finish. Her eyes wandered to three men leaning on the zinc bar drinking Beck's beer, with too much energy to actually occupy stools.

They looked college age, tall, athletic, handsome, with their hair a little longer than was fashionable, dressed in polo shirts and jeans. A thin man in a black suit discreetly took some shots with a serious looking camera. They must be from a professional sport team, Kendall thought. She wondered which one. Two couples occupied the other end of the room, having an after dinner cognac and coffee, and at the other end of the bar a group of dark-suited businessmen drank Scotch. In all, a quiet night. Kendall watched the musician's fingers on the strings of his guitar.

"Is the seat next to you taken?" an accented voice asked.

Kendall looked up. It was the tallest of the young men from the bar. His friends and the photographer were gone.

"You've been abandoned by your teammates," Kendall said, with a half smile. "I'm guessing you are on a professional team, perhaps soccer?"

"Yes, football as we say, and soccer as you Americans say. My friends are jet-lagged. They want to sleep. Of course I am wide awake," he said good naturedly.

"May I?" he asked and sat down. Kendall did not object. Up close he was even better looking, dark hair, dark eyes, with the accent. He could only be Italian.

"Piero Bracco." He extended his hand.

"Kendall Taylor." Kendall tossed her golden mane, her movements like a panther stretching. "Where are you from?"

"I play for Modena in Italy. My teammates and I were invited to visit Los Angeles by the Galaxy team. Have you heard of the team?"

"I know nothing except horses and wine, and even those I find I know less each year." Kendall smiled quietly, finally relaxing.

"Not so many years." He smiled and his soft Italian eyes glowed.

Kendall felt weak inside. She knew this boy was just on the prowl, but at least he had some style.

"A woman is exactly like wine. A few years in an oak barrel is good, it softens the edges."

"You are precious." Kendall laughed in spite of herself. "Did you just make that up?"

"My father owns vineyards in Piedmont. He makes Barolo, of course. He worked me like a Roman slave, but running up and down the hills is how my legs became strong enough for football, so I attribute my father for that."

Kendall's blues were suddenly gone. "I invest in wineries, in Napa, mainly, but we've never aged anything ten years."

"Then we already have something in common," Piero decided. "Shall we have another drink together? The same?" He indicated towards her empty glass.

"Yes, I would like that—except now you've made me want a glass of Barollo. Lets go to the Culina down the hall. They have a floor to ceiling wine cellar. Surely they can serve us a glass of Barolo. It will be quieter, too."

Piero stood and held out his arm. Kendall was pleased. This handsome young athlete had some sophistication.

Culina was gracious, though it was late and the kitchen was winding down. They had a bottle of Barolo, pizza and salad. Piero lightly touched her arm as they talked. He was funny and relaxed and made Kendall laugh. It had been a while.

"Have you ever been in love?" Kendall asked, her voice trailing. "I've only been in love once and that was many years ago. We've been apart now twice the years we were together, but I can't seem to forget him." Her speech was beginning to slur. "I'm trying to figure out if I want to keep remembering, or if I just want to forget." Kendall sighed.

Piero leaned back, his arm slung around the back of the booth as he lightly played with her hair.

"I gave him my heart, unconditionally. And he left me for another woman. A Korean woman at that," Kendall wrinkled her nose. Her beautiful face, flawless from a lifetime of staying out of the sun and using only the most expensive face creams, was creased now. She tilted her perfect face upward, and smiled at her companion. Young. Not complicated. Wolf had been way too complicated.

"I don't understand why a young handsome guy like you wants to be here drinking with a lonely woman."

"I don't know why you are lonely when I am here with you now." His tone was soothing. Piero looked around, the place was almost empty. "What do you want to do tonight that would make you feel better?" he asked, smiling with his eyes.

"No woman can really know what truly goes on inside a man's mind, now can she?" Kendall purred as she slid closer to him. "I married twice for money, and the third time for love to a man who was as charming as he was insincere. When I met him he was desperate. There were signs. I ignored them because he made me laugh and I loved him like I have never loved a man. Was I so foolish?"

"He was foolish to leave you."

"You are so very sweet," Kendall said. "I thought I could change him." She stopped, abruptly, and turned to face him. Her next words were earnest, searching.

"Piero, dear, can you kindly explain something to me about men that I simply don't understand?"

"Ask away."

"Asian fever," Kendall said, shaking her lovely head in bewilderment. "Can you please explain the appeal of Asian women to a man? Because quite honestly, I don't get it at all."

CHAPTER 43

Hermés. Chanel. Trezzo, that was it. Something with Zs in it, Mick thought. He sped past and turned into the alley that ran behind all the stores parallel to Rodeo Drive. He parked beside a dumpster and put his cop plaque on the dash. He folded down the visor and adjusted his tie and instinctively reached for his gun. He always packed heat.

Mick Chang squinted at the sunlight. He put on his sunglasses and walked up to the back door. A male attendant in a black suit and a clipboard stood with the guest list.

"What?" Mick said defensively.

"Your name, sir."

Mick's face registered slight surprise when the attendant found it.

"Right this way, sir," he said, motioning for Mick to pass through.

Inside was cool, the ebb and flow of quiet conversation, the clink of Champagne glasses, many guests milling around with hardly any room to move. There were no chairs.

Mainly there were a lot of really hot looking, but skinny, dressed up women of all ages. He tried to find Heather, but no luck, and he worked his way further up. A young caterer in a black T-shirt passed with a tray of Champagne and Mick snagged one. He was thirsty. A pretty girl also in black offered him a tray of what looked like baby wontons sprinkled with black sesame seeds with a black toothpick sticking out of it. It looked like a lot of trouble for something so tiny. He took one then snagged a few more and put them on a tiny black and white napkin and ate. He wished he'd hit the drive-thru on the way here. Heather had said there would be food but this didn't count. Seriously.

Then he spotted Heather by the front door, in another throng. He worked his way there; it wasn't easy. It would have made him happy to be able to clear a path by firing a shot in the air, but he had been written up enough times already.

"Thank you for coming," Heather gushed. Mick just stared at her. She had rocks around her neck that he just couldn't believe, they had to be real, he just knew. She wore impossibly high heels and a poufy black skirt and sequined black top that showed off her rocking hot body. There was more black here than at funerals. "You look amazing."

"You're too sweet." Heather pecked him on the cheek.

"When is the show?" Mick wondered and Heather read his mind.

"See some of these tall girls walking around?"

"Yes. Yes, they are really tall," he said. And hot and skinny and young, and that one is not wearing a bra, and neither is that other one, but they are wearing way too much makeup—only he didn't say these thoughts aloud.

"They are the show. Instead of a runway they walk around and pose for the guests. It's more intimate this way, don't you think?"

"It's more fun than I thought, babe." Mick finished his Champagne and magically another was handed to him and the empty glass disappeared.

"How much is one of his outfits?" he asked, curious.

"Outfit?" Heather thought for a second. "Trezzo's lines run starting from $5000. Fur trim and fancy beadwork doubles or triples the price. Any sales made today, 15% goes to the Italian earthquake fund."

"Dollars?"

Heather nodded and touched his arm but Mick was distracted by a waiter carrying sliders. He snagged three of them and asked, "What's the noise?"

There was a strange loud squawking coming from outside and the shriek of electrical feedback.

"You came at the perfect time." Heather touched Mick's arm. "It's protesters — they worry me, but only a little." Heather pointed him to the store display windows looking out onto Rodeo Drive where the protesters were chanting and carrying signs. "They're from PETA." Heather sighed. "Protesting fur in the—"

Before Heather could finish, Mick bolted out the door. Heather reached out to grab his arm but Mick was too quick.

Mick marched across the sidewalk into the crowd blocking the street, and headed towards the head yahoo with the megaphone. In half a second, the leader was on the ground after a discreet rabbit punch to the kidney. On his way down he swung the megaphone wildly and caught Mick by the edge on the forehead. Instant blood.

"Let go of the fucking megaphone," Mick hissed, "or you'll think you're back in prison—on date night." Mick squeezed. After a few seconds the leader coughed and went limp.

Mick grabbed the megaphone and took the batteries out of it. The lined-up guests behind the velvet rope waiting to get in broke into applause. The protesters shrieked and waved their signs. A TV news van rolled up and a female reporter ran towards Mick.

"Was that force necessary?" she asked.

Mick put his hand over her mike. "Fuck you, bitch," he whispered and walked away. Heather ran up.

"You're bleeding!" She reached for a black and white napkin off a tray.

"Really?" Mick touched his forehead with his fingers and looked at the blood. "Sorry."

Several of the male guests patted him on the back. Someone else brought him a glass of Champagne.

"I'm an attorney," a voice said, and handed Mick his card. "Call if there's a problem with this. We're big supporters of anything Heather Hart does and appreciate you helping out."

Mick turned to Heather. "If you're good, I'm going to disappear. I don't want to be a distraction. Beverly Hills cops will be here. I can hear the sirens. They're used to dealing with these clowns."

"You are so exciting, darling. Some of my friends were scared, and you took care of it," Heather gushed. She leaned forward and whispered in his ear. "Can you still have dinner?"

"Text me, babe. I'll go out the back." And he was gone.

Heather looked out the front window of the store. The cops were clearing out the protesters to the far sidewalk. The storefront of Trezzo would make the news, and that was never a bad thing. The guests had some excitement. All in all, a great day. And damn that Mick was sexy when he got fired up. Heather sighed at that thought.

CHAPTER 44

"Pick up! Pick up! Please!" Heather whispered into the ringing phone. Heather sat on her favorite couch. Her husband Gordon was upstairs. He spent his days feeding his neuroses only. The rare meetings or social events he attended were both preceded and followed by massive anxiety attacks. Heather looked around the room and quickly placed a call.

"Hello," Holly answered on about the sixth ring.

"Holly! It's me! I have to see you and I can't talk about it on the phone." Heather was frantic. She loved Holly like family. Strike that. She didn't like anyone in her family as much as she liked Holly.

An hour later Holly was in Heather's living room, drinking cappuccino, eyeing a small plate of almond biscotti and leaning on silk cushions. The room was pale yellow and turquoise with huge potted palm trees and a very large cream-colored Persian carpet with some sort of floral design.

"You look so good," Holly said, with utter sincerity.

"I've been only eating raw almonds," Heather offered. "And quinoa and ahi... I hate this room. Actually I hate this house—but this room has the most privacy. You quickly learn that the servants always have an ear out."

Holly nodded. She could see the blue glitter of the pool outside.

"I've been trying to get a hold of you," Heather whispered urgently. "I don't want to alarm you but the Feds are planning huge raids and American Legal Services is on the list!"

"Wh-what...?" Holly stammered, the color drained from her face. "Are you sure? How do you know?"

"Gordon had a sleepover at his mothers — again," Heather whispered. "So last night, I went out to dinner with you-know-who."

"The cop?"

"Yes!" Heather whispered urgently. "He always has his phone on the table during dinner. Well, it pinged while he was in the restroom so I looked — I mean any girl would look, right?" Heather's eyes went wide and Holly nodded.

"Anyway," Heather continued, "I looked over and saw American Legal Services pop up. Isn't that where you work?"

Holly nodded.

"Well, that's what I thought. So I picked up the phone and read the text because that's just the kind of person I am," Heather confessed. "And it was confirming the logistics to raid the place next week. Why are they raiding, Holly? Are you in trouble?" Heather asked, earnestly.

"I don't think so! Did you see my name?" Holly asked, frightened.

"No, no, not your name. You-know-who has no idea we are friends or that I know you. When he came back, I poked around and asked what he was doing next week. He said he was working on a big raid. You know how the cops are on those raids. They take everything and ask questions later. You are my dearest friend in the world so I have to tell you."

"What should I do?" Holly asked, her heart already pounding.

"Move your office, quickly. Once the warrant is signed you don't know when they'll hit. It's a big raid. And be careful what you say on the phone."

Holly sat up straight. "Now as in today?"

"Yes. The sooner the better. Now go!" Heather said, gesturing with her hands. "Before it's too late."

CHAPTER 45

Holly H. Park—Attorney at Law

Holly peeled the sign off the door. She pushed the door closed and threw the sign into a cardboard box, which in turn sat on top of a stack of other boxes. Exhausted, Holly went to her desk and put her head down and fell asleep.

Then, someone was knocking at the door. She stood up and looked at her watch. Who could it be? Holly opened the door hesitantly.

Detective Mick Chang stood there with a police badge around his neck, wearing jeans and a black T-shirt, which exposed his heavily tattooed arms. Her heart was racing so fast she put her hand on her chest. How did he know she was here? It was after hours and the office was closed.

The detective took in the boxes, desk, case files and nearly empty bookshelves. It was a tiny office, but there was enough.

"Going somewhere?" Mick asked, challenging her. "You know you just messed up my warrant. Now I'm going to have to go back to the station and write up a second warrant and find a judge to sign off on it. None of which is gonna make me happy. So why don't you start co-operating and tell me why you are moving in such a big panic?"

"I know my rights. If you have something on me arrest me now or you can leave and come back with a proper warrant."

Mick stood in the doorway a moment, his eyes moving up and down, brazenly. "Let me guess. You like to party and go drinking which is why you came to this side of town. Lawyers don't usually leave a fancy downtown firm for a ghetto place like this. Most people want to go up-market—not down."

His eyes definitely registered that he had done his homework on her. Mick brushed past Holly and walked into her office without being invited. "Don't you know that obstruction of justice is a felony and I could cuff you and take you down?" Mick asked in his toughest cop voice.

Holly held out her wrists, a gesture which Mick ignored.

"I know more about the Dumok than you do," Mick bragged. Holly just stared at him, so he kept talking.

"Yeah, he wears nice suits, but a punk is always a punk. Yeah, I know all about him." Holly blanched.

"Bingo," Mick thought. He had stabbed blindly, but Holly's face told the tale. Mick's eyes narrowed, suspicious. "That woman you work for—Kate Hong—there's probably enough dirt to get her into court. She didn't look so pretty in prison denim back in New York. Put it this way, if she ended up dead, nobody would be taking up a collection for flowers. Did she tell you about that? Kate Hong got smart and got out of the game, but maybe now she's back to her old tricks." Mick put his foot up on a stack of books.

Holly consciously slowed her breathing and tried to not react. "Where's your warrant, detective." He ignored her.

"Personally, I don't give a rat's ass," Mick continued. "I'm just trying to put the pieces together. There's Kate. She's dirty. There's been a long list of lawyers she uses and you're just the most recent. The dead but not mourned councilman was dirty for years, too. I wouldn't care if he was fucking a dog as long as he wasn't knifed to death in the process. How does the American Legal Service dream team plan on defending little Naomi Linser, the virgin whore? Did you know that she had bloody hundred dollar bills sticking to her like Post-it notes at the crime scene? What's your defense, Counsel?"

Another million dollar question, but the more Mick talked the more it proved he had nothing solid, so Holly decided to hold her tongue. Maybe he would say something interesting.

"And then there's the Dumok. The dirtiest of all. A rich man getting richer off the poor Koreans who do his illegal activities."

Mick didn't bother to mention that his own father had run parking services for the Dumok's nightclubs, and when Mick's father had died, the Dumok had paid for the funeral. To this day his mother kept a newspaper photo of the Dumok on her fridge, which infuriated Mick to no end. Mick only remembered what suited him, and what suited him now was to rant and try and unnerve Holly.

"The common denominator in all this filth?" he continued. "You. How do you fit? Or is it that the Dumok likes you because you are a dirty girl, too?"

Now Holly was getting annoyed. The sexual innuendo made her sick.

"Are you the FBI?" Holly taunted. "If you're not, you can just leave."

Mick walked over to the plant holder, looked down and spit. He didn't speak right away but only stared at Holly in that stoic, detached way cops have.

"I don't waste my time wearing suits and hanging out in offices. I'm from the streets. I like it up close and personal. People like you, who sit behind a desk, you don't know shit," he spit again and put a leg up on the plant holder. Mick leaned against the corner of her desk with his legs crossed. This one was pretty hot, with a fiery spirit, too. Impressive. She wasn't backing down so he walked over to Holly and stood deliberately close to her. He was wearing some men's cologne, Polo, or Aramis, a fragrance that Holly hated.

"If you can't piss with the big dogs, stay out of the tall grass." Mick turned and slammed the door shut.

CHAPTER 46

If there were ever a day when Holly needed her father's calming voice, it was today. She pulled into the church parking lot and slipped into the last row of the pews. Just sitting there calmed her stormy seas. Her father was a charismatic man, ageless in his vigor. Finally, Holly could feel herself relax as she listened to the comforting familiar resonance booming from the speakers.

"Do you have time to talk?" Holly ran in. Her father listened, then said words, as Holly knew he would, that would comfort her. It was everything he said. And some things he didn't say, too. His experiences growing up in North Korea under the Japanese occupation and escaping the North Korean communists during the war had forever shaped him. Even after many years in America, he suffered no fools.

"Be careful, Holly," he warned. His tone was somber. "You don't know Koreans."

Holly thought about his words as she drove home. It was true. The more she was drawn into Korean culture the less she knew.

The next morning Holly stood in front of the refrigerator and drank orange juice and grimaced. She looked out her open balcony door. It was everything a Monday morning at six would be. Nobody moving, nobody lurking in cars, no sounds of gardeners with their leaf blowers, nothing. She hadn't slept well and felt like hell. She applied fresh lipstick and put on a brave smile, picked up her briefcase and left.

Outside, Holly looked around carefully, but there was nobody who seemed out of place. Detective Chang had spooked her, but damned if he was going to break her.

Thank god Logan Burg hadn't held a grudge and had agreed to sublet an office on short notice. Kate Hong had not been happy but all Holly could do was mumble a short apology and leave. She did not give a reason.

Holly almost went to her old office out of habit. She already missed the annoying Mi Rae and her unsolicited takes on everyone and everything. As she was unpacking, a head popped into the doorway.

"Nice digs!" Mi Rae took an appreciative glance at her surroundings. "I can't believe you left this for Koreatown. There are so many good-looking lawyers, too! Anyone single?" Mi Rae asked, cocking her head prettily. Mi Rae was so impressed her excitement could not be contained.

"Perfect timing, you can help me unpack."

"I don't want you to be lonely so I brought lunch—bento boxes," Mi Rae said proudly, handing her a bag, which Holly put on a side table.

"Plus, I needed an excuse to get out of the office."

"Why?" Holly asked, frowning, immediately wondering if Mick Chang was poking around.

"Kate is in a foul mood, that's all."

"It's supposed to rain, that makes everyone grumpy," Holly suggested.

"Oh, Kate is more than grumpy! She's in full bitch mode," Mi Rae offered cheerfully. "Even Neil refused to stay and went out for an early lunch."

Mi Rae sat down and began organizing the food. Holly went to the kitchen for water and came back a few minutes later.

"Mi Rae, did the old court files on the Wolf Linser case ever show up?" Holly asked, as she opened the bento. There was yellow tail and tuna sushi, California rolls, and shrimp tempura. "What a feast," Holly said gratefully.

"Ta-da!" Mi Rae ceremoniously announced and handed over the papers like a magician. "The messenger service brought it this morning. That's really why I came, of course."

"Thank you, Mi Rae. Yummy," Holly said in between bites.

"You will pay me back for the lunch, won't you?" Mi Rae asked, sucking her chopsticks and smacked her lips. "You make more than I do."

"Of course I will—and I'll give you money for the parking. You'll cry when you see what they charge."

After lunch Mi Rae left. Holly cleaned up then walked over to the kitchen for fresh coffee and returned to her office, and carefully placed her green shaded lamp on her desk and turned it on. Then rain spotted the windows. The weatherman had been right after all. The rain was coming down hard and flowing along the curbs in rivulets.

Holly turned to the file on her desk, waiting for the coffee to kick in. She reached for the manila envelope that contained Wolf Linser's file. The public defender's office had handled the case. Holly opened the file and began reviewing it when she noticed something. Officer Mick Chang had been the arresting deputy? Her heart started pounding and she read the file.

The sound of the rain pounded against the glass window as Holly slowly turned the pages of the file. The arraignment, plea and sentencing were taken only two months after the arrest. Wolf Linser had caved with no fight at all. The public defender had done almost nothing. She picked up the photos and absentmindedly flipped through them. It was then Holly saw the photo. At first Holly thought it was a photo of Naomi then realized it wasn't.

The girl in the photo held two fingers next to her eyes in the double V-sign as she smiled, her head tilted girlishly to one side. Her large beautiful eyes had an artful innocence as she stared into the camera—eyes that gave away nothing. She wore a necklace around her long and slender neck, the kind you would only see in a very expensive catalog or *Vogue* magazine and not the kind of necklace a young girl would wear. The necklace was two interlocked circles of gold and diamonds resting in the hollow of her throat. She was wearing a halter top, which with the slightest touch would fall from her slim white arms and shoulders.

Holly turned the photo over. "Honeymoon at Jeju Island." The inscription was in English, in the faded, schoolgirl-careful cursive script she had seen before.

Holly felt a strange cold chill wash over her and her breathing became difficult. It was a copy of the photo the Dumok had shown her on his first visit to her office. The one that had disappeared. How did it end up in this file?

Holly grabbed the envelope and read Office of the Public Defender. How did the Public Defender get the photo? This could not be the lost photo, that one had not had a stamp on the back. It had to be a duplicate but why was it in Wolf's file?

Holly quickly scanned the other family pictures, her eyes searching as she scrutinized them. Holly gasped. It was so clear. It was plain and obvious and had been under her nose all along. Alexis Linser was Nara Song. She had changed her identity. That meant Naomi was the Dumok's daughter. Naomi was not dead. Grabbing the photos, Holly rushed out into the rain.

CHAPTER 47

The next night Holly left work early and stood on the corner. "Johnny!" Holly waved.

Johnny Gee quickly opened the passenger door and stood by the car, waiting for Holly to get in. They drove west to the end of the freeway and then up the Pacific Coast Highway and ended up at an outdoor eatery without tablecloths, barely visible from the highway. The restaurant was adjacent to an upscale restaurant with white lights wrapped around the trunks of the palm trees. From where they sat, they could hear the band.

"Isn't it nice that we can enjoy the music from here?" Johnny said, inhaling the night air deeply. He smiled, quite pleased.

They ordered beer, which was very cold and had a slight sour taste. Holly didn't have much experience with beer, but she gamely took a longer sip. Holly sat quietly, her eyes wide, stirring the remnants of her drink with a little black plastic straw. She felt her shoulders relax, and finally she was able to feel the merry-go-round in her head slowing down. Each of the riders on the merry-go-round was one of her clients, but each time the merry-go-round stopped, they changed horses.

Be careful. You don't know Koreans. The words echoed in her head. Both the Dumok and her father had warned her. And now Johnny was warning her too.

Holly told Johnny how she had been hired by the Dumok to find Nara Song. Then subsequently by Kendall Taylor to find out why her ex-husband, Wolf Linser, had left her for another woman, who turned out to be Wolf's ex-wife, Nara Song, now living under the identity of Alexis Linser. She told him about Kate and Choi—even about the morgue visit.

"I don't know why Nara Song lived under the alias of Alexis Lee, or what this Choi person's involvement is about," Johnny began. "Your job for the Dumok was to find Nara Song. You did. Your job for Kendall was to find out why Wolf left her for Alexis. You did. That's it. I think you're a little too close to the flame, Holly, if you want my honest nickel's worth." Johnny leaned back in his chair and flagged down a server and ordered another beer and a basket of chicken wings. "Our job as lawyers is to fulfill each client's instructions as best we can, though I admit when the instructions are so broad, it can make you crazy."

"I think the Dumok really just wants to know if Nara is alive," Holly said slowly, remembering New York.

"Then go tell him, Counsel," Johnny said, pressing the tips of his fingers together. "That you found out by accident doesn't matter. Client doesn't care how you did it."

"Will you come with me?" Holly squeaked.

"Holly," Johnny scolded. "You just need to take a deep breath. It's like muddy water. If you take a glass of muddy water and leave it alone long enough, the crud will settle on the bottom, and the water on top will be clear. If you keep picking it up to see if the mud has settled, it never will."

Holly nodded. Muddy water. Johnny had nailed that one. She would go and see the Dumok. She would go alone.

CHAPTER 48

The next night Holly again drove up the winding Pacific Coast Highway. It brought to mind many apocryphal stories of gangsters, serial killers, suspicious car wrecks and celebrity homes lost in mudslides.

Driving through the canyons now, after the rain, the heavy scent of sage and eucalyptus filled the air, the hills were shadows, except for a golden half moon in the east. The traffic had thinned out. Holly prayed she wouldn't get lost. "Just keep the ocean on your left," everyone had joked. She had a sudden shivering image of coyotes huddled in the brush. She checked the address before pulling off the main road and onto a private road. There were signs that said Private along the single lane road. Dense wild foliage finally gave way to palm trees and manicured landscaping. She now saw bursts of magenta, lilac and white bougainvillea vibrated with color, even as the light was fading.

The moon was higher and fading now. Holly stared out the window straight ahead, wondering whether there were hidden cameras in the Private signs lining the road, trying her best to beat down the urge to turn back. The mounting fear and climbing dread left her short of breath.

Holly continued driving without stopping until she reached the beach house. It was right on the ocean. A cracking sound filled the air—she thought, perhaps, the breaking of waves crashing the shore. She pulled the car into the circular driveway behind his black Mercedes.

Holly could see him, the outline of his form looming over the water, on a flat plane of damp sand, in a brilliant white shirt with his sleeves and pants rolled up. The sunset formed a silhouette of the Dumok's body, his height and broad shoulders unmistakable.

Holly heard the sharp crack again, punctuating the waves crashing against the rocks. It was then she noticed the white and bloodied corpses of a half dozen sea gulls and pelicans that littered the sand around him. The Dumok didn't turn as Holly walked up to him and instead remained focused, tracking a bird with a revolver. Holly felt sick to her stomach and stared at the horizon line as she walked. The ocean looked like it was on fire as the sun sank into it.

He must have been aware of her but made no acknowledgment. The gun cracked and Holly jumped, she couldn't help it. Fortunately he'd missed the shot and the pelican continued its low course over the water.

"I didn't realize you kill your own dinner," Holly said. She knew she was on dangerous ground, and tried to keep the fear and criticism out of her voice. The Dumok barely nodded his head then, in a forced, stiff bow not taking his eyes off the swarming birds above him. He tracked another bird, followed it, fired, then watched it fall.

"Do you know how pelicans die, Holly, in the wild, in the care of Mother Nature, in the arms of our Christian god?"

"No."

"They feed by diving for fish, and they have a protective clear membrane over their eyes to protect them from the impact of diving into the salt water. But as they age the protective layer gets cloudy, and they slowly go blind. Then, they starve to death." He paused. "Perhaps I am kinder than Mother Nature."

Holly didn't know what to say. She tried to read his mood.

"I've learned to identify the old ones..." He stood there reloading. "As for the sea gulls, they're just rats with wings."

"It seems merciful," Holly said as calmly as she could manage. "But the decision is not ours whether we live or die."

"No, but we choose how we live," the Dumok responded feelingly. "Darwin preached the survival of the fittest. The theory is that natural selection will enable the strong to survive and not only preserve but improve the species. I will give you an example. A deer hunter will stalk and try and kill the finest example of the herd. An animal predator will usually attack the weakest example, because it is easier and of less risk to itself. A wolf's priority is to eat and survive the hunt. So which predator is better for the survival of the herd, and the species?"

"The wolf, because the strongest deer surviving to breed will produce a stronger herd in the next generation," Holly answered.

"I agree. I am a predator, in Darwinian terms, and therefore not always in harmony with the human society we live in. But nature proves me right. Mother Nature is much crueler than I am."

Holly stared out at the horizon line. All the strength was leaving her knees.

The Dumok bent to carefully pick up the spent shell casings. When he had them all he put them in his pocket, and walked towards the beach house, motioning for her to follow. He remained silent on the walk back. When they reached the deck he finally turned to her. Searching her face with eyes that were dark and flashing, he took her face in his hands and kissed her. She rested her head on his shoulder and closed her eyes, listening to the waves.

"I would invite you in, but I sense that you have your business face on," he said softly. "Shall we deal with that first? Is it too cool for you out here?"

Holly sat in a white wicker chair. She found his politeness and formality comforting.

She was really glad it was getting dark so he couldn't see her face. The brightest things were the moonlight reflecting off his white shirt, and the sea, and the flashing of his eyes and teeth when he smiled. He was quiet for a long time. Holly sipped her wine and waited, enjoying the cool breeze. She could happily have slept, she in her chair, he in his, holding his hand. It would have been enough for her. But, she had a purpose. She had come for a reason. She had a job to do.

The Dumok smiled again and took the glass for a longer sip. So, Holly told him in the only way she knew how. She had practiced in the car. A dozen ways, a dozen tones. Like trying out different keys and tempos for a piece of music. The notes were immutable, but the feelings they stirred... In the end she was pure Holly. She just blurted it out.

"I found her. Nara Song! Your daughter, too!" Holly blurted.

For the briefest of moments the Dumok paled. Or it could have just been the moonlight on his face. His eyes turned inward, and when he came back, his voice was hoarse. There was bitter and profound sadness when he finally spoke.

"So the rumors are true." The Dumok examined how the moonlight refracted through the wineglass held by his manicured fingers and how a slight movement of wrist changed the spectrum.

There was another silence. She looked at him squarely in the eyes and smiled, hesitantly. She wanted to say something kind, to comfort him. But before she could speak he spoke again.

"How?"

"Exactly like you guessed. Nara Song just walked into the American Legal Services office."

"What is the nature of her troubles?" the Dumok inquired, his eyes banked with a lifetime of slow-burning anger.

"Nara Song has been living under the alias Alexis Lee Linser, who is the mother of Naomi Lee Linser, who I'm sure you know from the news, is charged with Councilman Willie McClellan's murder."

"What did you say?" The Dumok reared his head back and said it with such force she let out a small cry as if he had struck her.

"Nara Song has been living under the alias of Alexis Lee Linser," Holly said it again. It wasn't any easier the second time. "She is the mother of the Naomi Lee Linser, who awaits trial in the death of the Councilman who was stabbed to death in that hostess salon in Koreatown."

Now, the Dumok seemed almost demonic.

"The child is dead!" he said with such savagery Holly let out an involuntary cry.

"She is alive!"

"The child is dead. I saw the graves!"

Then there was silence. Holly bolted up and watched in dismay as the Dumok stormed inside the house, leaving her alone with the moon and the crashing waves, her heart pounding. Finally, when he did not come back out, Holly went inside.

She found him on a different balcony overlooking the beach, with a thousand mile stare over the sand where the carcasses littered the shore, lost in the deafening crash of the waves. Holly stood behind him, wanting so badly to comfort him, to say something, anything, but there were no words. She reached to touch his arm when he turned, violently, wildly.

Under the moonlight, he looked both like a man and a beast—his athletic form looming, creating shadows on the half dark balcony. They were only a few feet apart yet the chasm was too deep and far and she could not reach him.

Holly drove home. She had done exactly what he had asked of her, she had found Nara Song. And in so doing she had lost the Dumok. All their closeness ... gone.

CHAPTER 49

Two weeks passed and still there was no news from the Dumok. Holly went about her day, going to court, meeting clients, drafting motions, working out, getting her hair done and waiting for him to reappear. She liked being back downtown, the energy was better than walking around on tiptoe dodging Kate's stormy moods. Logan was happy, and promised to have lunch with Holly soon.

Then one day the Dumok just showed up. He was wearing his usual dark suit and white shirt with a muted tie. He sat calmly across from her with his hands folded in his lap. Holly had steeled herself for this day, how she would be calm and poised and not show her aching heart and burning cheeks. Professional, waiting for her cool and detached lawyer persona to kick in. So of course, the Dumok took her by surprise.

"Do you have a passport?" the Dumok asked quietly.

Holly nodded.

"Do you want to see the world only through books?"

Holly shook her head.

"Do you want to read, only, or do you want to experience the world first hand?"

"Experience the world first hand," Holly squeaked.

The Dumok's eyes flashed, dangerous, challenging, then they softened. "Then be ready after work. I will send a car for you. You will accompany me to Seoul tonight. I need my lawyer to witness something."

CHAPTER 50

Although the Dumok had insisted Holly accompany him, the Dumok rarely spoke or acknowledged her on the nine hour flight to Seoul. His mood was somber, and he sat with his arms crossed and head bent, his eyes staring deeply into the chasm of a buried and dark past.

It was raining when they landed. They had coffee and a bun in the Seoul airport while the Dumok rented a car. Holly found that a little unusual, as he almost always had a driver. In fact, she had never actually seen him *do* anything, things in his world just happened, seemingly by the pure force of his will.

But the trip was sudden, and she didn't dwell on it. He stopped first to buy clothes and a shovel and some rain gear and rubber boots. He offered no explanation about these purchases.

Soon enough the highway changed to a country road. They were in a green and fertile valley and the terrain ahead was foothills with mountains behind. Finally they stopped with the Dumok holding a shovel, the rain streaming like rivers down his face. He stared at Holly as if he only just now realized she was there. What a sight she must have been, rubber boots, a clear plastic poncho, a soggy ponytail, makeup long gone, looking about twelve years old, not the savvy young attorney making her mark as she had imagined.

"Are you ready?" His voice was hoarse.

Holly had to half run to keep up with his long stride as he preceded her up the steep path. The path, such as it was, was steep, uneven and slippery. There were no guardrails or signs. Holly's heart was filled with dread and anxiety. She wanted to break the silence, punctuated by the sound of raindrops on leaves, and the pinging and ponging off the metal of the large shovel the Dumok carried across his large shoulders.

At a rock he paused for a moment, stripped off his poncho and then his suit jacket. He pulled off her poncho, and helped her put her arms into the jacket and buttoned her up, trying to protect her shivering body, her cheeks and fingers white with cold and an existential dread she had never imagined. Yet there was an endearing intimacy in his action, a tenderness that was somehow surviving in him.

He put his own poncho back on, too. They continued up the mountain. Holly carefully placed one foot at a time into his muddy footprints, not wanting to slip, not wanting to fall behind, not wanting to be another burden to him.

Holly gasped when he stopped. Two little makeshift graves. They were far above the rich farmland. The ground here was rocky. Even to have dug them would have taken an astonishing labor.

Holly just stared as the Dumok paused to strip off the poncho and his shirt. Then he began to dig. Holly stood under a large purple maple tree shading the graves. It was the only maple tree in a forest of pines. Holly was exhausted, and there were rocks, but she did not want to sit, so she stood poker straight and watched. She was the sentinel on the frontier, the night watch, the one and only witness. Worse, she somehow had the voice of Logan Burg in her head, repeating *exhumation requires a court order*, matched with the withering gaze he reserved for associates who were not quite getting it.

Ping, ping, ping, ping.

The staccato sound of the rain as it hit the shovel alternated against the sound of the sharp metal as the Dumok methodically sliced open the ground and tossed the wet earth aside.

Ping. Ping.

Chunk. Chunk.

Thud. Thud.

The rhythmic sounds of the rain and the slicing and tossing of the wet earth seemed almost hypnotic. Holly could see the muscles of his back, his shoulders straining as he dug.

Suddenly he stopped. She heard a low gurgle, a guttural moan. It took more effort than Holly had ever made to take the few steps needed. The effort needed to stare into the grave. Empty. Again the Dumok did not pause.

Ping. Ping.

Chunk. Chunk.

Shuck. Shuck.

Thud. Thud.

The second grave. Then a growl, half man, half animal, as if the Dumok was about to turn into some mythic creature and merge into the forest forever.

She caught his gaze, he stared back, wildly, violently, backing up from the second grave, cursing his father-in-law the Ambassador of Korea as he fell to his knees. He was covered in rain and sweat and mud, caked on his face where he had wiped his brow. Against the drowning rain he stretched out his hands as he cursed the heavens, shouting. There was a great flash of lightning and then, a breath and the terrifying crack of thunder.

"Who dared moved the graves and where is my baby girl?!" The Dumok raged into the storm.

Then he broke down and wept. The little pile of bones, his only refuge from the world, was gone.

Who would move graves? Holly wondered. She looked up at the maple leaves blowing roughly above her and tried to imagine a greater or more profound cruelty, but she couldn't.

Maybe the Dumok had been right after all. Maybe she was not ready to leave her own watercolor world. She stood, helpless, doubting, wondering, utterly silent, but with tears falling and mixing with the rain as Holly stood on the violated earth.

Holly went to him, finally, inevitably. The Dumok collapsed as he reached for her, awkwardly, his great shoulders resting against her.

Holly felt the spasms of grief and fury move through his frame at he realization he had a wife and daughter he had not known existed. That he had been lied to with the most profound cruelty and that now his daughter was charged with murder. Somehow, the Dumok gathered his strength. Somehow, he took her hand and led her away from the empty graves, away from the abyss and down the mountain.

Thump.

Slosh.

Thump.

Holly tried to keep up as he led her down the mountain, clinging to his powerful hand against the icy cold rain. Strangely, down was almost as hard as up, because it was so slippery.

Ping.

Ping.

Ping.

The rain hit the shovel. And then they were off the mountain. Later, all Holly remembered of the climb down the mountain was that all the way he had held her hand.

CHAPTER 51

Holly woke wrapped in immaculate white sheets and a white duvet that seemed to float above the bed. Through a large window she could see daylight and a rich green pine forest, its infinite silence comforting. It looked like afternoon outside by the way the shadows fell from the trees. Shadows. That meant the rain had stopped.

A wood fire crackled and snapped in front of a long couch. Someone had perhaps tended it in the night and she had not even known. She stretched her body, feeling very relaxed, then bolted straight up and looked frantically at the bed, but the sheets on the other side were still tight and untouched. She looked around the room but there was no sign of the Dumok. Anywhere. Then she remembered the mountain.

They had come down, finally, to the car and driven only a short way. The Dumok had stopped at what looked like an inn. Stepping through white pine doors to a hot spring, the tranquil beauty of the spa waters had sparkled invitingly. The steam from the natural spring waters curled and disappeared. Holly remembered him murmuring something like orders to the women at the front. They had taken her through some doors and clucked disapprovingly over her before telling her to undress. She had wanted a towel but there were none. She lay down on a table, and while the ladies poured buckets of warm water and lathered her, she fell asleep. Holly remembered being woken up and taken to her room.

Holly had slept like the dead, but now she left the warm but empty bed and went to the couch in front of the fire. Her legs ached even walking those few steps. She wrapped a plaid cashmere throw over her shoulders and drank hot barley tea. This inn was magical. Where the fire and tea had come from she had no idea. As she thought of the mountain and what they had done she felt shivers and suddenly felt very, very small. As horrible as it had been, the idea of the Dumok having to do that alone was worse. She stared into the fire.

That night she ate alone in her room. The next morning a driver appeared and took her to a hotel in Seoul. At the front desk she was given a note from the Dumok which asked if she could have dinner with him that evening.

CHAPTER 52

Holly and the Dumok ate on the roof of the hotel from where they could look down at a black-tie party disbanding in the terrace garden below. The Dumok showed no physical signs of what they had done except where the palms of his hands were red and blistered from the shovel. Otherwise he was immaculate and showed only concern for her.

"Have you quite recovered?" the Dumok asked quietly.

"I slept well at the inn," Holly answered, regretting instantly having mentioned the inn. Her tone was formal to conceal the awkwardness. *Exhumation requires a court order.* The voice of Logan Burg still echoed.

"Perhaps I should tell you the rest of the story." His mouth was a tight thin line. His hard eyes caught the glint of the light from the window.

Holly nodded somberly with a calm she did not feel. But she was physically rested and smiled encouragement.

"I was told—late in the pregnancy—that Nara chose to terminate but it was too late. No doctor would agree. Nara was furious. She sought out the village medicine man and traded jewelry for a potion that would kill the baby. But it didn't work. The potion burned Nara's inside but the baby held on for months, fighting for life. The baby refused to die, instead kicking horribly while Nara was bedridden. I was told Nara suffered terribly and died while giving birth. My baby held on, choosing to die after she was free from the womb. The grave sites we visited were where I believed they were buried," the Dumok revealed. "I've lived these years in the fires of hell tortured by my own imagination. Not a day has gone by where I didn't think of my child, burning, helpless, hot and trapped inside the womb while I was in Taiwan, at dinner parties."

The Dumok spit out the words "dinner parties" as if nothing were more vile. Holly listened, afraid to speak.

"I imagined that my daughter would be alive today if I had just gone to the village, taken a knife and ripped my wife open and pulled out my child with my bare hands." The Dumok stopped, his voice dropping as quickly as it rose. "All these years I thought Nara had died a kinder death than she would have had at my hands. And now I learn the stories that have tormented me were all lies, fiction, artifice to some unimaginable purpose." He clenched his fists, his face contorted.

He turned to Holly, savage and animalistic. "Why all the lies? Why?!"

There was a bitter growl in his voice, his face slowly changing into a look she had never seen.

"Now, we are back at the beginning," the Dumok said. The rage having abated somewhat, he leaned back in his chair with the exasperation of a man who has just realized that he was played and turned into Sisyphus.

"You tell me my wife Nara Song, the Ambassador's daughter, is alive, living as Alexis Linser. My daughter is locked up, not in a poisoned womb, or coffin, but in a prison cell—a coffin of a different sort—awaiting trial for murder. I understand murder for I have blood on my hands, too. All this..." The Dumok spread his hands, a gesture to convey the enormity of it all. "All this..."

They sat, silent for a long time.

"The tree..." Holly said, abruptly, her brow furrowed. "At the graves... the beautiful red maple... you planted it, didn't you?"

"Yes." His voice was hoarse.

The rushing sound of the waterfall was soothing as Holly and the Dumok made their way across the lobby towards the elevators. Holly forced a smile and said goodnight as she fumbled with her room key, then showered and crawled into bed, exhausted. Outside the city had barely paused, even though it was three in the morning. Her thoughts tumbled as she lay on the white sheets and she couldn't help but think about Naomi in her hard, cold cell. How frightened she must be.

She realized that she could help the Dumok most by going back to Los Angeles for Naomi before it was too late. Something told her she had to hurry.

CHAPTER 53

Neil Cooper adjusted the knot in his new tie. He loved an audience and had one now with Kate and Holly. Holly had gone straight from the airport to the restaurant with no time to either shower, change or see the headlines.

"The Judge's face turned red, then white," Neil continued the story he had begun while they waited for their table. "His eyes bulged open, fixed on Naomi. He swallowed, hard, lips tightening into a hard line. The entire courtroom filled with silence." Neil paused for dramatic effect. "Nobody dared move. The only movement in the courtroom was the loose flesh of the judge's neck as it jiggled, as he turned his head from Naomi back to the prosecutor and then to me," Neil boasted. "I had spoken to Naomi before court, and—get this—she said, 'But I didn't murder him!' That's what she said! Can you believe that?" Neil's voice was loud, even in the crowded restaurant.

"What did you say?" Holly asked, trying to keep her voice neutral.

Neil snorted, and took a gulp of his martini before answering, palms up, in an exaggerated manner. "Honey, you killed him! No one else was in the room. You were still holding the knife. You just reminded all the men in America to keep their eyes open next time they get a blow job in K-Town," he snorted, throwing back his shoulders.

"Oh, that's righteous!" Kate cried, laughing, clapping her hands.

"You don't want to hear what the judge said next, do you?" Neil paused, sipping his drink and sawing at his rib-eye with a knife.

"Oh, we do! We do!" Kate exclaimed, her bright, animated voice echoing off the walls.

Holly was as pale as the moon, she felt sick to her stomach. But she pushed around bits of an excellent Caesar salad, half listening while studying the decor of the restaurant. Waiters walked around wearing long white aprons in the French tradition carrying savory dishes and brightly colored pastries.

"The judge wiped a tear from his eye before taking the plea. Kind of gave me a lump in my throat," Neil said, pulling his tie, and pausing dramatically, sipping his drink, watching for a reaction.

"You're a natural orator!" Kate squealed in delight, her eyes on Neil now, with a kind of restless glitter.

Kate had engineered it all, of course, while Holly had been in Korea with the Dumok. Neil was a publicity hound. He had allowed Kate to prop him up in front of the media, making statements, doing interviews. Then, behind closed doors, badgering Alexis, Naomi's mother, hands outstretched, reading from the police reports that the Councilman was stabbed through the heart, how Naomi's screams were heard, how the Councilman couldn't talk, and had tried to get up but then slumped over, covered in blood. Rumors swirled that he had tried to reach over to hold Naomi's hand, and in his moment of death, that Naomi had pulled her hand away.

"Neil is practically a statesman," Kate was saying, wagging her fork in between bites of butternut squash ravioli. "Isn't he, Holly? He is skilled and experienced. And respected. Respected by all the judges."

Eyeing Holly she laughed, her quick, high fevered laugh, and she looked away, but not before catching Holly's eye in a swift, mocking glance.

"The plea was life in prison without the possibility of parole but thanks to *moi*," he said, pointing his thick fingers at himself, "she avoided the death penalty."

"Neil, the last woman executed in California was in 1962," Holly said as calmly as she could manage.

"She avoided the death penalty! Neil boomed. "You never know when the government might change, like in Texas."

"That's the best you could do?" Holly asked, putting down her fork. "You pled her to life?" The table was suddenly quiet.

"Yes, Holly. Yes. Under the circumstances, yes."

Neil was defensive. He took some bread and spread butter on it.

"How about defending Naomi?" Holly cried.

"How? It's the most open and shut case in history. I avoided the death penalty. She didn't kill just anyone. She killed a popular politician, Holly—not some John Doe Kim Schmuck who owns an acupuncture clinic out in Arcadia."

Holly folded her napkin on the table and stood up.

"Holly." Kate leaned forward, her voice ugly. "Naomi couldn't afford to go to trial. Her mother gave me a ring. It was a fake. Worth only a couple of thousand dollars. I should have taken her handbag. That was worth a good twenty-five grand. Psshh," Kate exclaimed, disgusted.

"Don't you know anything, Holly? There's no such thing as a free lunch."

Neil swallowed his bread and washed it down with the rest of his martini and plopped more ketchup on his plate.

"What, Holly? What would you have done? What would your defense have been?"

Holly sat, wordlessly facing them.

"You see, you have no defense. None. You would have strung it out and in the end done the exact same thing. Well, here's what they didn't teach you in law school. It ain't moot court out here with the grown-ups," Neil reached for another piece of bread. "The client pretty much gets what they pay for.."

Holly stared at Kate and Neil as if seeing them for the very first time and spun on her heels and left.

Kate wriggled her nose. "I knew she didn't get it when she showed up with that cheap Louis Vuitton handbag," Kate said, mimicking Holly storming out of the restaurant, her high pitch laughter resonating loudly off the walls.

Holly sat in her car in the parking lot. She would never go back to American Legal Services again. She felt sick. Life without parole. The Dumok's daughter. The next day Holly mustered the courage to tell the Dumok.

"Sufficient funds have been wired to your trust account. Withdraw the guilty plea and prepare for trial," the Dumok texted back.

CHAPTER 54

Naomi Linser shivered in her cell and somehow made herself even smaller, a tiny quivering ball, wrapping her thin arms around her legs, hugging herself tightly, trying to stop shaking from the cold.

She listened to the sounds of a jail at night, intermittent and indecipherable. She had grown up on a ranch, where the wind in the trees and the rain on the roof were comforting. This was very different and terrifying.

And now there were footsteps, the heavy plodding of cheap work boots worn by men who are paid by the hour, who have no incentive to hurry for anything. There were two deputies on the night shift. The taller one had spiky brown hair and a short, pug nose and his eyes were a pale, cold blue. The other one was younger, shorter, hard and dark. The tall one walked over and eyeballed her. "

Gone was the beautiful, petulant party girl who had caught the attention of the American public when she made the front page, handcuffed, with a half smile, being pushed into the back seat of the police car wearing a sequined dress and clutching a Chanel handbag. In her place was a shell, as fragile and tentative as a drawing made with a broken pencil on onionskin.

"There's a rumor," the tall guard wheezed in a nasty tone, "that you aren't comfortable here. And a complaint, that you talk too much to your imaginary friend."

"My chest hurts so much, it hurts every time I breathe. And I'm so cold. Can I get a blanket please?"

"Call room service," the short one snorted, "like at a Holiday Inn."

"Where does it hurt?" the tall guard asked in a mock sympathetic voice. "Show me."

Naomi pointed at her chest. "Right here," she whimpered. "I have a huge bruise. I can hardly breathe."

Naomi looked away. She rarely made eye contact and when she spoke it was to the wall or to the floor. The shorter guard followed behind, rubbing his chest. "Right here! That's the spot!"

"Ohhhh, you're making fun of me," Naomi wailed. "I need to see a doctor."

"It's count-time, little killer," the short deputy sneered. Naomi's head snapped up.

"What did you say?" Naomi's voice had a raw texture. "What did you call me?" Naomi stood up, too calm. She walked over to the deputy and faced him, her body rigid. "Did you call me a killer?" she repeated. Her voice trembled and her eyes caught fire. The words hung in the air. "I loved her," Naomi sobbed. "She suffered so..." Naomi's voice broke. A hiccup turned into another sob. Her face contorted. "It was an accident. An accident!" Naomi shrieked.

"Snap out of it." He grabbed Naomi by the upper arm. Immediately Naomi twisted and squirmed.

"Let go of me. You're hurting me!" she cried. It was an accident. An accident! Get your hands off of me!" Naomi twisted out of his grip and fell to the floor. "I'm not a killer... I loved her. I loved her..." Naomi curled up on the floor in the fetal position, rocking and moaning.

The guards looked at each other and shrugged.

"Psycho," they both said under their breaths as they walked away, leaving Naomi in a heap on the cell floor.

CHAPTER 55

For the next two weeks Holly interviewed lawyers. By process of elimination, the Dumok had narrowed it down to, well, no one.

The Dumok liked Holly, only. She knew her way around the system, and nothing intimidated her, not even him, he thought with a smile. She found pressure energizing, but the Dumok knew she was inexperienced and needed a strong lead.

The Dumok had explained that the big firms would take your money, then stick some junior associate on the case and double the billing. Ivy League lawyers were brainy but arrogant, which could put off a jury. The lawyers on the west side were condescending, patronizing, and too old-boy. Beverly Hills was the same.

Koreatown had the best of the worst. The white lawyers who occupied this part of town had weak stomachs and chins. In contrast, the first generation Korean lawyers had strong stomachs and chins but their English was not good enough, leaving them unable to read the subtext of the court proceedings. Plus, nobody paid a lawyer to speak Korean in American court.

Finally, the Dumok settled on a lawyer on Sunset Boulevard who had experience with high-profile Hollywood clients. Eli Behr had just made headlines after winning an acquittal for Doghouse Riley, a black rap star whom the pundits had all described as "utterly unsympathetic" to potential jurors, black or white.

Eli Behr walked and talked with a swagger. He strutted into the diner and slid into the booth across from Holly. He wore an Italian suit and cowboy boots and a big gold pinky ring. Holly had got there early and watched him get out of his car—a conservative enough black 7-Series but with slightly blingy after-market wheels. She was keen to meet the first of seventeen lawyers who had caught the Dumok's interest. Eli Behr was stoically built, with a physique that had come from hours in a gym versus from a sport, which meant discipline rather than passion—that had been the Dumok's analysis.

Holly tilted her head and studied him, wondering if it were true. Eli Behr was on the light side of forty and wore his blond hair slicked back. His blue eyes were intense but with a friendly twinkle. He was handsome enough and manly, but he had the appeal of looking like anybody's brother or son.

The only question was would a jury like and trust him? Yes, Holly thought. He was also ambitious, ready to cut the strings from his mentor, an old-Hollywood lawyer who had treated him like a son and taken him along to absorb—incrementally—the fantastic chaos of Hollywood, partying in penthouses and back alleys with drug dealers, prostitutes, celebrities, and petty criminals and charming his way into celebrities' inner circles.

Holly asked Eli about the Doghouse Riley case, which she had not followed. Eli described Doghouse as a fatherless boy who had crawled out of the gutter through hard work and musical talent, but the scumbags from his past just wouldn't let go. He had convinced the jury that the prosecutor had overcharged the case to make himself a name on the back of a celebrity. Thanks to Eli Behr, the jury found Doghouse not guilty. And Eli showed some modesty, explaining how Riley had been cooperative about toning down his rap persona for the middle class jury and had been appropriately frank and honest about his troubled past. Working together, they had made Doghouse Riley sympathetic and credible.

He impressed Holly with his analysis, and his understanding of how juries thought. Now, the young lawyer on the Sunset Strip was ready to put down his shot glass and grab the spotlight on his own. Yes, Eli Behr was perfect.

He leaned forward, his eyes twinkling. "Where I'd like to start on your case, is by finding out if I order pie, will you order some too—so we can relax and get to know each other—or are you going to order some scary green thing and push it around on your plate while the whole time staring at my pie and wishing you'd ordered it?"

When he spoke it was slow, methodical and borderline monotone. Holly held his gaze and answered, "Apple, but no ice cream."

"Fine."

"And coffee. Straight up."

Eli leaned back in the booth and smiled. "So what do I need to know that I didn't read in the tabloids and see on the entertainment channels—aside from the fact that she's innocent."

"That you are going to work harder than you've ever worked in your life until you curse me and the day you were born. That your job is to blur the racial lines completely until nobody remembers the color of skin. I want the jury to forget who was black, white, yellow, rich or poor. It is not race or class warfare on trial, but guilt or innocence."

Eli nodded, he was intrigued. He leaned forward and lowered his voice. "What is our defense, Counsel?"

"I don't know. That's why I need you." Holly slunk down into the booth, drained. "And if all that doesn't scare you, the client will. But with any luck you will never meet him." Holly paused and looked up. "Shall we order?" she asked brightly.

"I should have held out for ice cream," Eli said, his gaze penetrating hers, as he chewed slowly, savoring his pie.

Two hours later, outside while waiting for their cars, Holly had one final thing to say—and this was verbatim from the Dumok. "For the record, Eli. No plea bargain. No scandals. We can't afford to see headlines that you are sleeping with the D.A. or caught photographed leaving a bar with her one night. Naomi Lee Linser walks—or we both go down in flames and there will be a short, cheap funeral." Holly paused. "Did you win that buckle or buy it?" she asked, pointing to Eli's big gold belt buckle.

"Calgary Stampede. Summer of 2001. Cracked a rib." Eli grimaced at the memory. "Still hurts when it rains. The longest eight seconds of my life—so far."

CHAPTER 56

"Holly?" Naomi mouthed her name as she approached the plexiglass window, her large eyes staring with some curiosity. Holly slowly rose to her feet and stood to face Naomi in the attorney visitation room. Holly felt the shivers. Naomi hesitated, then took a seat on the other side of the glass.

She sat and tucked her feet under herself, and wrapping an arm around her knees, she reached up for the phone. Holly stared back, feeling as though she were looking into a void, but she could feeling the suffering that came with every breath Naomi took.

"I remember you from church," Naomi said, and Holly just stared at her. "Maybe that's why my mom hired you." Her shoulders relaxed as her mind wandered off to some scrap of happy memory. "Do you remember me? You were always so nice, and gave us snacks in Sunday school."

"Church?" Holly waited, stunned, the way you almost stop breathing when you are sitting outside and a humming bird dances on the flowers close by. The voice was strangely familiar; it was not an ordinary voice. Holly did not remember and she shook her head slowly. Naomi's eyes drifted in and out of focus.

"My Korean name is Sari. My sister is Sara. We used to wear ugly green plaid coats and carry pink Hello Kitty backpacks. We came to your church when I was little." Naomi was insistent. "You were our Sunday school teacher."

Then, suddenly, Holly remembered. The strange looking sisters. Holly's memories came to life. Her lips moved but she barely breathed the words. "Father, forgive me for I have sinned."

There is a place in hell for every sinner. In the Los Angeles First Korean Church it is the third row in the middle pew where eleven-year-old Holly Park sat. His eyes were on her. She could feel it. Holly shifted her weight and pressed her small hands over her heart as she kept one eye glued to the pulpit. The earmarked paperback book hidden between the pages of the Bible lay unread and forgotten. Holly shifted her eyes without moving her head. The flock had nothing to fear. It was only her. She was the only one who would burn in the fires of hell. She was the only sinner. Now, he was looking directly at her.

"Repent!"

Holly jumped as the voice thundered from above. She froze. "Yes, I will, oh, I will!" she cried and jumped up she ran down the aisle as fast as her legs could go and out the back doors of the church.

After the flock had gone, Pastor Park went searching for Holly. He found her hiding in the closet of the Sunday school room. She was curled up like a puppy, sleeping. Her long hair was tangled around her tear streaked face. He reached down and gently stroked her cheek.

Holly's eyes flew open and when she saw her father the tears welled up instantly as she climbed out of the closet and into her father's arms.

"I was being dra-dragged to h-h-hell by the devil!" she cried with a fresh burst of sobs. "It was me, it was me and not little brother who broke the teacup last night! I dropped it on the floor when I was drying the dishes," she confessed, hiccupping between sobs, feeling that whatever punishment lay in wait at the hands of her father would be gentler than what punishment awaited in hell.

Pastor Park was a strict man. He was a dogmatic preacher and conservative in his teachings. He followed the black letter of God's law and expected no less from his flock. But looking at his daughter's tear stained face he felt she had suffered enough at the hands of her own conscience.

His eyes were gentle and kind as he lifted his daughter up and carried her. Holly threw her arms tightly around her father's neck and scrambled into his arms, nestling her head in her father's shoulders. She was tiny for her age, and Pastor Park easily carried her down the stairs.

Finally, in her papa's strong arms she was safe from the devil at last. As she clung to her father's neck, Holly saw two little girls standing at the bottom of the stairs. She peeked from her father's shoulders and glanced at two toddlers standing behind their mother's skirts. The girls peeked back. They were very small, their bare shoulders and arms thin as chopsticks in their strange foreign dresses, their disproportionately large eyes round that stared back at her. These girls looked different. Korean? American?

Holly stared curiously. They were such exquisite creatures! They were like out of one of her storybooks, only one faded and one vibrant with color. The one with the fair pale skin and large grey eyes met her gaze and gaped at her. The other child looked away shyly and buried her face in her mother's skirt. Holly peered at the girls but soon her curiosity got the better of her.

"What is your name?" Holly asked.

"They don't understand you. They speak only Korean," Yong Kim, the church clerk said, as he came in with their luggage "They are Sari and Sara. They are *mugunhwas*—beautiful Korean national flowers who just arrived from Seoul."

Holly slowly climbed out of the well of memories "Sara?" Holly asked slowly.

"That's my sister. I am Sari. Do you remember us now?" Naomi asked, a tiny spark in those otherwise lifeless eyes.

A strange chill shivered Holly's spine.

"I liked Sunday school," Naomi said in that little girl voice.

The familiar faces and voices from her childhood—Sari and Sara. Always the subject of gossip and whispers, but Holly was too young to understand. Painfully shy girls who rarely spoke. Skinny, hesitant, and withdrawn. It was their voices that stayed with you. And Holly remembered the green coats. The sisters who were inseparable, holding hands or walking with their arms encircling each others waist, one always dressed in tights and coats and the other in sun dresses. The pictures in Holly's memory faded then, and she realized she had never seen the two girls separated.

"Shall I call you Sari, or Naomi?" Holly asked softly.

"Naomi... Sari? Sari... isn't here anymore," Naomi said wistfully.

"Naomi, it was your father who hired me, not your mother," Holly began carefully, keeping her voice low, soothing.

"Wolf?" a tiny voice asked hesitantly, hardly daring to speak.

"No... not Wolf," Holly murmured carefully.

Naomi's face went as white as a field of new snow. Her eyes were blank.

"Your real father," Holly began. "He was looking for you all this time."

Still Naomi gazed back with wide eyes and said nothing. Softly, patiently, for the next hour, Holly explained as best as she could how her real father had come searching for her and was paying for her defense.

It was a lot for Naomi to process. She kept her arms around her knees and rocked softly.

"I need to ask you some questions about the night of the Councilman's death, is that okay?" Holly began slowly. Naomi nodded.

"How did you meet the Councilman?" Holly asked.

Naomi bit her lip, looking down, and her chin quivered as the next words tumbled out.

"I went to his office."

"Why?"

"I wanted his help."

"For what?"

"I wanted his help to get some public records."

"What records?"

"A death certificate."

"Whose?"

"Sara's." Her voice barely a whisper.

"Sara's?" Holly looked up, surprised. "Your sister Sara is dead?"

"Yes—Sara drowned." The words were so soft Holly strained to hear. Naomi was more agitated.

"When?" Holly asked.

"When we were little, in the pool."

"What swimming pool?"

"A plastic backyard pool."

"What happened?"

"We were just playing...and she drowned," the tiny voice whispered.

"How?"

"My mom said it was my fault."

"What did she say?"

"That I shouldn't have pushed her head under the water," Naomi whispered. "After that, I think God forgot all about me," she breathed.

Holly was shaking inside and had to force herself to inhale.

"Mom stopped going to church after... the... accident," Naomi continued, and the tears began. She lifted her head and met Holly's gaze. "If I pray, like we used to in Sunday school, will Jesus forgive me for what happened? I didn't do it on purpose. Do you think Jesus forgives accidents, too?"

"An accident is just that. An accident," Holly said, her heart racing.

"But, Holly, once is an accident, but twice?" Naomi whispered. "Sara and now the Councilman? How come everybody dies who comes near me? Do you think I'm cursed?"

Holly shook her head vigorously.

Naomi wailed, "I used to pray... but... I gave up. I know it looks really bad... but if you see my mom can you tell her this time it really was an accident, too?"

Holly promised, like you would promise a child, then excused herself to the washroom, merely washing her hands, not looking in the mirror, trying to remember. She stood outside the door, her fingers wrapped tightly around her briefcase, so she could gather her strength and have something to give Naomi. Holly came back and Naomi stood, swaying, biting her lip.

"Will you tell my dad thank you for me, please?" Naomi pleaded as tears streamed down her face.

Holly nodded yes.

"What is my dad, like, Holly?" Naomi summoned all her courage to ask.

"He is exactly what a dad should be like, Naomi," Holly answered with utter conviction.

Holly sat in her car for a long time. She drank some of her watered-down ice tea. It was warm. She wanted to think but all she could do was cry. She told herself that she couldn't help Naomi if she fell apart, too. That gave her the strength to start the car, fix her makeup and head for the church.

"Hi, Dad." Holly burst in and plopped herself in the chair across his desk.

"Dad, do you remember two sisters named Sari and Sara? Little girls, from a long time ago?"

"Yes. The twins...sure, I remember."

"What happened to them?"

"They left the church."

"Why did they leave?"

"The mother remarried."

Pastor Park thought of the day the fancy black car had pulled into the church parking lot. The fair daughter standing next to her mother, more beautiful than ever, but less alive.

"I remember now, when she came back. She had changed her name. She introduced her daughter, Sari, as Naomi Linser."

"What about the other sister?"

Pastor Park thought back about that day. He frowned. "There was no mention of Sara. Nobody asked. It was as if she had never existed."

"Why did the mother come back?"

"Nara's father was dying. The twins' grandfather. They needed to leave for Korea right away, but Naomi didn't have a passport. They asked me to sign a witness affidavit regarding her identity because her name had changed from Sari Lee to Naomi Linser. It was required by the Consulate to issue the passport under a different name."

"Did you sign the affidavit?

"Yes. As I said, only one. No one mentioned the sister."

CHAPTER 57

Daisy Moreno was not happy. In the six years she had worked for the freshly buried Councilman she had never been questioned by any person of authority. Until now. She straightened her too tight skirt and slipped her feet out of her pumps and examined the red semi-circles on the skin of her feet where the top of her shoes had created a painful welt. Reaching up, she nervously patted her hair.

"Thank you, Ms. Moreno, for seeing me. I'm truly sorry for your loss and the loss to the public," Holly said. "The Councilman had a long and illustrious record of public service. I join the public in mourning his untimely demise. I know you are concerned that the Councilman's political legacy is remembered, " Holly continued, "not the scandal of his death.".

She is smooth, this one, Daisy thought. "His murder," she said stiffly. "But yes, that is my concern."

"There is the presumption of innocence until proven guilty, Ms. Moreno."

"The girl got life, is what I heard. That's not innocent where I come from."

"You may not have heard that the guilty plea has been withdrawn and vacated. Naomi Linser has new lawyers and will stand trial."

"At great public expense!" Daisy exclaimed.

So many people loved to decry public expense until it was their turn at the trough, Holly thought, but she was gracious.

"Actually, the defense is privately funded."

"A lot of trouble to go to, missy," Daisy sniffed, not liking this answer at all. "Naomi Linser stabbed the Councilman to death, is what she did. Cracked his sternum like a roast chicken. Don't see a lot of wiggle room there."

Daisy's harsh perception matched that of the general public and Neil Cooper.

Holly tried again. "I'm sure it will be quite difficult for the next Councilman to fill such big shoes."

"There are a lot of pressures. Some days I just throw up my hands."

"That's true," Holly agreed. "I'm lucky. If people want something from me, they have to pay."

Daisy laughed in spite of herself. She didn't much like defense lawyers but she was starting to warm up a bit to this one.

"Sometimes men under a lot of pressure have to blow off some steam," Holly suggested evenly, thinking if she could get Daisy Moreno talking, she might learn something valuable.

"The Councilman was an attractive and charming man, in the prime of life—and he liked the ladies, and the ladies liked him. It never needed to make the papers," Daisy sniffed.

"So he engaged in casual relationships, to help manage the pressures of this job?"

"Don't think your precious Naomi Linser was the first, not even close." Daisy shook her head.

"And never any problems?" Holly queried carefully.

"We covered up for his indiscretions. We got good at it, we had the practice, but this Naomi girl was different. She was the kind of girl who marries the richest boy in town and hangs out at the country club all summer. She wasn't one of those nightclub girls, if you know what I mean. But he saw her and liked her."

"So you had met her?" Holly asked, surprised.

"Yes," Daisy said. "That Naomi was beautiful, but scrawny as a chicken wing. Don't understand that at all. A man usually likes some meat on the bones."

Daisy was on the plus side of voluptuous, mid-thirties, and her dress left little to the imagination.

"How did the Councilman meet her?"

"Actually, Naomi just walked into our office one day like a regular constituent. At first, the Councilman assumed she was from Club Kiki. Turns out she wasn't."

"Why did she come?"

"She came in looking for some public records," Daisy answered.

"How is it that you remember her? There must be so many constituents that contact the Councilman."

"She stood out."

"How so?"

"She was classy, that one. She wasn't like those other girls from the club. And the Councilman saw that and liked her. And I don't mean 'blowing off steam' liked her. I mean, 'leave-your-wife-and-kids-and-move-to-Costa-Rica' liked her."

"Did the Councilman frequent Club Kiki?"

"He was a VIP there. He was crazy for the Korean nightlife. He enjoyed the hostess bars and room salons. They made him feel like a big shot."

"If Naomi wasn't from Club Kiki, how is it that she was there the night of the murder?" Holly asked.

"The Councilman's repertoire was the same. And it worked every time with these young girls. He always started by inviting a girl to accompany him on functions. The girls were always easy, willing, you know, the novelty of it and all. Naomi was no different. The problem was he developed feelings for that one, that Naomi girl. But her feelings did not reciprocate. She stopped accepting the Councilman's invitations, always making up an excuse not to go."

"Was he upset? Did his behavior change?"

"Yes. I could tell by his mood something was wrong. He was preoccupied, less enthusiastic about his work which was not like him," Daisy said. "It wasn't my place to say anything, but of course now I think maybe I should have."

"How did they end up together that night at Club Kiki?"

"Geez." Daisy frowned. "I don't know. They were on the phone and arguing that morning. Then the Councilman left the office which was unusual."

"What were they arguing about?"

"Those records. He had promised her the records she had originally come looking for."

"What records?" Holly persisted.

Daisy sighed. "Naomi wanted a copy of her sister's death certificate, is what it was. I had asked her what year because the application is different if it's before 1995. I looked it up for her and wrote it down and gave it to her. It was the most I could do. I remember it's sixteen dollars, the fee. I wrote it down for her that first day she showed up, I remember now," Daisy said. "He promised her he'd obtain a copy."

"Did he?"

Daisy shook her head. "I tried to get the records but couldn't find them. I thought maybe she died in a different county, which would means we couldn't access it. We can only access Los Angeles county records. So I asked Naomi to double-check the venue where the accident occurred. That was the only time I spoke to her about it."

"Is there any way the database is wrong? Did somebody personally check the archives?" Holly persisted. Daisy was annoyed.

"The database is accurate. If the sister died in Los Angeles County, we would have record of it unless, of course, they buried the body in the backyard and nobody knows about it," Daisy joked. She stopped and looked up. "Are you okay, there?" Daisy held one of those small cylindrical paper water cups.

"Thank you," Holly said and drank the whole thing.

"Somehow Naomi ended up at Club Kiki that night. Do you know if it was at the invitation of the Councilman or do you think Naomi found out he would be there and she just showed up?"

"Well, the Councilman came back to the office late in the afternoon. I guessed Naomi and the Councilman made up because he was in a good mood and he gave his driver the rest of the evening off which meant he drove himself to the Club." Daisy stopped. "Is that helpful?"

"Yes, Ms. Moreno." Holly pulled herself together and stood, using the back of the chair to steady herself. "Thank you. If you think of anything else, no matter how unusual or insignificant, please call me. And thank you again, I'm so grateful."

CHAPTER 58

"Naomi, try to remember, please. Tell me, what happened in Seoul?" Holly pleaded. "I spoke to Wolf and he said something happened to your mother in Seoul. What happened? Can you tell me?"

Naomi's eyes went far away as she remembered.

"Your grandfather is very ill, so don't say anything," Nara told Naomi in the cab. "He may call you a different name so just answer normally. If grandpa says anything to you that seems strange, just bow down your head and don't correct him."

They had gone straight to the hospital from the airport because Nara's mother had said that time was short. Wolf went to the hotel with the luggage.

"Who are those men?" Naomi whispered to her mom, pointing to the dark suited men with earpieces outside the hospital door.

"They're here to protect your grandfather."

As arrogant as ever, Nara thought. Even facing death he thinks assassins are lurking. Nara's mother emerged, her lips pursed and tight. She had aged. Perhaps they all had.

It was a large single room. The Ambassador lay on the bed with wires and intravenous tubes extending from both wrists like a puppet. How ironic. The master puppeteer puppeted.

The sight of her father made her blood cold. His eyes were closed.

She noticed the IV drip with the morphine, the heart monitor and other colored lines which ran across the screen. The monitors beeped and buzzed incomprehensibly. A nurse stood at full attention with her hands clasped tightly without moving.

Nara was not afraid. She knew he was arguing with God—using his inevitable courtesy as a weapon—making his case that he be allowed just a moment more and the strength to lash out his great bear claw at her one last time. She who did not exist.

He had erased her—her school records at Ewha University, excised from the family records, burned the photographs, forbid the very mention of her. Cut from the will, displaced, disinherited, disowned. Nara stared at her father silently.

Beep.

Beep.

Beep.

Who let *her* in the room without his permission? Why had she come? He certainly had not summoned her. Her mother conceded every time to avoid a fight yet this time she had insisted, despite his wishes, that Nara come.

Nara had not come for her mother, either. She was angry over her mother's weakness, for refusing to answer any of her letters all those years. Only after her father had become gravely ill did they develop a superficially cordial relationship—as long as it was at a distance.

Why had she come? To defy him? No. To upset him? No. Perhaps, even after all these years, it would be nice to pretend she still wanted her father's forgiveness and approval, which is why Nara had agreed to go along with her mother's story. Or maybe she just wanted closure. But those were just lies to be socially palatable.

The utter truth was that she would not have trusted news of his death. What she needed was to see the head in the basket before she would truly believe and be free of his judgment.

Nara angrily wiped away hot tears from her cheeks. When she had returned from her brief honeymoon at Jeju Island, the Ambassador had horsewhipped her for shaming the family with her out-of-wedlock pregnancy. Her forearms black and purple with defensive wounds. The following day he removed all her belongings, everything that was reminiscent of her from the house and forbid anyone to ever speak of her again. It was as if she never existed.

He ordered Nara's exile to America, thrown away like trash. But Nara could not travel until her wounds healed, and by the time she was ready to travel, her belly was too big.

Her father was considered a great man. He had fought the communists. He had fought the Japanese. He had stood up to the Chinese and Americans when it had been politically difficult. A hero to everyone, but harsh and unrelenting in his judgments of his own daughter.

"I'm going to take your child and get tea for everyone." It was her mother's voice, frozen in formality, not even willing to breath Naomi's name. "Your child," not "Naomi" or "my granddaughter."

Nara shuddered and turned and watched her mother depart with Naomi, leaving her standing there alone with the nurse. Nara walked over closer to the bed to look at her father. He immediately began to softly moan and twist a little. Nara jumped back, startled. The nurse quickly adjusted the dial on one of his drips. "Is he in pain?" Nara asked, trying not to sound hopeful.

"No, ma'am. The medicine is very strong, but he seems to know you are here."

Her heart pounded in her chest. Nara had prepared herself as best she could for this moment. Strange gargling and gasping sounds were coming from the Ambassador's throat. She badly wanted a cigarette. The nurse made another adjustment on the oxygen and pressed a button.

"*Abonim*, father, I have come from America. It is I, Nara." The Ambassador lay with his eyes closed, breathing laboriously. Perhaps Naomi could have a relationship with her grandmother after this monster was dead because Nara had done what was asked of her. Nara rested her hand on the side rail.

"Father, I know you need to rest now. I'll come and visit tomorrow."

She said this only for the benefit of the nurse. The truth was she wanted a smoke, and the other truth was if she stayed in that room another minute she was at risk of ripping the oxygen tubes from his face and hurrying his trip to hell.

Nara backed away from the bed and turned to leave, but at the door she turned back to thank the nurse only to find her father's head turned towards the door, his hard eyes open, coldly staring at her.

Nara left the hospital room and leaned against the wall, panting. She had not eaten or slept on the plane. She surprised even herself at how raw her anger was, after all these years. Over time she had formed it into a wall of icy and implacable rage that was her confidante and comfort, but it had melted into flames just seeing him.

Wolf was walking down the hall. He had just come from the hotel. Seeing how pale his wife looked, he took her elbow and they joined Naomi and her grandma in the tearoom.

"Who is watching Sara?" The grandma asked in Korean, sipping her tea. "Is she alone in the hotel room?"

Wolf looked up, curiously. His Korean was nominal but he knew Sara very well from Naomi's many stories about her imaginary twin sister.

"Is she asking about Sara, Naomi's twin?" Wolf asked innocently.

Nara froze. She turned sharply and glared at Naomi who withered from the mean eyes of her mother. Wolf caught the whole thing. He had seen it too many times. The poor thing, always at the other end of her mother's wrath.

It was all too weird. The food, the land, the customs, the smells and now the family asking about Naomi's pretend sister. Now Nara was upset. In fact, he had never seen Nara so upset. She was an icy flame, that one. Wolf didn't know what to do so he stood up.

"I'm going to go pay my respects," Wolf said, getting up. "Then go to the hotel room and take Sara out for some ice cream," he joked and pointed at the grandma. "Someone translate for me what I said. Ice cream for Sara."

No one translated anything. The grandmother stared at Wolf as he left. He could feel her eyes on his back. The rock didn't fall far from the tree. Meeting the grandmother made that plain enough. Poor Naomi.

The Great Ambassador had obsessively planned his death for the ten preceding years, determined to have his power reach beyond the golden, velvet lined casket that waited. Whether years, days or hours or minutes, it didn't matter. The time was short. He had arranged every last detail of the funeral including the release of doves and the firing of a canon at the burial site.

Naomi looked up and met Holly's gaze. "It was right after we returned from Korea that Wolf got arrested," she whispered.

CHAPTER 59

Heather had been right to warn Holly about the raid. The agents stood in groups of two and three with hands on their hips talking to each other. Their anonymous cars had taken the last of the metered parking. Another agent stood blocking the exits. More FBI agents were staked out across the street as a visual reminder to the Koreans that this was not Seoul.

Holly brushed past an agent and pushed her way inside the building. "Ninth floor. They're still there," the security guard whispered. "They're not here to get you, too, are they Miss Holly?"

"Of course not!" Holly laughed as her heart pounded. "Any other floor?" she couldn't help but ask.

"No."

Holly took the elevator to the ninth floor. The double doors of American Legal Services were wide open and more FBI agents walked out carrying computer hard drives and boxes of files.

"Holly!" Kate rushed over, both hands outstretched and her face flushed. "Listen, you know I always cared about my clients, don't you?" Her voice rose sharply, she raised her hands and clasped them to her chest—imprecation, remorse, benediction—it was all of those things.

"Time to leave." The FBI agent clapped his hand on Kate's shoulder.

"Don't touch me!" Kate shrieked, her voice eerily loud. She

wrenched her thin, delicate shoulder free, withering from his touch, her face dead white, eyes poised and haughty to the end. Ever the fashionista, she fumbled around looking for her platform heels and checked her face in the tiny mirror hanging on the wall. Voices rose and fell around them.

"I...I don't understand. What did you do?" Holly cried, her eyes full of hurt, pleading. Across the room there was a low snicker of laughter.

Kate whirled around, a bitter half-smile on her face. Her eyes suddenly seemed small and narrow.

"You're so stupid, Holly. Don't you know anything? Everything is right under your nose and you're the only one who can't see it. If you haven't figured it out, you can read about it in the papers!" Kate turned again and faced the agents. "You'll make sure it's a nice photo of me, won't you, boys?"

Holly watched as Kate Hong was led away.

***

In the parking garage downstairs, Neil Cooper threw the thin Naomi Linser file in the trash. He loaded his trunk with his belongings, a rolling briefcase holding a few framed photos, diplomas and mementos from his office along with a nearly full bottle of Johnny Walker Blue, and the spare shirt and tie he had kept on a hanger on the back of the door. He had come to the office to pass the Naomi Linser file back to Kate, but when he walked in, there was yelling coming from Kate's office down the hall so he had left, moments before the FBI had showed up.

It was an excellent time to go out to Palm Springs for a few days and play a little golf until the heat died down. If it didn't, he could always sell his Harley-Davidson and set up out there. Life was short, he should enjoy himself.

CHAPTER 60

Eli Behr spun a quarter on the tabletop. It was late and quiet, a smattering of people at the counter. He loved diners. A cheerful waitress, a club sandwich or bacon and eggs for dinner, coffee you could use to clean a carburetor. In a drive-thru world, there was a continuity that was comforting.

The woman slid into the booth. He took off his baseball cap and ran his hand through his slicked back blond hair.

"Thank you for coming, Joan. You must be tired," he said. "This shouldn't take long."

"Apple pie and coffee, black please," she said, to the waitress. "It's nice to be sitting for a change." Her voice was soft. "I feel a bit deflated, I haven't eaten all day. The café was busy."

"Eat some dinner, take your time. Keep your strength up — I'll join you, I was in court all day."

Eli ordered a roast beef and American cheese, lettuce and tomato, and a top-up on his coffee, then encouraged Joan to order something more substantial.

"Club sandwich, then, please, easy on the mayo, with fries."

"Good, you'll feel like a new person."

"I'd like to feel like a new person. It's been a while."

Joan had once been a beauty, but the blonde hair was streaked with gray now, and the cut was out of date, the eyes wary and tired, lines beginning to show. Deflated. Her word. Life had taken the wind out of her sails.

"On the telephone you said you wanted to talk about William?"

"Yes. Are you up to it?"

"Oh, sure," she said, not sounding sure. "I went to the funeral, stood in the back, dark glasses. Didn't want to intrude on the family, but I wanted to be there."

"What was he like when you knew him?"

"Fun. We laughed all the time. Some of my friends said I was just a trophy to him, an arm piece. Every man's fantasy to have a blonde on his arm—that was a big deal back then. It wasn't that long ago, was it?"

"I can see that you were a beauty," Eli offered, sincerely, then leaned forward. "Did William ever exhibit any aggressive behavior?"

"He was sweet. Attentive. Romantic, liked those soul songs by Marvin Gaye, gentle as a lamb until he started drinking. As he drank more and more, he would start reminiscing about his glory days and pretend he was back on the football field rather than in bed. He would then become angry and sad at the same time. When he got like that, his lovemaking could become fiery and aggressive."

Joan took a big drink of water and pushed a cold French fry around with a fork. She was so drained. Joan looked at Eli and smiled. She understood from television how lawyers wore you down by making you tell the same story again and again and again. Eli sat pensive, watching her.

"Does that help?" she asked softly, wanting to please him. The waitress brought more coffee, which Eli stirred relentlessly, though he'd put nothing in it.

"Yes, Joan, thank you. It helps. You never know which piece is going to be the one that works. It's like a jigsaw puzzle. Those ones that are snow scenes or sky and you can't tell anything? But you just keep working it and get a couple of pieces together and then maybe you get some traction."

Eli threw a couple of twenties on the table and stood up.

She stood, too. "You single?"

He could hear the wistfulness in her voice. The invitation. She was still good-looking, but not a good idea. He needed her as a witness. He shook his head, glad he wasn't drinking.

"I roam alone when I'm in trial," he said. "But maybe after..., that would be nice."

Eli watched her go. Some people live in the shadows of their past and can't let go. He thought of Holly instead. Now there was a firecracker that would burn your fingers.

CHAPTER 61

"A hypnotist may be able to unlock Naomi's mind," Holly's mother had suggested over lunch. "To find out what really happened that night."

So here Holly was. It was five minutes before noon and she was already having second thoughts. The office building looked like the sort of place where businesses go to die. Older and dirtier than its neighboring buildings and nearly as tired as its tenants. Professionals with creaky credentials, practitioners who needed more practice, marginal specialties like chiropractic, language schools, acupuncture, oriental medicine, and paralegal services.

There were a few making money, comfortable in the protective coloration of the seedy old building.

Holly sighed and stepped over a sticky over-sized soda cup and read the sign on the door: Dr. Perry Koo, Certified Master Hypnotherapist.

His door was next to an office where the sour smell of herbs fermenting lingered behind a sign that said Oriental Medicine. Holly wrinkled her nose and pushed open Dr. Koo's door and went inside.

In this building, anybody in a white coat, glasses and a clipboard could pass for a doctor, including Perry Koo with his piercing eyes. He not only had the white coat and glasses, but an alphabet soup of acronyms and titles that took up the space of an entire business card.

The reception area was empty.

"You can call me doctor."

The deep and sonorous voice came from the back. "It's almost lunchtime and I'm closed in five minutes." Dr. Perry Koo appeared.

"Thank you for seeing me, Dr. Koo," Holly began.

"I close from noon to 1:30 p.m. You can join me for a drink or come back later. I do my best thinking in bars, so you are welcome to tag along. Let me grab my coat," he said, pulling on his white lab coat.

Okay, Holly thought. *This is already going so well. He drinks in the middle of the business day.*

Holly followed him to an old hotel off Olympic Boulevard. It didn't look too clean. It was hot and sticky outside, and the hotel was old so the air conditioning blew hot air. In fact, it was not much different from the building they just left, only this one had bar stools.

"I need to impress this young lady, so I'm going to teach her how to make a special drink," Dr. Koo announced to the bartender cheerfully. "Two shots of gin, Tanqueray, not that scary stuff you have behind you with the gummy worms in it, a tablespoon of Rose's lime juice per, shake it like dice, very cold, an egg white if it's fresh. Two."

He turned to Holly. "This is called a gimlet—you're paying right?" He leaned back. "I'm kidding. But you can if you want."

"Of course I'll pay," said Holly.

The drinks came. The doc took a slow sip, nodded approval and stared into the glass as if looking into the past.

Holly took a sip. It was excellent. Sharp and sweet. Like a painful memory you were still somehow fond of.

"Okay," Dr. Koo began by raising his glass. "You have questions, I have a drink."

"Can it hurt the person, the subject, to have traumatic memories awakened?" Holly asked.

Dr. Koo steepled his fingers and thought. "There are no absolutes. In a secure setting it is possible but not entirely reliable. But an unreliable memory may be better than no memory at this point. The priority is to find out what happened. From what you told me on the phone, you have nothing."

"I have to know what happened in that room." Holly's tone was grave. "Will you—or more importantly—can you unlock Naomi's mind so we can find out what really happened?

"I can try." Dr. Koo nodded, slowly.

"You are our only hope," Holly spoke softly. "The problem is that only two people know the truth, and one of them is dead."

CHAPTER 62

"Still no text?" Holly asked Heather with concern.

Heather Hart shook her head and looked down at her phone. "He always says I can't compete with the streets," Heather said wistfully, looking to her best friend to calm her storm.

They were at the Rose Bowl in Pasadena for their weekly run. Holly parked the car and the girls got out. It was just starting to get dark, their favorite time to run.

Heather could feel the familiar anxiety rising within her. The stress that had started the year of her engagement. She had just thought it was bridal nerves and ignored it. But the feeling wouldn't go away and the bad feeling just got worse and worse. Eight years later, all she knew was that something was terribly terribly wrong and if she thought about it too much she felt like screaming. The only way to control it was to ignore the cause. It was getting harder and harder though, and Heather relied more and more on Mick to help her get through the day. Just a text, a connection. That's all she needed. The run would help.

Holly was stretching when Heather looked across the way and spotted Mick. Did he know she was here? Maybe he was tracking her by her phone and came to surprise her. The thought made her giddy inside.

"Mick—" Heather started to call out, but stopped as an old Honda pulled up and a girl got out of the driver's side of the car and walked towards Mick. She wore a midriff bearing T-shirt and jeans cut very low, showing a tramp-stamp tattoo on her backside. An informant?

Heather watched as Mick playfully tugged at her long hair, whirl her around in a bear hug then slap her bottom before grabbing her hand and swinging their arms as they walked. When they reached the beater car, the girl tossed Mick the keys. Mick got in on the driver's side and drove off. He had not seen Heather. Heather turned to say something to Holly, but she had seen the whole thing.

"What a piece of shit—" Holly said, grabbing Heather's arm. "Let's run."

"A long one tonight, Holly, so I can sleep. Tomorrow is mother-in-law day."

The tea was served in lovely Wedgwood cups. Heather took a sip and said, "I'm sure you remember the Westons. They're getting divorced. They endowed the library as Edith and Tony Weston and now the fight is over whose name goes first on the plaque."

"What an embarrassment for the family." Her mother-in law put down her tea, not finding any humor in the story, then added, "trusts were set up to bar divorces, like anyone with significant wealth would do."

"You mean like my situation?"

The mother-in-law sat up stiffly and examined the girl that sat across from her. Heather was the worst of all possible combinations—beautiful, highly intelligent, and ill-bred. They should have held out for pretty and dumb for Gordon. She sighed. It made Heather difficult to control at times. And now she was starting to ask questions—difficult questions.

"Trusts guarantee that nobody in a wealthy family will ever become poor as a church mouse. But you know that, dear." Her thin lips pressed together tightly as she spoke. She looked hard at her daughter-in-law. Heather had not been through war, displacement, economic struggle, social upheaval. She had only known American prosperity. Her carefully planned marriage into the Hart family had been to provide her with a secure economic future in exchange for preserving to the grave the Hart family secret.

Gordon's mother had hand selected Heather when she was too young to know any better and still mourning the loss of her father to question or challenge anything.

Mrs. Hart was always aware of Gordon's emotional frailty. As a child he was sickly and spent many days in bed. While his friends went to summer camp and sporting events Gordon read books. Hundreds of books which educated him in theory and deprived him in practice. His occasionally bizarre or off topic public outbursts were accepted as the result of his prodigious intellect, which is how the family was able to fool everyone and keep the family secret. Unprotected by family, servants, doctors, specialists, therapists and pharmaceuticals—and vast walls of money—Gordon would have been as vulnerable in society as a child playing in traffic. The secret had been kept even from Heather whose youth and innocence had been used against her up until she married Gordon. After that it was too late. Gordon's mother's plan had worked beautifully.

The mother-in-law sighed. She had discouraged Heather from bearing offspring, without telling her why, and bought the Labradoodle to be a third wheel in the wedding bed, knowing full well her son's fondness for dogs. To end the family curse once and for all. There had been four generations of half-wits and Gordon was the fifth. Whatever difficulties his frailty brought into the marriage, her daughter-in-law didn't realize the side benefit of his timidity, and that his emotional attachment to Heather saved her from having to endure the pain and humiliation of girlfriends and mistresses that the men in the Hart family had long been known for. In short, Heather didn't know how good she had it.

Heather put down her teacup and stood. "I'll let you know how the museum opening goes. It's not likely that Gordon will attend."

Half an hour later, Heather made her frustrations clear at Neiman-Marcus. On the first floor—shoes and handbags—on the second and third floors — fashion and more fashion. Only the fourth floor was spared, because that was the men's floor.

"Bill everything to Mr. Gordon Hart," Heather cheerfully told her personal shopper, who could barely stand, holding Heather's selections.

CHAPTER 63

The trial of the People of the State of California versus Naomi Linser was underway. Holly loved the acoustics of the old courthouse. Her heels clicked on the marble floors of the fifteenth, floor as she raced towards Department N-9, past the rows of long, lacquered wooden benches where lawyers sat, pensive, waiting for the courtroom doors to open. She admired the double doors of the other departments as she hurried by, marveling at the tiny windows cut into the doors of the windowless courtrooms where so many battles had been fought. Win or lose, the rule of law elevated man out of the swamp.

Last night Naomi hadn't cared about Holly Park, the lawyer. Naomi had wanted Miss Holly her Sunday school teacher to pray with her, as they had done when she was a child, a simple child's prayer.

"God be with you," Holly whispered as she finished.

It was the sound of someone clearing their throat, loudly, that broke the quiet hush of the hallways and made Holly stop. She listened. She heard it again. The sound was coming from the stairwell. Holly pulled open a side door off the corridor and peered into the stairwell

"You can't smoke in here!" Holly said frantically, looking around. "You're going to set off the alarms!"

Eli Behr took a last drag of his cigarette and dropped it at his feet and crushed the butt with the tip of his cowboy boot and watched as the red glow turn to ash. He turned to face her, thumbs hooked in his pockets and his shoulders hunched. Beads of perspiration lined his forehead and there were blotches where his moist skin had soaked his once-crisp white shirt. Holly stared, the color draining from her face.

"Pre-game nerves," Eli explained, leaning away from her. Eli put his fingers between his shirt collar and neck and pulling the fabric away from his skin, ventilating his neck. "Once I throw up, I'll be fine." He smiled weakly.

"I'll go in first." Holly tried to sound calm and encouraging, though inside she was horrified. "Come in when you are ready."

The courtroom was packed. The media hovered, setting up equipment in the back. It seemed like half of Los Angeles was gathered in the hallways waiting to pick the flesh from the bones of Naomi Linser.

Holly nodded to the bailiff as she walked past the wooden bar and into the well where she took her seat beside Naomi, who, dressed in prison blues, was somehow magically beautiful, though if one could look closely, her eyes were frightened.

"It's time," Holly whispered, her eyes bright, eager, lit with anticipation, her nostrils flared. Naomi stared straight ahead but saw nothing. Her pale face was filled with fear. In a few minutes they would begin. It would be okay. Holly was ready. She did not fear the judgment of men.

When Naomi Linser was arrested for murder, the Koreans were afraid, and rightly so, that the crime would cause uninvited scrutiny upon Koreatown and its practices. The Koreans were private and reclusive people who didn't want outsiders poking around in their affairs.

During those long months while Naomi sat in a cell waiting to stand trial, the District Attorney, Blake LeBlanc had methodically built up his case with Koreatown's cultural and business practices as virtual co-defendants. By office policy death penalty cases were supposed to be staffed by two D.A.s, but LeBlanc had not been assigned any help and had never asked for an explanation.

Blake LeBlanc stood military straight as he strolled in, with a pretty law clerk close behind carrying black trial binders under her arm. Aside from her own experience having lost to him once, Holly had heard stories about him. She hoped he would like Naomi, but Holly was clutching at thin straws. Her optimism was wasted.

LeBlanc was in a classification of his own. He took great exception to the intrusion of women in the workplace. He believed there were only three places a woman belonged—in bars, kitchens or in the bedroom.

In the privacy of his own thoughts, Blake secretly believed the system was too lenient, and would happily have dispensed with it so that he could mete out punishment as he saw fit.

Though he was cordial and did not say so, it showed in the coldness of his eyes. The extreme formality of speech and excessive politeness with which he spoke, devoid of emotion, whether he was addressing adverse counsel, law enforcement or witnesses was all a mask. A formidable adversary if there ever was one. LeBlanc walked up to the jury box where the jury pool sat and casually dropped his briefcase on the counsel table.

It was just another morning in court. Another case. Another trial. Another murder, his body language said. His tie hung loose around his neck, which he tied while chatting with the potential jurors as if he were at home in the kitchen waiting for the coffee to brew. LeBlanc cheerily waved at the cameraman, calling him by name. If his casualness was meant to have the effect of unnerving Holly, it worked.

The buzzer sounded. One short buzz indicating that the judge was about to take the bench. The crowd quieted to a hum then silence as the judge entered.

"All rise! The court is now in session," the clerk announced. "The Honorable Christopher H. Marshall presiding."

Holly froze. The light seemed too bright as it buzzed and hummed overhead. The courtroom seemed to pulsate with unfamiliar sounds. All Holly heard was:

First degree murder.

Homicide.

Naomi Lee Linser.

Premeditation.

Special circumstances.

Death penalty.

And so the trial began. For the rest of the day, Holly and Blake LeBlanc alternated questioning the potential jurors of whom twelve plus two alternates would remain to sit in judgment of Naomi, the accused. Naomi, ever so emaciated, so beguiling, sat staring ahead in wonderment. Somehow Holly got through it. The court reporter smiled encouragingly. That one gesture, that single unexpected act of moral support, strengthened Holly, who turned and smiled at Naomi and gave back, squeezing Naomi's hand. The next morning, headlines blazed:

Counsel and Murderess Hold Hands

Oh, Naomi! She became the most photographed woman that summer from the moment she stepped into the courtroom and throughout the trial. Oh, how the cameras loved her, capturing her soft, smoke grey eyes time and time again as they glowed in awe, watching. It was as if she were sitting in the VIP section of a show, not understanding that in fact the crowd had gathered to watch her—the main attraction.

Naomi Linser was beguiling, vulnerable, innocent and provocative. Often Holly wondered if Naomi even realized this was all about her. The lamb being led to slaughter. Looking like a virgin, and accused of being whore. The public rushed to judgment like it was an open bar.

During LeBlanc's case in chief, the jury found themselves being pulled into the underbelly of Koreatown, presented as a theme park ride, thrills and horrors interchangeable, and the jury was hooked. LeBlanc wove a majestic tale of how Councilman William McClellan had entered Koreatown by virtue of position, power, affluence and chance, as a good-hearted mover and shaker, working to give the Koreans a second chance at rebuilding a community that had been burned to ashes in the 1992 riots.

While the good Councilman's focus and good intentions were on public works, he had been unsuspectingly lured into a culture he did not know, a dark, seamy—and illegal—culture which used beautiful girls as lures into traps as certain as a hunter's snare. The Councilman had been guilty only of naiveté and romantic innocence and did not deserve to die with his pants around his ankles and a knife through his broken heart. This was the portrait LeBlanc so deftly drew.

Yet LeBlanc was perhaps no different from the Councilman. He, too, had been lured into the underbelly of a culture he neither knew nor understood. A little bit of knowledge is a dangerous thing, and LeBlanc was vigorous and diligent. Yellow pad in hand, he had forced himself into the hostess salons and hostess bars interviewing *domis* under the threat of contempt and the power of the subpoena. The little known truth was that Blake, too, succumbed to the hospitalities of the very establishments he would later vilify and put on trial. The women were too tempting, too beautiful, too deferential for him to realize what was happening. Had he been more broadly educated, he might have recognized sirens when he saw them.

But that summer, the public attention was on Naomi.

Trial lawyers are great storytellers, puppeteers of words. Blake described Naomi as a child of privilege, spoiled, petulant, whimsical. A reversal of fortune had caused her to lose her upper-class equestrian lifestyle of dressage shows and circuit jumping, and she had turned to slumming in the streets of Koreatown, partying in the underworld run by gangsters and brokers on payroll where she lived a double life as a *domi*.

In a world of excess cash where any indulgence could be had for a price, Naomi was spoiled, driven around like a diva in illegal taxicabs, entertaining men while emptying their pockets. The Councilman never stood a chance.

"The evidence will show that the defendant, Naomi Linser, knifed him to death simply because she didn't get her way. She simply threw a tantrum of colossal proportions, a spoiled, vindictive girl," was how LeBlanc ended opening statements that first day.

Daisy Moreno, the Councilman's longtime secretary, took the stand and Mr. LeBlanc had first crack at her.

LeBlanc: Have you met the defendant, Naomi Lee Linser before today?

Daisy: Many times.

LeBlanc: When did you first come to know of her?

Daisy: It started with the letter. I remember the letter because I opened it. It was written on thick creamy paper with neat schoolgirl script.

LeBlanc: Why was this particular letter so memorable?

Daisy: Because she ended the letter with "xoxo" and a hand-drawn smiley face, with one of those gel pens. The Councilman liked it. He felt she was coming on to him. He kept the letter in his special drawer in his credenza. And his journal, which I read—after he died, of course.

While Daisy Moreno was trying to be helpful, one thing became immediately apparent. She was not about to give up her few minutes of celebrity. For the next forty minutes, she described Naomi as the subject of the politician's growing obsession and laboriously began all over again, recounting the very private thoughts of the councilman.

LeBlanc: How would you describe her relationship with the Councilman?

Daisy: She was like the other girls. She often came to the office. And he would shut his door for an hour and we knew not to disturb him when she was there.

The inference was clear. Naomi sat quietly, frowning, as if she were trying to remember, her mouth a small "o", her body bent forward, legs crossed daintily at the ankles. Holly had warned Naomi that jurors would be watching her and not to react, no matter what, but Naomi couldn't help it. Naomi sat at the edge of her chair, listening to Daisy's account of how she had become the object of the Councilman's affection. Naomi listened as if she were listening to a story about somebody else.

Daisy: He invited her to a function, and when she walked in he messed up part of his speech, which was not like him. I saw her, too. The Councilman was fond of the ladies. Particularly the Korean ones.

Daisy wrinkled her nose when she said that.

LeBlanc: What about the night in question?

Daisy: That night was different. I saw Naomi lock eyes with the

Councilman and watched his eyes follow her around all night. She was scantily clad—completely inappropriate for a political function.

Daisy Moreno sniffed.

LeBlanc: Did the Councilman fall in love with her?

Daisy: Yes. The Councilman said he found love that he neither could nor wanted to prevent. He needed the young girls around.

LeBlanc: Did you like her?

Daisy: Not at all.

LeBlanc: Why not?

Daisy: Because she thought she was better than the others. But she was just a higher priced whore—just one of those girls.

LeBlanc: Can you explain who "'those'" girls are?

Blake LeBlanc asked this with a deliberate weary patience, leaning with both hands pressed hard against the podium.

Daisy: Fine. I'll say it! She had sex for money. I'm not afraid to call a spade a spade.

Daisy crossed her arms and tossed her head. She harrumphed, her voice a half octave higher than a moment before.

Daisy: Wearing expensive clothes and driving a white Mercedes don't make her a lady. Just a cleaned-up whore is what *she* was.

"The State calls Mimi Hwang to the stand."

Blake LeBlanc grinned. He was just getting warmed up.

CHAPTER 64

Holly looked around the packed courtroom and saw Eli slipping into a seat in the back. She caught his eye and gave him an encouraging smile. He would come to the counsel table when he was ready. If he wasn't ready, she did not want him.

The investigator had staked out Mimi Hwang's apartment and dragged her to court, half asleep, a creature of the night. She was the prosecution's star witness.

Mimi came to court wearing a baseball cap which the bailiff made her remove before taking the stand. She stumbled taking her seat. Mimi rolled her eyes and dropped her oversized designer handbag in her lap, looking more like a pampered and sullen child than the prosecution's key witness. She stifled a yawn as she raised her hand and took the oath.

Mimi Hwang squinted at the light like a vampire, her knees neatly pressed together, back perfectly erect from hours of daily yoga. The male jurors shifted uncomfortably, an involuntary sniff from the female jurors who sat and pressed their knees together, unconsciously imitating the body language of the sleepy beautiful girl as they scrutinized the hair, skin, perfect body, the perfectly manicured nails and pretty feet of the witness. She was young, with a long slender neck and a slight gap between her teeth. Her hair hung in wisps framing her pretty face.

LeBlanc: What is your job?

Mimi: I'm a *domi*.

LeBlanc: What is a *domi*?

Mimi: A hostess, a companion.

LeBlanc: What type of hostess?

Mimi batted her eyelashes and looked up shyly then looked down again.

Mimi: We help men relax. We pour drinks.

Mimi smiled and gestured to illustrate in that Korean subservient way how she poured drinks with one hand behind the other, with girlish embarrassment, eyes downcast, eyelashes fluttering shyly, with their delicate wrist movement, never spilling a drop.

LeBlanc: Do you get paid?

Mimi: Of course.

LeBlanc: So your job is similar to a bartender?

Mimi: Not at all. Korean places only serve liquor by the bottles. That's why it's so expensive. A waiter brings a bottle into the room and we pour it. You can't buy a shot in a Korean place. You can only buy the bottle.

LeBlanc: Is it part of the job for the girls to drink with the men?

Mimi: Yes. But we have tricks, like placing extra ice cubes in our own drink and waiting for the ice cubes to melt. We pretend to drink, but really just pour more Crown Royal into their glasses. The more bottles the guys consume the more the house makes and the higher our tips.

Her voice danced with a playful inflection.

LeBlanc: Do *domis* do anything else other than pour drinks?

Mimi: We sit next to the men and listen and laugh at their stories and sing and dance for them.

Mimi looked up, innocent and helpless, cupping her mouth with her hands, suppressing giggles. There was a smattering of laughter from the gallery.

LeBlanc: How is the hostess salon set up?

Mimi: The rooms are all private with karaoke machines, lights, booths, tables and tambourines.

LeBlanc: How much do these private party rooms cost?

Mimi: Thousands of dollars.

LeBlanc: Thousands?

Mimi: Yes.

LeBlanc: What does a customer get for thousands of dollars?

Mimi: The pleasure of our company, of course. If a customer likes a particular girl, she is never allowed to stay in that room too long so that she is asked back. The way to get a girl back is to order more expensive liquor and hand out bigger tips.

LeBlanc: Were you working the night of the Councilman's murder?

Mimi: Yes.

LeBlanc: Did you see Naomi at Club Kiki that night?

Mimi: Yes. I was already there and saw her when she came in.

LeBlanc: What is the primary purpose men go and spend thousands of dollars at these hostess salons?

Mimi: They come to escape their wives. They come to relax and to spend time with pretty girls. We are sexier, younger, and more fun. The wives are a drag and put on weight. The guys say their fat wives just sit there complaining, putting them down, and demanding money.

Mimi paused and looked up at the ceiling. There was a lot of muttering in the gallery.

Mimi: We want their money, too—but at least we stay skinny, wear short skirts, show a lot of cleavage and ask nicely.

Mimi smiled coyly. Murmurs again from the gallery. The jurors leaned forward, captivated by what else Mimi Hwang would have had to say.

Mimi smiled at LeBlanc.

LeBlanc's face reddened. He shifted his legs and tried not to stare down her cleavage at the perfect swell of her young breasts. No bra. He was flustered. Blake LeBlanc prided himself on his cool. He never missed a beat, but her smooth, moist skin, her perfect lips—he wanted to reach over and touch her.

Mimi badly wanted a cigarette. She yawned.

LeBlanc: Is there anything further we need to know about the job of a *domi*?

Mimi thought, her head tilted up, doe-eyed.

Mimi: Only that the wives shouldn't be mad at us. It's better their husbands come to us than get a girlfriend. With us, they just pay for one night and go back home. We don't text or call their husbands like a date or girlfriend would. We leave the guys alone unless they come back looking for us. We are just always there, waiting.

Holly sat, frozen, having listened with a climbing dread. She closed her eyes and deliberately sat up straight, trying not to show her dismay. How could this be evidence? It was ridiculous. Blake's strategy was clear: first hang Koreatown, then tighten the noose on Naomi.

Maybe the testimony was not enough for a murder conviction, Holly tried to convince herself. All Mimi had really done was place Naomi at the crime scene, which no one was denying in the first place.

Holly watched as Mimi delicately swung her long legs around, eased herself off the witness stand and waved shyly at the judge and jury. Holly bit her lip.

Naomi sat with her head bowed, her fingers pressed together, looking thinner, tired, her eyes larger and translucent, wide, even more fragile than before as she was led out when the court adjourned for the day.

CHAPTER 65

The next morning, as Holly and Eli Burg huddled outside, Detective Mick Chang was in the courtroom hallway milling with the crowd. He always showed up to court in a flak jacket and a leg holster while other law enforcement wore the standard blues or khakis. Holly's stomach churned as he looked at her, his eyes mocking.

Holly walked past him, braced herself, and walked into the courtroom. There were two alpha dogs and only one fire hydrant.

Outside the courtroom Mick sat away from the others, hunched over, elbows on his knees with his head down. He looked at his phone. Still no text. He hadn't heard from Heather lately. His thoughts turned to Naomi. In court with her. Again. A victim before and now the defendant. What were the odds of that?

Mick hadn't thought of Wolf Linser in years, but he remembered every detail clearly. It was the case that got him promoted to detective and he hadn't looked back since. It had been open and shut—hadn't it?

Naomi Linser was even more beautiful than he remembered. How many years had passed? Five? Six? Seven? Open and shut, right? The detective felt uneasy. Something didn't seem right. He tried to remember.

His first week on the force and he was working as an investigating officer when a third party had called it in. When he pulled up, all the lights were on in the house. A knockout beautiful Korean woman was standing over an equally beautiful teenage girl, shrieking, Korean style. It was 2 a.m. He had flashed his badge and walked in the same way as he had seen the cops do when they had arrested his stepfather so many years ago.

Then a tall, older man with longish wavy blond hair wearing a sports jacket and jeans pulled up in a Range Rover and sauntered in moments after the detective arrived on the scene.

"Arrest him! Arrest him!" the woman screamed in English. "You ruined her!" she snarled at the tall blond man. "I'll put you away in prison forever!"

"Mom, please." Naomi stood up, pulling her mother back.

Mick took Wolf Linser into custody that night. The ride to the station was silent. When they got to the station, Mick knew he should only book Linser for having sex with his fifteen-year-old stepdaughter. But fuck him. Instead, Mick booked Linser under rape and sodomy, knowing it was overcharged and wouldn't stick. But inside, the charges would go viral, and if nothing else, the arrest record would follow Linser for the rest of his life.

It was his first case since making detective. He wanted a good one. A week later, the case landed back on his desk for further investigation. Mick had gone back to the house to interview the girl. Naomi was home alone, her face ghost white.

"My mother never came home," Naomi said. "It was always the two of us alone. We spent an awful lot of time together. The sex started on my sixteenth birthday."

Naomi hid her face as she spoke so that he could barely hear her. It didn't take too much trickery after that. Mick went back and interviewed Linser, who caved.

On the day of sentencing, Mick squirmed. He was used to girls with no status, girls from the streets he called hood rats behind their backs, and this one was such a classy girl he wanted to do right for her.

Mick looked down at his shiny boots. When the case was called, he crossed his arms and watched Linser shackled and led out through the side door. He turned around again towards Naomi but she was looking off into the distance. He had expected to see vindication or relief in her face. But neither was there, only darkness and clouds. Something about her expression bothered him. He couldn't explain it but he couldn't shake it, either.

For his work on the Wolf Linser case Mick received a commendation. He went to the ceremony alone, received his award and threw it in a box. That year he was promoted to detective and never gave Naomi Linser a second thought. Until now.

Mick shook it off. It didn't matter. It was just a weird coincidence. Then why did he have this bad feeling in his stomach? Worse than right before kicking in a door at 4 a.m.

"Detective Chang?"

"Yes?

"They're ready for you now."

"Thank you."

CHAPTER 66

Blake LeBlanc stood up and buttoned his suit jacket, unconsciously smoothing it as he walked up to the witness stand. LeBlanc was a perfectionist. He strongly believed that if he presented an officer on the stand, the officer should have a deep grasp of the case and conduct himself in such a way as to live up to the billing. Detective Chang always came prepared. LeBlanc smiled inwardly. Again, the detective came through.

LeBlanc: Did you respond to the call the night of the Councilman's murder?

Chang: Yes. The call came in as an incident at the location. I was familiar with the location having been there on numerous occasions.

LeBlanc: How were you familiar with the location?

Chang: Part of my duties includes investigating establishments that solicit for prostitution. Approximately twenty of my cases have involved Club Kiki over the past couple years.

Chang paused, pressing his fingers together. He was patient, he'd given testimony hundreds of times.

Naomi and Holly looked at each other. It was clear that LeBlanc would spend the entire morning putting Club Kiki on trial as part of his overall plan of painting Koreatown black.

Holly sat back, not surprised, but still dismayed. They had a brief pause while the judge discussed something with the bailiff. She tried to shake the feeling of foreboding, that something bad was about to happen, but she couldn't. She looked at Eli next to her, he seemed okay, entirely focused. She looked around the gallery, trying to read the mood. It was then Holly noticed Choi in the courtroom sitting in the seat closest to the door. He had been there since the first day of the trial and always sat in the same spot. Holly hadn't realized before his hair was bright silver, his cheap pinstripe suit shiny with the passage of time. Holly had seen him earlier that week and felt him watching her now. Why was he interested in this case? It didn't matter, Holly had to concentrate on the trial and not let anything distract her.

It was late Friday afternoon before a long weekend and LeBlanc had given the jurors something memorable to think about. The gruesome crime photos and especially one of Naomi holding the knife.

Holly watched helplessly as the bailiff handcuffed Naomi and led her out the side door to the holding cell. Naomi turned. She looked more fragile than ever. With a flutter of her eyelashes she was gone. Holly couldn't get the horrific crime scene photos out of her mind. A picture speaks a thousand words.

LeBlanc had painted his masterpiece and certainly convinced the jury of the guilt of Koreatown, and by association the guilt of Naomi Linser. Had he convinced her, too?

Holly buried her face in her hands. She was the last to leave the courtroom, not wanting to face the cameras and the questions. She had sent Eli to face the horde. He owed her. As she walked out of the courtroom, she saw Choi again, looking like he was waiting for someone

"You have your father's fire," he began as he approached her, "and compassion."

Holly stopped reluctantly. "Do you know my father?"

"I know him well. Everybody knows him. He has the church near the freeway."

Choi clutched a plastic shopping bag tightly as he spoke.

"You would not remember, but I met you many many years ago.

You were just a little girl yourself, then," Choi said, sounding mildly astonished at what time had done.

"I'm sorry, but I don't remember," Holly answered quietly. "So many people came to Dad's church in those days."

"Naomi went to your father's church when she first came to America. Did you know that? Ask your father, he will remember."

"Yes, I know that." Holly bristled. "How do *you* know that?" she asked.

A courtroom door slammed and Choi jumped.

"I'm sorry," Choi said, his voice trailing off. "I did some good things in my life and I did some bad things, too. I only intended to scare you at the mortuary... and... and... it was a bad idea."

Holly nodded slightly, waiting. She knew that wasn't why he had come. Korean men of his generation did not apologize to girls of Holly's generation. He sat on the ancient oak bench with his hands folded, and when he looked up, he stared at the ceiling. "Would you sit with me a moment? I'd like to tell you something."

Holly sat and folded her hands in her lap. He would tell her in his own time.

"Did you ever want to do the right thing, but it was so—hard?"

"Many times."

"I came to speak to you because I want to do the right thing." Choi spoke softly. "I am not trying to claim virtue, or excuse myself. I am just weary...weary of doing wrong things that never work out. I want a good life, now. I want to do right."

He mumbled something else, incoherent, then he pulled a crudely wrapped brown paper packet out of the plastic bag and pushed it into her hand. With that action he stood up, bowed and left.

Holly went to the restroom to freshen her lipstick. She didn't want to leave before the press scrum had cleared, so she opened Choi's package mechanically, expecting perhaps some long incomprehensible written rant, but inside the envelope was an old-style Korean passport with a black and white photo of an unsmiling young mother with two girls. Holly read the names on the biographical page. Sari and Sara, born on the same date.

There were some other papers inside. Curious, Holly unfolded the paper. It was a yellowed church bulletin from her own church. Her father's church. Her eyes quickly scanned the announcement portion, which showed the baptism of Sari and Sara. Two old passports fell out. Holly slowly went to the biographical pages. The passports of Sari Song and Sara Song. They were twins. Holly quickly flipped through the pages. There were no exit or entry stamps. The passports had never been used. Holly went back to the biographical pages and studied the faces, then looked closer. The birthdates were off by two years, two years older than the court documents. Holly walked slowly and thought. If the passport was a true identity document of Naomi Linser, born as Sari Song, she was eighteen years old, and not sixteen, when she first engaged in a sexual relationship with Wolf Linser. That meant he was not guilty of sex with a minor as convicted.

There was also a business card: Tomahawk Club—720 Rush Street, Chicago, Illinois. Tommy Hawk, Proprietor.

What was this? Choi had all Holly's attention now. She tore open the last envelope. There was a plane ticket to Chicago and ten thousand dollars in cash. The bank notes were worn and old and wrapped in a rubber band.

"Please use for Naomi's defense," the note read.

Holly stuffed the packet in her briefcase and ran out to the parking lot, but there was no sign of Choi.

Holly jumped in her car and sped to the church. Holly handed her father the documents. "Who is Choi? Why does Choi have these passports? The birth date is two years different than what is in the court file. And there is no entry stamp in either of the passports. What does all this mean?"

Pastor Kim smiled at his daughter. She always came to church short of breath.

"They came in with a different passport." Her father shrugged and did not appear the least bit surprised or concerned. "It was not easy for a woman with young children to get a visa back in those days. I'm sure they all entered with a fake passport with altered birth dates, usually younger by a couple of years."

"But, why?"

"It made it easier to get a visa. Once the children were school-age, the government wouldn't issue the visa. It was common in those days."

"Then Naomi is really two years older than what she was told," Holly said slowly. "Which means that she wasn't sixteen years old, but eighteen at the time she became involved with Wolf," Holly said, slowly. "Naomi was of legal age—it means Wolf Linser was wrongly convicted."

CHAPTER 67

It didn't take Holly long to pack. She dialed the number to an illegal cab driver that Johnny Gee had given her. An unmarked black sedan was waiting as soon as she walked out of the lobby. The driver stood and opened the back door.

"LAX, please," Holly said. She loved how the driver had the latest fashion magazines lined neatly in the seat pockets and the car was impeccably clean. She chose Korean *Vogue* and flipped the pages without really seeing them. Soon, they were at the airport.

"May I get you a blanket, miss?"

"Yes, please," Holly said, blinking from the dry air.

She must have fallen asleep on take off.

Holly stared out the window as the plane made its ascent towards darkening purple clouds. A storm was approaching. It would be a bumpy midwest-style ride. She must have fallen asleep again because the next thing she knew they were announcing the descent.

At O'Hare airport Holly quickly wolfed down a Chicago hot dog then took a cab, checking into a tired brownstone hotel downtown. She could see Rush Street from her window. The hotel was next to a transit station in a part of town near the river, where the original train tracks were elevated high above the one way street. The Tomahawk Club was actually underneath train tracks near to Gene & Georgetti Steakhouse.

The original red and yellow neon sign, a graphic of a chopping motion of a tomahawk remained high above the two story red brick building on a corner lot. The marquee read *Slow Train Lexington — This Week Only*.

The sidewalk out front was already lined up. A massive doorman, the shape and color of an eggplant, stood behind the velvet rope with a racially mixed crowd milling around excitedly, waiting to get in.

Tommy Hawk was a former homicide detective who had made good without being bad. His twenty-five years with the police force had ended when an ill-run jazz club underneath the train tracks had come up for sale. He had bet the family farm on it. While he had loved being a cop, he loved the idea of owning a jazz club more.

That night, Tommy was leaning on the vintage oak bar, busy on the phone with one of his lady friends. Tommy loved the banter as much as the romance, maybe more.

"Babe, tell me you're in town and I'll get my handcuffs out of the evidence room."

"I'm not in town, but I could be," the female voice purred. She was calling to ask for something, Tommy thought. It was the only time he ever heard from her.

"I don't need money. I can read your cop brain from a thousand miles away."

"Those are almost my four favorite words—I don't need money. Gotta go, babe. Got some bum in here says we're watering the drinks. Call me later."

Tommy took the new call. A few minutes later he put down the phone, reached over the bar and pulled a mini-bottle of tonic water and a couple of ice cubes in a glass.

Joey walked up to him. "You good, boss? You look like you seen a ghost."

"You can't see ghosts on a telephone, dummy." Tommy's laugh sounded forced. "But I guess you can hear 'em."

Holly worked her way through the crowd up to the bar and stood patiently until the bartender noticed her.

"I'm here to see Tommy Hawk, please?" she said over the honks and toots of the band tuning up on stage.

"Are you Holly Park?" It was a voice from behind, and a nice Italian-looking waiter came up to her.

"Yes."

"Tommy got hung up on a call but he'll be right out. Just follow me."

He led her up some stairs in the back where a few café-style tables were set up on a balcony overlooking the stage from one side. These were obviously special tables.

"What's the drink of choice here?" Holly asked, just trying to make conversation.

The waiter smiled at her. "In the Chicago summer, beer, and in the Chicago winter, potato vodka. Colder than fog. Colder than a woman's heart."

"I hope you don't feel that way about all women." Holly laughed.

He laughed along with her and pointed to a table. "I sense that you are cappuccino and biscotti kind of girl. We make our own. I will be right back."

Holly sat up straight and looked around. She was watching the band setting up on the stage when a man slipped into the chair across from her.

"Choi!" Holly said, in complete surprise. This made no sense. She had just seen him yesterday in Los Angeles.

"You came." His voice revealed neither surprise nor pleasure. He smiled but his eyes were grave.

"Why did you invite me here?" Holly asked. "Couldn't we have talked yesterday?"

"No," Choi said flatly, then added, "you will see."

Choi flagged down a waiter and ordered a draft beer. Holly waited patiently. She enjoyed surveying the crowd, the happy energy a relief after the nervous tension of the jammed courtroom.

Choi sipped his beer and looked over the crowd too, but saw nothing. Like a prisoner who has bonded with his jailer, he now hesitated in the last moments before freedom.

"I have been burdened with a story all these years," Choi began. "I have decided to share it with you. Two can carry a rock more easily than one."

Holly nodded encouragement; she didn't want Choi to change his mind.

"Koreans say that a woman should be as discreet as two ships passing in the dark night." His eyes flashed. "But when those ships collide, the wreckage is great and spreads far and wide. Years will pass, but the debris remains." He took another sip. Choi's eyes closed, and he paused, the lines on his face deepening.

Choi nodded to himself, lost in memory. "The Dumok and I were classmates. Friends and rivals. He was my rival although now I know it was all in my head. Perhaps he did not even know. I was an introvert and an intellectual. He was known as Young Chun in those days. He was handsome, muscular, thrilling, charming—and top of our class. He was on top of his game and he knew it. He was brilliant, successful at everything. He broke rules and got away with it. How I admired him as equally as I envied him. We both applied for the same government positions after graduation. He beat me at everything. He became the senior aide, I was given a lower position. I was both happy for—and bitterly jealous of—his success. Yes, I was jealous of him, a fact of which I took no pride. How I wanted to be exactly like my classmate and rival. I wanted to be him!"

Holly nodded her understanding.

"Several years later, the Ambassador came to the United States, where I was posted in Los Angeles. He came alone. A personal matter, the Ambassador said. Finally, I thought, a chance to show my abilities without being in the shadow of my rival."

Choi continued, "The Ambassador was seeking diplomatic clearance for his newly married daughter and family who were scheduled to arrive in the States in a month. Diplomatic clearance for three, he said. He asked that I handle the matter personally, down to the smallest detail. Of course, I had heard that the Dumok had married the Ambassador's daughter. As the Ambassador spoke, I detected an unease in his speech. I secretly could not have been more pleased at my own good fortune. An important chess piece had been taken off the table. I would be the replacement, I was certain."

Holly sat back in her chair. The ambient sounds of the jazz club, which had been so loud, were gone. She might as well have been in a field somewhere, or in a silent room.

"I made the necessary preparations." Choi gestured with his hands in his animated way. "I also received a cable that a package would arrive at the embassy to be turned over to the arriving family. You can imagine that I rehearsed in my mind how to play the scene to come. Sincere welcome to the family. Both judicious concern and encouragement to my friend at this twist of fate. My sincere pledge to render any possible support and encouragement in the days ahead... Yes, with my ascension imminent, I was ready to be gracious."

"You paint it so clearly."

"I have had time...to contemplate—" Choi pressed his lips together—"that fateful day."

Holly nodded, leaning forward, afraid to miss a word.

"I went to the airport. I had reasonably assumed that the clearance for Young Chun, Nara, and their children would be expedited. While I was waiting, I opened the package and two passports fell out and $10,000 in cash. In that moment I knew, with the utter and absolute certainty of the damned, that the twins who came off the plane were not the offspring of my good friend and rival."

Choi hesitated then, his brown eyes clear and certain, but not even seeing Holly. He was back at the airport, staring fate in the eye.

On the stage below, seated at the grand piano, Slow Train Lexington looked towards the stairs at the back of the club. It was time.

Holly remembered to take a breath. "How? How, Choi? How could you have been so certain?" Holly asked in bewilderment, confused.

Choi smiled then, and indicated casually with his chin to look below, to the girl wearing a wireless mike and slowly walking down the stairs and across the club floor.

"May I present Naomi's twin sister," he said. "Ms. Cherry Lexington, formerly known as Sara Song."

Then Holly heard a voice, a cappella, from the back of the club. It filled the room and she turned to look. This was no ordinary voice.

"The nights are long, the dice grow cold... My lucky number, bought and sold... I turn the cards, they never lie..."

Holly's eyes followed, until hers, too, rested on the girl. A single spotlight. She had cat eyes and mocha colored skin and moved like a panther. If her dress were any tighter it would be paint.

A hush fell over the crowd as she made her way to the stage.

"...but fate is cruel, yet still I try... alone and dressed in blue... alone I wait... for you."

The drums, stand-up bass, piano and electric guitar kicked in now and the beat turned aggressive.

"I wait longer, than time itself... to turn the cards that I was dealt... only clubs and spades are mine, no hearts or diamonds, cards never lie... the cards are red and black, I dress in blue... one more time, to wait for you..."

The club filled with a burst of wild applause and hushed appreciation as Cherry shyly bowed and made her way to the piano.

"Was I good, daddy?" she asked, kissing him on the cheek.

"You know it. Thank the nice people," said Slow Train. "You feel up to doing another?"

"Yes," she beamed.

Mr. Lexington nodded to the band. They were all so in synch that the new tempo, more upbeat, swinging, seemed entirely natural.

Slow Train Lexington had, with the assistance of his friend Choi, adopted Cherry. He and his late wife had raised Cherry as their own in Chicago's jazz community.

Her voice had a texture and melancholy well beyond her years and she connected with the audience one-on-one, making each patron feel as if they were alone with her. That was her gift. He had nurtured but not created it. She was born with it.

Though her musical talent didn't come from him genetically, he had groomed her raw but astonishing natural talent and took pride in her ability as if he had passed on his own. He loved her as a gift from the Lord. If only he could make the nightmares go away.

Up on the balcony Choi sat silent, his eyes pressed tightly shut. Holly waited until the set had ended, enjoying every moment, but also stunned and in shock. Choi came out of his trance.

"She's half...black," Holly whispered. "and half Korean."

"Do you understand why you had to come?"

Holly nodded numbly.

"I didn't know until after I saw the girls myself," Choi said. "I learned the real truth later, much later, from Nara."

Choi resumed the story. "Apparently, Nara had an indiscretion with the son of a South African diplomat. When Nara took to her bed moping after the boy left, the mother was instantly suspicious. Only the mother knew the identity of her daughter's lover, not daring to tell the Ambassador whose child Nara carried. Nara had two younger brothers and any illegitimacy in the family line would have destroyed the family's reputation and caused a political scandal. They needed to cover it up for the sake of their sons' future marriages. They needed someone to blame—a scapegoat."

"The Dumok!" Holly cried.

"Yes. He was, to the Koreans, a foreigner, even though his mother was Korean, and he was raised in Europe, making him double the outsider When he came to Korea to study, he was unaware of the prejudices of the Korean people against half-breeds, that they would never fully accept him.

"The Ambassador was terribly fond of the Dumok. Young Chun, as he was known then, was handsome, big, smart, and had a love of the Korean culture. He was a perfect choice. The public would not suspect anything if the Ambassador married off his daughter to his trusted aide."

"Nara was given secret marching orders by her mother to seduce Young Chun before the pregnancy showed, so that they could pass the pregnancy off as his child. The identity of Nara's lover was kept a secret from the Ambassador. Nara's mother planned to send Nara to America to finish out the pregnancy. But the plan did not work. The rumors reached the Ambassador of the identity of Nara's lover. The Ambassador lost control and beat Nara so badly she could not travel, so Nara was sent to a remote village to heal." Choi swallowed, hard, then took a sip of his beer.

Holly sat, silent, the enormity of it gathering on the horizon.

Choi continued, his voice raspy. "The pregnancy was difficult. Sari, who we know as Naomi Linser, was born first, followed by Sara—who is Cherry Lexington. As Sara was pulled from Nara, the screams of the midwife could be heard throughout the village. Nara's womb produced two children, one black and Korean and the other, entirely Korean."

"Dig the graves," Nara's mother ordered grimly, without hesitation or discussion.

"The graves!" Holly cried. "The little graves!"

Choi nodded.

"That was the fate of children with mixed ancestry. *Twigis* they were called, a very derogatory word for children of mixed blood. Often, they were left in the streets to die, or drowned in the river."

Holly scarcely dared breath as Choi continued. "It was survival to many women then. They could not remarry with such a child tethered to them. Nara was in a different position. She was well-bred and educated. And in the end, it was Nara who refused to let her babies die."

Holly's eyes were the size of dinner plates as the horror washed over her.

"Nara fought hard for her babies' lives," Choi continued, "threatening to make a public scandal if anyone harmed her babies."

"Choi, it's not so long ago, is it? One generation only?"

"The old families in Korea are not modern, Holly. For all their veneer of sophistication, they are slow to change."

Holly nodded in understanding, but the truth was she did not understand at all. Holly raised her eyes to Choi, encouraging him to continue.

"I was charged with informing the Dumok that both Nara and his child—one child—had died in childbirth and they were buried on that mountainside. Yes, the Ambassador used the Dumok. But with the lie, it was actually his intention to set him free to go on with his life. To forget about Nara and the dead child."

Holly's memory flashed back to the wet graves, the watchful maple tree, the drowning, freezing rain, and the gaunt figure of the Dumok brought to his knees, raging against fate. She shivered, her eyes focused on Choi.

"What surprised—and infuriated—me," Choi continued, "was that even in his trickery, the Ambassador was still fond of my rival and took great efforts to mitigate any harm against him."

"'With time, he will forget about Nara and the baby,' the Ambassador said." Choi sighed. "I was fueled with jealousy that the Ambassador showed only concern over my classmate and rival. It was then I realized I was nothing to the Ambassador but a tool and nothing more."

Holly nodded. Not trusting herself to speak. Silently willing Choi the strength to keep going.

"And I tell you plainly, what I have told no one, that jealousy made me twist the knife. I, of course, did as the Ambassador ordered. But I added a lie—what I thought then was a small lie. I told the Dumok that Nara had gone to the medicine man in the village, and had traded her jewels for poison to kill the child, and that the poison ended up killing the both mother and child. I never imagined what happened next. The Dumok went to the village to confirm with his own eyes the graves where his wife and child were buried. A villager saw him climb the mountain," Choi said, a new quiet in his voice. "When he came down the mountainside, he was like a raging bull. He ran into the village tearing open the huts."

"The medicine man!" Holly gasped. "He was looking for the medicine man!"

Choi nodded. "The Dumok killed the medicine man with his bare hands, and almost lost his own life in the battle."

Holly's hand involuntarily went up to her throat. "The scar," Holly whispered.

"The medicine man struggled hard and the Dumok was almost decapitated, but he was the one who came out of it alive." Choi sighed. "Gradually, Young Chun became comfortable in the dark places and his anger grew at becoming an outcast of the only world he had ever known, that of privilege and accomplishment. It was then he became the Dumok, setting out to build his own world, where he would be the predator and not the goat."

Choi took a slow sip of his beer. "I have studied his rise over the years, and can say with certainty that no man ever turned cruel fate into a flaming sword as he did."

Then Choi's mood darkened. "There are always two aspects of tragedy. First, the tragedy itself, and secondly—and this is perhaps worse—the moment when you become reconciled to it."

Choi's voice resonated with the bitter authority of experience. "I realized, too late, of course, that we had both been played by a master. I had betrayed my friend to gain favor from the Ambassador, only for the Ambassador to betray me in turn. It was as if the devil himself had pushed my neck into the earth with a pitchfork."

Choi reached for a cigarette. Holly waited patiently.

"Have you ever been desperate, Ms. Park?"

"Honestly? No." Holly shook her head. "Not in the way you describe."

"Even desperate men can be shocked by how desperately they act," Choi continued. "Yet...sometimes even good can come of it."

Choi looked over the balcony at Cherry. Applause swelled below them as the band came out for another set.

"Of course, as fate lives to twist the knife, I later ran into Nara with her girls. I realized that even in America, prejudice was too deep against Sara because of the color of her skin. I was no better. I can't deny it. But like a coin, fate has two sides. It was a twist of fate that I met Train Lexington when I did." As Choi spoke, his eyes glistened in memory to twenty years ago when he first arrived in America.

Jazz kept Choi going in America. That, and Korean saunas where he went to relax. Choi turned off the music and parked his car and went to the lobby of the men's spa, took the elevator that went down one floor to the basement where he was handed a robe, towel, flip flops, a razor, and a toothbrush and pointed down the hallway. He walked past several dozen men watching the Korean news channel in the communal area, lounging naked or in towels on leather couches and chairs. He knew many of them by sight and exchanged nods of greeting with a few.

Choi ate a bowl of seaweed soup before heading for the sauna, which was empty except for a black man, heavy set, leaning his head against the wall, his eyes closed, maybe asleep. He looked a little familiar, maybe a retired athlete, maybe a football coach. The Americans had discovered the Korean saunas a few years before and now they were a common sighting.

Choi poured a scoop of water on the glowing rocks, trying to do it quietly, but the sizzling sound of the water hitting the hot stones woke up the man.

The heat hit Choi in a soothing wave. The seaweed soup had been good. He tapped his fingers and hummed a few bars of a popular jazz tune "Adam's Other Rib" that he hadn't been able to get out of his head.

"Adam's other rib... caught me by surprise... the other woman came... in a soft and pale disguise..."

"Don't step on the beat, brother."

Choi's eyes flew open at the sound of the deep voice. The black man was sitting straight up now, a crooked smile on his face. Choi was about to tell this fellow he knew nothing about jazz, when he realized he knew the voice. He stared, it really was his idol, Slow Train Lexington. Besides his music, he had heard him interviewed on jazz radio.

"You can call me Train." Lexington held out his hand.

"I'm...Choi," he said, awkwardly.

"Do you know where I can get some good Korean barbeque?"

"Certainly." Choi nodded.

"I'm out here with my wife seeing doctors at the UCLA Medical Center and Cedars-Sinai for in vitro treatments." Train sighed. "She wants a baby. You'll do any crazy thing your woman wants, right?"

They chatted for a while in the heat, opening up in a way that sometimes only strangers can. "I will take you to a good Korean restaurant tonight," Choi offered. "The best. Very best."

"I think I will take you up on that!"

Train's enthusiasm was genuine. Over Korean barbecue and a few glasses of soju, an unlikely but lasting friendship was born. The nervous Choi and the mellow but sophisticated Slow Train Lexington had both lived their own versions of the blues, and fate had brought

An Empirical Analysis of the Effects of Climate Change on Agricultural Output in Nigeria

them together.

Holly watched Cherry in fascination. Choi watched Cherry, too, but his thoughts were of the past. The greedy and unrelenting past that refused to let him go. He sighed and continued his tale.

"I knew Nara could not survive on her own, so I convinced her to give Sara to my friend Train Lexington—the man at the piano. He and his wife had been trying everything to have a baby to no avail. At least save the life of one child versus destroying the lives of two."

"But...Naomi..." Holly's voice quivered plaintively, she could barely squeak out the name.

"Exactly." Choi pushed his cigarette butt into the ashtray. "The other horn of the dilemma presented itself. We needed to keep Naomi from searching for her twin, so we told her that Sara had drowned, in that little backyard pool—and it was Naomi's fault for not watching her sister."

"That's *so* wrong," Holly whispered.

"Nara insisted. She didn't want Naomi to go searching or to ask questions."

Choi looked at Holly with an unusual, for him at least, calm demeanour. Certainly the horror on her face was plain. But Choi could be calm because he was far past looking for forgiveness or even understanding, just simple acknowledgment that he wasn't the only one who had looked into the abyss. Choi opened his hands in surrender, with the expression of a man welcoming the blade, asking only that it be sharp, and the executioner strong.

Then he jumped as he felt an arm go around his shoulder. He looked up. It was Cherry Lexington standing beside their table.

"Daddy promised you would come this time, thank you," she said shyly. Cherry reached over and kissed Choi on the cheek and beamed.

"Choi is my godfather," she explained to Holly, smiling at him.

Holly couldn't help but stare. Virtually identical pages of a child's coloring book only one was uncolored and the other, colored in. They chatted quietly for a few moments, then Cherry walk away with a smile. Her affection for Choi was apparent.

Choi spoke first. "The adoption was done here in Chicago, privately, so nobody would be able to trace the records. I had become friends with the family. Many strings were pulled to hide Cherry's past. I was good at that. Nara blamed Naomi, saying that the authorities must never find out, and that she would protect Naomi from being charged with the drowning as long as she never mentioned Sara to anyone, " Choi said. "Then, in Korea, as the Ambassador lay dying, Wolf Linser innocently mentioned Sara's name and Nara assumed Naomi had told him...and we know what happened to Wolf after that."

"Nara had to get rid of Wolf," Holly realized, "so nobody would come around asking questions. Wolf had to disappear."

"Yes," said Choi somberly. "Nara had her own self-preservation in mind. You understand now why you had to come here and witness the truth made flesh."

Holly nodded but no words came as she pondered the enormity of it.

Choi knew Holly was taking it badly. He had played the cruel cards he had been given. Choi had never told anyone the whole truth before, and he had astonished himself doing it. Choi had told Holly in order to set himself free from the rocks that hid between the waves. Their voices faded, like people leaving shore in a small boat. Soon the sound of the soft waves was all that remained. He had passed his burden, though he could scarce believe it. Finally, in telling Holly the truth, he was free.

Brad Chisholm & Claire Kim

CHAPTER 68

Holly took the first flight back home on Sunday morning. She jumped out of the cab hastily and slipped into the last pew of the sanctuary of the church as worship service was ending.

Holly looked up at her father singing, his booming voice had always been her anchor in the storm. She felt helpless. She just didn't know what to do. The trial would resume tomorrow. She knew Naomi's acquittal was dependent upon an expensive defense. Fees that only the Dumok could afford.

A dilemma always has two horns and Holly was caught on both of them. If Holly told the Dumok that Naomi was not his daughter, the Dumok would pull the defense fund, the original plea would stick and Naomi would get life without the possibility of parole, but... she would have the benefit of her twin sister's visits, and be released from the terrible guilt of having drowned her beloved twin sister Sara, now Cherry Lexington.

If Holly didn't tell, Naomi had a chance at an acquittal but could never learn that Sara was alive, and continue to believe that she had been responsible in the drowning.

There was only one absolute. Holly had jumped to conclusions and been wrong. Holly looked down at the church bulletin. It said "The truth shall set you free."

267

No it won't! It won't at all! Holly thought angrily. *I've just made it worse!*

Pastor Park watched his daughter sitting in the last pew at the back of the church, weeping. But, when he finished the benediction, he turned and discovered the pew empty and Holly gone.

Holly parked and walked into the diner. It was usually easy to spot Eli Behr. His presence filled a room, but not today. Eli reached for the sugar and poured a scary amount into his coffee. Gone was his signature confidence and easy banter. He folded his arms across the table and leaned forward.

"So, how was Chicago?" he asked, trying, but without his usual grin. "Did you at least get some deep dish pizza?"

Holly wordlessly slid Naomi's passport across the table. The old vinyl cover cracked as he opened it.

"Who's Sari Song?" he frowned.

"Sari Song is Naomi Linser. Sari Song is the name she was given at birth."

"What about it?" Eli asked, tossing the passport back.

"Naomi Linser was not underage when Wolf Linser had sex with her. She was eighteen, not sixteen. Detective Chang blew it," Holly announced. "Can we use this information tomorrow to discredit Detective Chang, saying he botched this investigation liked he botched the case against Wolf Linser?"

Eli Behr's skin had always been pale. Now the blood pumped into his face. He forgot to stir his coffee, or even drink it. He smiled. Tomorrow, Detective Mick Chang would take the stand. What would the jury think of the detective now?

CHAPTER 69

A glance over to the gallery and Holly knew Detective Mick Chang was there. She didn't want to look at him. Like two dogs peeing in their respective corners, lawyer and cop faced each other.

The judge made a surprise ruling that the cameras would be allowed to film and the crew was setting up. The long benches on the right side of the courtroom quickly filled up with a group of *Free Naomi* supporters wearing pink.

The morning passed with Detective Mick Chang on the stand, describing how Naomi had clutched the murder weapon and confessed to the crime. "She had bruises, breastbone was blue, purple, orange and green and extended horizontally onto her second pair of ribs creating the image of a cross from the knife.

"It's mortification of the flesh," one juror stage-whispered to another. "It's the physical manifestation of suffering or psychological stress."

"Silence!" the judge ordered but it was too late. The press ran with it. A photographer happened to capture Naomi with her hands folded as in prayer and the next day a headline appeared next to the new photos: *Stigmata Appear on Virgin Whore*.

Would Naomi Linser be the first woman to get the death penalty in the State of California since 1962?

"I trust the jury to make that determination," Blake LeBlanc had told the press with a thin smile.

Holly adjusted herself and stood from her seat and began the cross-examination.

Holly: Isn't it true you were the deputy who responded to a domestic call at the home of one Wolf Linser, about eight years ago?

"Yes."

"Were you the investigating officer assigned to the case?"

"Yes."

"Were you responsible for the investigation against Wolf Linser, charging him with have sex with his then sixteen-year-old stepdaughter, Naomi Linser?

"Yes."

"For that offense, isn't it true Mr. Linser received fifteen years imprisonment, of which he has served eight years?"

"Yes."

"Is it true that if Naomi Linser had been eighteen years old at that time, she would have been of lawful age for consensual relations?"

"Yes."

"And no crime would have been committed?"

"Yes."

The detective rolled his eyes. Where the hell was she going with this? How he hated defense attorneys. They always picked some irrelevant detail and then just beat it with a stick.

Holly let the detective's answer hang in the air. 'Yes'. The smallest detail was the difference of two years. The smallest detail between unlawful and lawful, consensual sex. The difference between freedom and fifteen years incarceration. The difference between crime and no crime, and the difference between the competence and incompetence of an investigating officer.

"I would like to mark the passport of the defendant as defense Exhibit 1. May I approach the witness, your honor?" Holly addressed the court. The judge nodded.

Holly walked up and handed the detective the passport. "Were you aware Naomi Linser was eighteen years old, which is the age of consent for sexual relations in the State of California, when you arrested Wolf Linser?" Holly asked.

Detective Mick Chang swaggered out of the courtroom. Holly Park. She was the exact reason cops hated defense attorneys. Any day a cop could walk out of a courtroom with his badge and job, it was still a good day. Mick Chang spit on the ground then kicked the trash bin as hard as he could and stormed out of the courthouse.

CHAPTER 70

On the last day of trial, the Dumok walked into court and took the last empty seat. Holly turned, her elbow knocking her papers onto the floor at the sight of him. She bent to scoop them up and dropped the trial binder, which of course sprang open.

Naomi was brought in wearing a blue prison jumpsuit, wrists shackled, but looking even more stunning than ever, if that were even possible. She possessed the unalterable faultless symmetry of a top runway model. Naomi took her seat and looked around, curious, as if she were a spectator and not the accused, and when she saw the *Free Naomi* T-shirts, she blew kisses to her supporters which caused opponents to hiss and start name-calling and heckling.

Holly didn't see him arrive, but Dr. Perry Koo also entered and greeted Naomi, wearing glasses with his hair neatly combed back. He wore a gray suit and a shiny purple tie and carried a bottle of water.

Holly winked and gave him the thumbs up as he took the stand.

"When a client in hypnosis remembers a trauma," Dr. Koo began, "she is likely to remember it more vividly than if she were awake, if she can remember it at all. It is quite common for the individual in hypnosis to describe what is occurring with extensive details, many of which would be known only to an individual who was really there."

"As evidence, in a limited legal context, can such memories be relied on as much as a regular witness?" Holly asked.

"Hypnotic memories are sometimes frozen in time, at the point of the original trauma, but layered over and tinted and colored with other fears, memories and experiences. Certainly useful in therapy—but as historical fact? No. Even very experienced therapists can be fooled. And with the truth, there are no guarantees."

"Did you hypnotize Naomi Linser?" Holly continued.

"Yes," Dr. Perry Koo answered. "And I unlocked her memory as to what happened that night inside Club Kiki."

There was a murmur in the courtroom. The Dumok and Naomi locked eyes and he slightly nodded. Naomi turned and motioned for Holly and whispered something into her ear. Holly stood up and addressed the court.

"The defense would like to call Naomi Linser to the stand."

A nascent lawyer should not be handling murder trials, Blake LeBlanc thought, smirking, and looked at his watch. The jury deliberations would not take long once he finished tearing Naomi apart and he could start his weekend.

Naomi took the oath and sat, like a princess taking a throne, yet with utter humility. All watched her, enthralled, leaning forward to capture every word. Naomi's eyes were bright, her voice was soft but clear.

The defense team had done little to prepare Naomi, mainly because of her emotional fragility. Putting her on the stand was, as they say a "game-time decision." The smug look on Blake LeBlanc's face said it all. I win, you lose.

The Councilman had been drinking before she got there, Naomi began. She knew because there were half empty bottles on the table. When she arrived, he told the other girls to leave the room. They were alone, and he drank more and more. His mood darkened as he began reminiscing about his glory days of being back on the football field. She drank with him and listened to him, waiting. She had come for a reason that night. She wanted the document he had promised her, but his conversation was rambling, almost as if he were alone. Then, suddenly, he said he loved her. Naomi froze. He pulled out a diamond necklace, and again said that he loved her. Her stomach climbed into her throat and she was really frightened now. He was out of communication. It was very strange, almost like she wasn't even there he was so preoccupied.

Scared, she reached over for the service buzzer on the table and pushed it. The waiter was supposed to come. Once, twice, three times but nobody came. She didn't know why.

Naomi faltered only slightly, then gathered her strength and went on.

The Councilman had started to touch her, pull at her shirt, which is when Naomi knew it was time for her to leave and got up. But the Councilman wouldn't let her go. He chased her around room calling her a tease. Naomi went to open the door but it was locked from the outside. Trapped and panicking, she ran into the kitchenette. She had seen the waiters put the fruit and sushi knives under the counter so she ran and pulled one out. The VIP suite was large, and in his inebriated state the Councilman couldn't find her. He was shouting, belligerent. She remained hidden, crouched in the corner. She was sure someone would come, or if he saw the knife it would shock him to his senses. She gripped the knife tightly in her hands with the handle against the middle of her chest. Finally, he spotted her, crouched in the kitchen.

It was dark. The Councilman perhaps did not see the knife although the outside lights had bounced off the blade as she held it tightly on her chest. Tugging at his belt he came after Naomi. He hollered for her, pulling at his pants. In his inebriated state, he still did not react to the knife; he may not have even heard her voice screaming to stop.

The Councilman lunged at her, impaling himself on the razor sharp knife, his weight crushing Naomi, matching the description of the position Detective Chang testified he had found Naomi, pinned under the Councilman. Naomi finished with her face in her hands.

"The death blow was inflicted by no one other than the honorable Councilman himself," Holly calmly explained later in her closing argument. "Tragedy? Yes. Murder? No."

Blake LeBlanc was right about one thing. The jury deliberations came back in record time.

"We the jury...find the defendant, Naomi Linser, not guilty of the crime of murder upon William H. McClellan, a human being."

"Thank you, oh, thank you!" Naomi whispered. She hugged Holly, and then started to cry, and looked around the gallery for the first time. "Daddy! Daddy!" she cried, searching for the Dumok. A long second passed, and as each member in the courtroom absorbed the verdict, cries of relief and joy filled the courtroom. Somebody cursed.

In the commotion, there was the Dumok. He rushed towards Holly, then past her to Naomi's waiting arms. The Dumok held Naomi's bright sobbing head, murmuring something Holly could not hear, speaking softly, with a tenderness she had never seen. And that's when Holly saw it. The pain that was etched in stone was no longer there. The media caught it too and ran a photo of the Dumok smiling down at Naomi under the headline:

Jury Acquits Crime Boss Daughter in Murder of Councilman

Naomi was laughing, inviting the media to share in her gaiety with the Dumok tenderly holding her hand as they were led out the back way. Then they were gone. Holly stood a moment watching. Then she picked up her briefcase and looked around the empty courtroom. The lies told twenty three years ago and halfway across the world that had strangled the lives of so many and had crossed continents to end up surfacing in an American courtroom. Finally, it was over. They had won the trial. And now the hard part would begin. Now, Holly would have to tell the Dumok the truth.

CHAPTER 71

There was not even a tree. Wolf Linser sat in the sun on a concrete curb outside the prison with a small canvas duffel bag. He wore jeans and a denim shirt that still draped as if on a hanger, and cheap canvas shoes. His hair was quite silver now, grown out and combed back behind his ears. His skin was paler than he could ever remember, even paler than back in the days when he had prowled the casinos for a living. That was a long time ago. He lit a cigarette he had rolled himself, a long way from the Davidoffs or Dunhills he had once favored. But they had given him back his Dunhill lighter, and amazingly it worked. He took a long drag and contemplated his freedom. Holly's black BMW pulled up and she set the passenger seat back for Wolf's long frame.

Wolf saw a flash of long flowing hair, the sunglasses came off, and the million dollar smile that had kept him going this past year. He had been the envy of the facility, the prettiest lawyer—and the smartest. She had won his freedom. Everyone asked for her phone number. And of course there had been Naomi's case in the papers. He had read every word, prayed each day for her and for Holly to prevail, and finally, on news of the acquittal, he had wept stones.

"So," Holly asked, once they were comfortably on the road. "Where to?"

"What I would love more than anything is to go to this little barbecue place, the Bluebird, in the hills. The meat falls off the bone."

To Wolf, the strong black house coffee was like a drug and he could feel the life flowing back into his body. The food was served family style—baby back ribs and chicken with coleslaw, corn and beans that almost collapsed the paper plates.

"The horses—that's what kept me going—besides you. They know nothing of our world, and that's a good thing." Wolf hesitated. "I'm not so good with words, Ms. Holly, but I want to say, without you..." He shook his head and started again. "I used to smile at your energy and faith, but you made me a believer. I will never be able to thank you. And as far as Kendall . . ." Holly just poked at the coleslaw. Wolf paused. "I just want to be with the horses and trees and breathe air again, but...I would like to see Kendall and apologize to her for what I put her through." Wolf leaned back in his chair. "What do you think?"

"I think that's a great idea."

Wolf nodded and picked up a piece of corn bread.

The road to the ranch brought back memories. The road was the same. The dust was the same. Wolf's friend Travis was the same, except the beer was already cold and in a bucket and the horses were in the show corral. A bucket of apples and carrots stood ready. Simple things but life itself. The men embraced, but said nothing. Clinked their beer bottles and looked at the horses. Holly was puzzled. How can men who have hardly seen each other for years have nothing to say, yet act like they had just seen each other the day before?

Holly watched Wolf and Lightning. Now this was a reunion between lost friends. Even to Holly's utterly untrained eye Lightning responded to Wolf in a way which she found fascinating. Then Wolf went over to a young, pure black stallion, a yearling that stood to one side, pawing the ground.

"That's Lucky Strike," Travis called out. "He's out of Lightning and a filly from Utah, Smoke Dancer. Needs your magic, Wolf. A tree horse ever there was one."

"Okay, we'll start tomorrow," Wolf said. There was a confidence in his voice she had never heard.

"Holly, come here."

Holly gingerly walked over the dirt and took the carrot from Wolf's hand. Lightning snuffled and nudged against her.

"He likes you, Holly." Wolf laughed. "I think I have to give him to you."

"I don't think he'll fit in my apartment."

"I mean it, Holly," Wolf said. "I can't afford to pay you. I have nothing. But I can give you Lightning. Sell him to Kendall and recoup your fees or you can board him here. Travis has the papers. I'll sign him over. He's yours."

"I-I don't know what to say," Holly stammered.

"Lucky Strike needs me now. I don't need them fighting over me like jealous girls."

"But…" Holly stroked Lightning's nose and he snuffled.

"Walk around the ring with him. No one is in a hurry anymore."

Holly did that. The late sun filtered through the trees and she felt the offshore breeze coming up. Lightning was particularly interested in rubbing his nose against her shoulder.

He was such a boy.

CHAPTER 72

The invitations were printed on thick stock with a letterpress, and the envelopes sealed with red wax. The quality of the invitation was such that it was kept as a cherished keepsake for years by the partygoers.

Holly's cheeks paled when she saw the invitation. The usually elusive, reclusive and quiet Dumok surprised the Koreans with his next move. He wanted to celebrate his happiness over finding Naomi. On the bottom it stated in very small script, Black Tie.

The people all received the invitations on the same day. First there was puzzlement, then sheer delight at the extra enclosure—an American Express gift card—intended for new clothes for the gala. Nobody in Koreatown was left out.

There was gaiety, joy and excitement—feelings foreign to the hardworking first generation immigrants. They were the generation of suffering and hardship, who knew nothing of life and leisure.

But for one magical night, the Dumok changed all that. The Dumok would have it his way and make a gesture to the community they would never forget. Both men and women, single and married, the people always working would walk out of their shops, offices, and businesses for one night to, well—simply enjoy.

It was a fabulous party. Everyone was beautiful that night. But the beauty everyone remembered and talked of for years after was Holly.

Holly, who a week before had slumped in her closet, thoroughly discouraged, almost crying, wanting to wear something other than a suit so that the Dumok would see her as someone other than his lawyer. It was that simple. But Holly had no experience with nightclubs or parties or dressing up. She was a pastor's daughter who had not been allowed out at night. When the time came to have fun, she didn't know how.

Kendall Taylor came through at the end, perhaps seeing a little of herself in Holly.

Kendall took Holly under her wing and for next three days they trolled the spas of Koreatown where, under Kendall's watchful eye, Holly was washed, poked, cleaned and scrubbed until her skin turned two shades whiter. Top hair designers cut, conditioned and colored Holly's hair until it fell softly like a cloud around her face. The biggest surprise was the dress. Not to be outdone by the Dumok, Kendall marched Holly over to Chanel in Beverly Hills.

"The first thing is this. The last thing you want is to see someone else walk into the party wearing *your* dress," Kendall explained in her sand-papery yet feminine growl. Kendall was wrapped in Missoni that day, and Holly always envied how she looked so effortless.

Several hours later, they settled on a black silk vintage Chanel cocktail dress with a demure scoop neck. It draped like a waterfall over Holly's body—she starved herself for days before the party. The vertical pleats began below the bustline, and a pleated wrap around her hips provided visual contrast. Most dramatic was the back, which was entirely sheer. Even the buttons on the wrap were finished in silk.

"The design works because it promises sin but delivers grace," Kendall said with a smile.

Holly, who was only comfortable in business suits and workout clothes protested at first then gave in with a laugh. The last stop was a lingerie store where Holly picked a pair of lace stockings hand-embroidered with small white pearls, but when she walked up to the counter to pay, Kendall raised an eyebrow. Nope. They were not done yet. Kendall spread out a selection of black lingerie, and the salesgirl was smart enough to get out of the way, recognizing that a master was in the house.

"But, but..." Holly bubbled, "no one will see it!"

"Then we're not doing our job," Kendall sniffed.

Four hours later, they were back at Kendall's house. Holly put everything on and slipped her feet into new black strappy heels, the ones that flashed red from the soles when she walked. Kendall lent her a small black clutch purse and her own Tahitian black pearl necklace.

"There." Kendall was pleased, having wanted to make Holly over from the first moment they'd met. "Now you are appropriately dressed."

Holly looked in the large full-length mirror and a woman she didn't know peeked back.

"And you need to smile," Kendall insisted. "A woman's most important accessory is her smile."

Holly tried to smile into the mirror, but it just wasn't happening. She turned to Kendall. "You made me so b-beautiful!" Holly said, a tear forming.

"Don't cry! You'll ruin the dress!" Kendall hurriedly reached for a tissue.

CHAPTER 73

"Kendall, my turn!" Holly announced. "We're going for a drive." Holly was all smiles as she sped along the Pacific Coast Highway and into the canyons as the afternoon faded.

Holly glanced at Kendall who sat, relaxed, wearing large sunglasses and a scarf wrapped around her hair to block the sun. "You reminded Holly of Grace Kelly with that look."

"I don't know where you're taking me, Holly," Kendall shook her head slowly, "but I don't want to see Wolf, if that is what you are planning. Truly, I've moved on."

"No, it's not to see Wolf, I promise." Holly looked over at Kendall. "But he did say he wants to see you and apologize in person. He also asked that I tell you it wasn't Asian fever that he got caught up with Nara who claimed to be Alexis Lee," Holly said softly. "Wolf missed his daughter who died, and when he met Naomi he got caught up playing house. That was all."

"Did he really mean that?" Kendall said, softening.

"Yes."

They were deep in the canyons. "We're here." Holly had called ahead to meet with Travis, who was working with Lightning. Travis walked over.

"Wolf signed over Lightning to you, Miss Holly, before he left for the horse auction, and if you sign where I've put the 'x' and put in Ms. Taylor's name, you'll have conveyed him to her. I'll go get the papers," he added and strolled off.

"Holly!" Kendall put her hand over her heart. "You got my horse back!"

"Kendall, it was sort of Wolf's idea," Holly said, beaming. "Why don't you go for a ride! I'll watch."

Kendall smiled. "Do you think he's sorry?"

"Yes," Holly said. "Really."

CHAPTER 74

The Masonic Temple on Wilshire Blvd was a brilliant piece of creamy Art Deco architecture almost exactly on the border between Koreatown and Hancock Park. It had been for sale for some time and then sold for eight million dollars. It was scheduled to become a private art museum. The dining room seated fifteen hundred and it was here the Dumok held his party.

Already the ballroom was filling up as Holly tiptoed into the main hall.

"Is that you, Holly?" Naomi breathed, taking both Holly's hands between her own. "You are exquisite!"

Both Holly and Naomi were lovely. Holly was classic, Naomi was modern, wearing a backless silver Herve Leger dress handsewn with hundreds of silver and blue sequins that glittered when she moved, and she had somehow painted tiny flakes of silver glitter on her bare skin. She looked utterly magical. When Holly gushed, Naomi said, "Oh, this dress weighs about ten pounds, you can't imagine. I can hardly move!"

Guests were pouring in. Johnny Gee and Eli Burg arrived at the same time, strolling in like kings, handsome in their tuxedos, identical save Eli's cowboy boots.

Eli whistled a slow and appreciative one at Holly. Holly blushed but Eli was already scanning the ballroom for girls. Holly laughed. "Be easy on the hearts," she said.

"Detective Chang is outside. Taking pictures with a long lens," Eli yelled out, as he disappeared into the crowd. Holly smiled and shook her head. She would forget about Mick Chang for a night.

Holly looked into the crowd, and then turned as someone touched her arm. It was her sister, Christine. Finally, a face without secrets.

"I didn't even recognize you."

"I didn't recognize you!" Holly gushed. Her sister wore a pink and black beaded minidress with a simple Art Deco pattern from the 1920s with fringes. She had added elbow length gloves, one pink, and one black. For jewelry, she had ropes of alternating black and white pearls and matching earrings. She was radiant.

"Isn't that Mi Rae?" Christine asked, pointing. Yes, it was, radiating fun in her shortest skirt yet, dancing with both Eli and Johnny Gee, laughing.

Mix stood apart, watching the festivities. On his face, he had an expression of careful ambiguity, but he, too, was enjoying himself. Mix slipped outside unnoticed and walked over to a car and leaned against the open window. "You can get better pictures inside. It's a great party, lots of food."

Detective Mick Chang took a sip of convenience store coffee from the Styrofoam cup. Cold. He grimaced, shifting his weight uncomfortably on the vinyl seat of his car. "Naw. I'm good where I am."

Mix tossed him a beer and pointed. "If you need to take a leak, bathrooms are through those doors."

Mick nodded and smiled faintly, then in a moment, turned, lost again in his own thoughts, his mission. When he looked up, Mix was gone.

The lines were long for the linen cloaked buffet tables, which groaned with Korean favorites, plus a seafood station with crab and lobster, a prime rib carving station and a sushi bar.

Flowers, crystal and fine china decoratively sparkled on the tables beyond imaginable opulence.

Holly wandered through the crowd for the next hour. It wasn't that the Dumok was exactly ignoring her, but it didn't go exactly as Holly had thought. He was polite, warmly appreciative of her presence at the party, but with years of discretion masking his true feelings, he made no move to make her feel special that night.

The Dumok, clearly the most magnetic person in the room, lacked for no company as guests lined up to speak to him. As the party progressed, he excused himself from the crowd, and Holly watched him go over to speak with her father whom he had personally invited to give the blessing for the event. And wherever the Dumok went, Naomi was his beautiful little shadow. Holly's eyes followed him everywhere, waiting for the right moment, but she couldn't get her mother's disapproving words out of her head.

"Nobody said life was fair. He is—or perhaps was—a gangster. And you are a pastor's daughter. You cannot change that."

Holly could hear the music, the voices, but they seemed so far off in the distance. She nodded, but her eyes were on the Dumok. The crowd was larger now, standing in the buffet line. Holly saw the Dumok extricate himself and go upstairs.

It was on the balcony that circled the ballroom where Holly found him. A tiny island of peace from the chaos below. She watched him although he did not know she was there. He waved back to someone below and she saw the corners of his tired eyes crinkle and his jaw relax into a tender smile. Holly didn't need to look down at the crowd. Only Naomi could make him smile like that. It was then Holly knew with certainty she must never tell the Dumok the truth. Whatever the price. And she could only do that by giving him up, because to be near him, it would be impossible to have the lie in her heart. Quietly, she slipped away.

The Dumok would only dance one dance that night. Everybody watched as he took Holly by the elbow and lightly led her out on the dance floor. The Dumok did not speak but smiled his melancholy smile and brushed her hair from her face with his fingers and spoke to her with his eyes. Holly, self-conscious of the eyes on her, held him lightly as she danced.

Holly looked up at the Dumok. She had practiced a million speeches in her head to declare her love, but he had already said goodbye. This was their end.

"Sorry, boss." An assistant leaned in. "It's time."

The Dumok closed his eyes and held Holly close, for just a moment. Then he was gone. She looked at the time. Midnight had come so quickly.

The Dumok ascended to the stage with Naomi at his side. Then Christine was at Holly's elbow about to whisper something in her ear when the Dumok spoke and the room became silent. The lights dimmed and a single spotlight shone on him.

"I invited you tonight because it is our farewell party. I will be leaving Los Angeles tomorrow and will take Naomi with me." He said "Naomi" so tenderly. Someone coughed in the audience. From the back of the hall, another person cleared their throat as the guests listened.

Outside, a tuxedoed waiter stood there patiently with a hotel room service cart and a folding chair set up on the narrow strip of lawn. "Your dinner is served, sir. Prime rib—medium rare—baked potato with sour cream and chives, and sautéed carrots. Dinner roll. The wine is a Cabernet Sauvignon from the Napa Valley. Enjoy."

Mick tried the wine. It was excellent, but the best was the baked potato. He put more butter on it. He sighed and took another bite. The beef and potato together were awesome.

Later, when Mix came outside, Mick put down his knife and fork, clipped on his radio and got out of his car. The friends stood with their arms across their chests leaning against the car. In their silence they were aligned.

The dining hall was empty. Holly looked up at the clock. It was half past midnight. Only the Dumok and Holly were left. The party felt like such a long time ago already, Holly thought, looking around the empty hall. Tears welled up and she quickly wiped them away as the Dumok walked up and took a seat beside her.

"Did you have a nice time?"

"Yes." Holly nodded, trying very hard not to cry.

"I've come to say goodbye," he began.

"I know." Holly lowered her head as tears streamed down her face, choking on the words.

"Naomi has been through a tremendous ordeal and she needs all my attention now," the Dumok said gently. Holly nodded, unable to meet the Dumok's eyes.

"I understand," Holly murmured. "Let's not say goodbye. I hate goodbyes. I'm not good at them."

"I'll be back. Soon."

"No... you won't." Holly could not bear the falsity of those words between them.

"Holly, look at me," the Dumok said. "Look at me," he said again even more gently. Holly looked up, slowly, and their eyes met.

"Sit with me," he said, taking her hand. "I know the truth and you are such a dear for caring so much about me to withhold the truth for my feelings sake," the Dumok said.

"What—about what?" Holly asked.

"About Naomi," he said. "I see a father as someone who cares and nurtures a child—every day. It is not just the passing of DNA. Sometimes, a father may not pass on his DNA but that makes him no less a father."

Holly froze, the blood draining from her face.

"How—how did you find out?" Holly stammered.

"Your father told me," the Dumok said.

"My father?" Holly asked, disbelieving. "What did he tell you?" Her thoughts raced back to the image of the Dumok and her father, speaking quietly at the party. "And when?" she exclaimed.

"After you came back from Chicago. Holly, I went to your church looking for you—because I was worried."

A black Mercedes had pulled into the church parking lot. A tall, solitary figure in a business suit opened the driver's door and entered the church. The Dumok looked up at the ceiling. Would lightning strike? It was the first time in three decades he had been inside a church.

The Dumok stopped and listened at the sanctuary door. A child's voice, so plaintive and pure, singing a song from the Dumok's childhood. A song his mother sang to him to sleep each night. Curious, the Dumok opened the door. He stopped, surprised. Inside, was a beautiful boy, an adolescent child, of mixed ancestry like the Dumok, except his exotic eyes were a clear blue, singing a song. When the child saw the Dumok he stopped singing.

"Hello. My name is Cole. Are you lost?"

"No. Is the pastor here?"

"Yes, sir. He is my grandfather. Come this way," the child said, waving for the Dumok to follow.

"But how did my father know?" Holly cried.

"You are his daughter, Holly. He saw it in your face when you came back from Chicago. Your father knew something was wrong and guessed you must have seen Sara there. Remember, your father knew Nara and the girls when they first came to this country. Your father always knew Naomi could not be my biological daughter. Your father told me what he suspected and I flew to Chicago to see for myself. I saw Sara. And met Choi there, too."

"Choi?" Holly asked, surprised, almost choking on the name.

"Ah, yes, Choi," the Dumok said thoughtfully. "My old friend and rival." He chuckled. "We did it like in the old days. A grudge match in the back alley to settle the score." The Dumok laughed and Holly could not tell if he was serious or not. "After, we had a drink together."

Holly buried her face in her hands, unable to speak. "I'm—so—sorry, forgive me," is all she could manage.

"I know why you didn't tell me, Holly," the Dumok said, as softly as rain, leaning towards her. "God bless you for caring about me so much."

"Then just stay here. Don't leave!" Holly cried. "Do you have to go away? I'll care for you and Naomi."

"Yes, my dearest love. I have to go. This town is no good for Naomi, and you know the media will not leave her alone. When the publicity dies down we will be back."

Holly nodded, not trusting herself to speak.

"Naomi has been through too much. I want to give her a fresh start. But first I will take her to Chicago, where the other half of her heart will be waiting."

It was then that the Dumok pulled out a thick cream envelope with gold edges and handed it to her. Holly gingerly took the envelope, confused. "Read it when you are alone," he said. The Dumok walked Holly out to her car where they kissed goodbye.

When the Dumok was gone, Holly drove the long drive to the port near Long Beach. She parked at the wharf where she had once watched the cargo container load the Dumok's Bentley coupe. She stared at the smoke rising from the many stacks. Or was it steam? She'd had the same wondering thoughts the last time. She still didn't know. And now the night ocean air hitting the warm air on land was bringing the fog. Fog and smoke and steam. And now soft rain.

Ethereal.

Indefinite.

Transient.

Alone inside the car, Holly carefully opened the envelope, afraid. There was a card with words in a beautiful script. *Quartier Libre.* It was one of the Dumok's favorite French expressions. It meant "free time." Holly dropped the card and shook her head. "No, no no," she cried, over and over, tears falling again, not understanding.

The Dumok was so elusive, neither in his presence nor in his parting was there any certainty. She was reminded of the story Choi had told her about the two ships. That a woman should be as discreet as two ships passing in the dark night, or the wreckage would go on forever. Well, she thought, forever was not long enough for all her tears to fall.

Utterly drained, she became very still and sat for a long time watching the lights and fog reflecting and dancing on the water.

We hope you enjoyed reading this title from:

BLACK ROSE
writing™

www.blackrosewriting.com

Subscribe to our mailing list—*The Rosevine*—and receive **FREE** books, daily deals, and stay current with news about upcoming releases and our hottest authors.

Scan the QR code below to sign up.

Already a subscriber? Please accept a sincere thank you for being a fan of Black Rose Writing authors.

View other Black Rose Writing titles at www.blackrosewriting.com/books and use promo code **PRINT** to receive a **20% discount** when purchasing.